I0788123

BELVIDERE.

VIII

X
Sans Nom

Title: **Belvidere.**

Summary: *A mysterious man is sent to a dead-end town; to do what, and to whom, he simply doesn't know. It's all part of a game he neither understands, nor controls. He befriends those he will likely betray; there will certainly be trouble if he does not. A fantastical, mysterious journey; an ephemeral olla podrida of raw erotica, graphic violence, racism, heathenism, bigotry and vulgarity, all buoyed by the providence of friendship, love and kindred souls.*

1.   Fiction-General.   2.   Fiction-Fantasy.
17 18 19 20 21   j i h g f e d c b a
First Edition - American

TABLE OF CONTENTS - VIII

CHAPTER 364 – ON A COLLISION COURSE TO A BALLROOM BLITZ

A short black skirt, white cotton top and vermilion scarf queued vertical by the jukebox.

Lillian oozed aphrodisia, carnality; the hungry itch of raw sex.

The air around her was juiced; everyone in the place who knew Lillian, which meant everyone, sensed something bad was coming. They had all at various times seen Lillian fixated, a broil of emotions….and heaven help the unfortunate focus of her wrath.

And it was clear to all that Joan was in near-term trouble.

Carol stood tall, arms folded across her front in defiance, on the edge of the open circle which had materialized around Lillian; a respectful orb, just outside the range of a flying fist, or a swift high kick.

Everyone knew Lillian.

The vinyl disk dropped and Lilly pulled from God knows where the ultimate ace, a dagger she didn't know she possessed, the one she had taken hostage and worn all day….Carol's cheap black sunglasses.

Carol's eyes cue-balled. She gave C a look-to-kill and yelled.

"With my fucking shades?!"

C offered nothing but a helpless shrug.

Lilly caught the commotion and it *instantly* clicked; that third set of shades, C's ham-handed profession of a mistake in the glove box, was *no* mistake....none at all. And she realized her seat in the Mustang was Carol's all along. Her anger piked at the revelation; how could she *not* have figured? But as quick as the storm spiked, it melted and morphed to sweet satisfaction. Who had the day? The *best day ever!* Who won in the end?

What a fitting finale to a fourteen-year feud.

She slowly slipped the black plastics on, then slid them down, just a hair, and smiled provocative at Carol, her eyes cat-slit over the top.

It was a miracle the volcano didn't erupt right then, right there; but things happen, or don't, for a reason.

There is no such thing as an accident;
it is fate misnamed.

[Napoleon I]

And somehow, fate, and calm prevailed, as the story at the *Cabin* continued to unfold. Lillian come-on fingered her brother, as *The Sweet* began to sing:

Are you ready, Steve? Uh huh;
Andy? Yeah;
Mick? Okay;
All right fellas, let's go!

There was a sudden surge of adrenaline, and the *Cabin* crowd went crazy; they were all on a collision course to a *Ballroom Blitz*.

CHAPTER 365 – THEREIN UNFOLDED A WHOLE NEW LEVEL OF DIRTY

This was not just another regular in the repertoire; it was her absolute favorite.

Lillian lived for this song; the fight in it was the fight living in her for the past twenty-five years. It owned her as much as she owned it. And Earl had the routine cold; he had danced it with Lillian a thousand over a thousand more. Probably the only song the two had danced to more than the Joan ditty that just ended.

And if they weren't siblings, one would swear that he was slipping it into her, but good; the dirtiest of dirty dancing was cued up and on its way, for all the *Cabin* to see. God help them.

Jaws dropped as the scene made a sharp left, and arched erotic. If it had been anyone but Earl and Lillian, if any brother and sister had done anything close to what was happening, before collective eyes on that *Cabin* floor, rumors would have rocketed, Marty would have been called, and time behind bars would end the story.

Instead, the place went utterly unhinged.

Carol stood stone beside C, arms folded hard across her chest, fuming, not believing the scene unfolding before her.

"Take it easy, take it easy, I got something important to tell you."

C said, in a relaxed tone.

It didn't work.

Without warning, Carol unleashed, punching him hard in the shoulder, a real barn-burner.

"Way to be on time, shithead!"

"What, is this the new thing?!"

He said, stepping back, rubbing the impact.

"She can hit? So can I! *Harder!* And why didn't you show up a bit later? I've been stewing in the God-damn kitchen, sweating my ass off stuffed in this red leather sausage for four fucking hours!"

"I *told you* I'd be here by midnight, and I was, with two minutes to spare *[C held up two fingers in her face, and smiled]*. And why'd you dress in the leather gig so early? Anxious? Any panties on under there, by the way, I don't see any unsightly lines."

Carol was not amused (and she *was* sans panties, for the record; her sweaty crotch was fact-evidence).

"Did you string it out *just* to annoy me? That's what is seems like, all lovey-dovey with that bitch! And you said *no chance* she'll ever even go into the City! Nice guess, asshole; remind me never to bet on you - you ruined my whole fucking day."

"Oh for Christ sake, just relax; I think you're gonna want to hear this. You...."

That's all C got out.

"Just shut up and give me your fucking shades! I know they're in your jacket, I saw 'em. Give 'em up, *now*!"

She stabbed him in the chest with her pointer, holding it there, pushing hard. He gave them up.

Sweet's first stanza was coming to a raucous close:

And the man in the back said 'everyone attack!'

Carol flipped on the shades, shoved C aside and scampered stealth across the open dance floor, snatching Earl's arm from behind as Lilly was finishing her moves, mugging to the crowd, eyes closed behind black plastic frames.

Waiting for no one, the second stanza began.

Carol witnessed the goods and knew she couldn't out-dance Lilly, as much as it killed her to think it. That bitch was fucking good, too good for Carol. How could she be so good?

But she could do what Lillian couldn't. So she did.

And therein unfolded a whole new level of dirty.

CHAPTER 366 – EACH EYED THE OTHER, THROUGH DRAWN SHADES

Oh, I'm reaching out for something,
Touching nothing's all I ever do;
Oh, I softly call you over,
When you appear there's nothing left of you.

As the words ricocheted off the walls, Carol cinched Earl around the waist, quickly pulled him in tight and jumped up, wrapping those red leather talons around his midsection like a vice. Suddenly, ominously, she leaned way back, like she was bucking a bronco, and ready to eat dirt. Earl panicked; he instinctively grabbed her from falling, then clutching her, eyes locked, he froze.

Just as she planned.

Carol flung forward, wrapped her arms around his neck and kissed him, smack on the lips, long, hard and wet, sticking her tongue in his mouth, whether he was ready or not, as the music jammed. The ring of spectators let out a thunderclap of moans, hoots and rabid applause.

Lilly smiled and opened her eyes; she knew she was good, but was she *that* good? She must be. Until it became clear the boomlet was directed at the action *behind* her.

She spun to see she'd been swindled.

Before she could react, Cord flew to her side, ready to tackle, if necessary, squinting and bracing for the wrath, the fist or foot, which was surely on its way. But, with eyes half-closed, waiting for sudden impact, it never came. To this surprise, his delight, Lillian just stood silent, smiling odd, arms folded in front of her, just as Carol had done moments earlier.

But Lillian's wasn't an angry pose, or an evil-smile, not at all. It was different, much different....rather good.

And that is how Lillian stood, without moving a muscle, joining the crowd in ogling the pornographic peep-show unfolding before them, with an odd, satisfied detach.

C looked at her in disbelief, then cracked a small, crooked smile. It made no sense, but since it was Lilly, it made all the sense in the world.

Only Lilly.

And with Carol grinding hard her red leather crotch, an open-air, voyeur, not-so-dry-hump, on Earl's belly, kissing him boy-crazy, leaving a trail of smeared pecks and smacks, glossy fire-engine ovals of dishy lipstick on his face and neck, the second refrain was reeling to an end:

And the man in the back said 'everyone attack!'
And it turned into a Ballroom Blitz;
And the girl in the corner said 'boy I want to warn you'
It'll turn into a Ballroom Blitz;
Ballroom Blitz;
Ballroom Blitz;
Ballroom Blitz;
Ballroom Blitz.

And for the next twenty too-long seconds, the drums and guitars pounded out an ominous, stalking beat, sans words, and the *Cabin* went silent, wondering, worrying, just what Lillian Liddell would do to Joan Jett.

Carol dismounted her horse, throbbing with adrenaline, her wet crotch still warm from the furious friction. The briefest of smiles was there and gone as she tipped her shades to Earl, then turned stone to stare down her foe.

Lillian kept smiling; she had the feel of a feline, up to something, and that usually meant trouble. But what stew it was gonna be, no one in that room was quite sure.

And save the thump of the song, the room was silent....waiting.

With arms folded, standing tall, each eyed the other, through drawn shades.

CHAPTER 367 – ONE EYE ON THE PRIZE, THE OTHER ON THE OTHER

The crowd inched closer, ringing the threesome, three-deep; the third refrain about to begin. A Mexican standoff in the offing, with shades instead of pistols, and poor Earl an unwilling third, with the noose tightening.

In Mexico, the advantage was always to the second to act, at least it worked that way with a gun.

Carol stood possessive; closer to Earl than his sister. It was a challenge, more than a stance.

The crowd watched as Lillian stalked counterclockwise, taking up a position opposite her foe.

Lillian stopped at hour three on the clock; Carol at hour nine; poor Earl was smack in the middle....no-man's-land.

It was then that Lillian tilted her head down, flared her nostrils and stared bull-charge over her shades at the challenger, a flutter of the red cape.

The crowd erupted for the hometown favorite, as the third-stanza unspooled:

Oh yeah, it was like lightening!
Everybody was frightening;
And the music was soothing;
And they all started grooving;
Yeah, yeah, yeah, yeah, yeah.

And the man in the back said 'everyone attack!'
And it turned into a Ballroom Blitz;
And the girl in the corner said 'boy I want to warn you'
It'll turn into a Ballroom Blitz;
Ballroom Blitz;
Ballroom Blitz;

Sam stood with both hands over his face, peeking between fat fingers, waiting for the axe-scene in the horror movie, the one you knew was coming, the one you couldn't watch, but would, kind-of, anyway, afraid to move, not knowing, for sure, when the carnage would begin.

For once, Frank was smiling, through a drunken, slobbery stupor; he knew someone was going down and that alone was worth the effort to push and swing his big belly from the bar. For sure it wasn't going to be Lilly....for sure. *No one gets the best of Lilly, no one*, he murmured through a wet belch, as he chugged the last of the warm beer in his mug, lips smeared with suds.

Buck was scared. He always got scared when Lilly was riled, because that just meant trouble. And even though it wasn't directed at him, thank God, childhood memories of being locked in the dark of the basement, or the attic, tied to the back porch by anchor-rope or forced to eat fish-stink cat-food struck fear in him whenever Lillian was angry, and nearby. And his money was clearly on Lillian; in the end, when the chips are down, especially if the subject is Earl, no one gets the better of Lilly....*no one.*

And as the rabble ogled the ring, both cougars stalked their prey, circling slowly, one eye on the prize, the other on the other.

CHAPTER 368 – INSTEAD, SHE GOT AND EYEFUL OF *HER*

Lillian was the first to act.

She lunged at Earl in a mock charge; Carol instinctively recoiled, half-closing her eyes, expecting some sort of impact.

But it was just a dance-juke; Earl knew it and reacted rote, like a dog on a fetch; he had no choice, and the two began a series of exaggerated, coordinated moves, leaving Carol standing, dumbfounded, and embarrassed.

Earl quickly realized his sister's dirty trick and stopped mid-routine, turned and started to dance toward Carol, an apology. Carol knew what Earl did, smiled thanks, and began to dance with him.

Lillian figured Earl would catch on, feel sorry for Joan, like a sad-sack, and dump her; she was two giant steps ahead of her brother. Without skipping a beat, as if it was all part of the act, she moved into another routine, so seamless no one could guess the improvise. She swung around, her back to Earl's, and danced for the ring of faces around her, who were screaming and singing the lyrics at the top of their lungs.

Lillian backed up a bit into Earl, ass-to-ass. She knew exactly what he was dancing, even though she wasn't looking at him, and she began to mock his moves, so they looked in sync.

The crowd ate it up; the place was a pandemonium.

Carol saw Lillian saddle up against Earl, butt-to-butt, and couldn't let the challenge go. She immediately spun around, stuck her ass out back, and ground on Earl's crotch, her mouth open, licking her lips seductive, like she was in the middle of public sex. A reverse Oreo.

"

The crowd on that side of the room, clearly liking the scene, erupted their voyeur approval.

Buck got butterflies, the scared-shit kind. Without realizing, he instinctively inched away from the threesome.

Earl, not knowing who to appease, just stood there, whirligig in place, like a bad white-guy's groove.

Just then, without warning, someone, no one ever determined exactly who, although Belvidere-sized rumors ran rampant for years, cut the lights, and the dance floor went dark; the room aglow from the amber fire and neon jukebox back-light, in the far corner, behind the crowd.

The third stanza was coming to an end and the two girls, shades down in the dark, back-to-back, were each gyrating furious on their man, barely brushing ass-to-ass and ass-to-crotch.

A climax.

The song ended and chaos reigned; cheers, whistles, claps and shrieks echoed around the dance floor, mixed in a stew of laughter. Both girls were sure they won, huffing, hyper-ventilating post-marathon.

Both spun to Earl just as the lights kicked back on, and found themselves nose-to-nose, the closest they had ever been, breathing heavy on each other's face.

Earl smiled and clapped loud from the sidelines, arms over his head, nestled in the crowd beside his best friend.

And they were both laughing.

And before the girls could react, to the situation, or each other, the crowd quickly engulfed them in dance, the next song already in play.

Lillian was surrounded by a sea of familiar faces, kissing and hugging her, laughing and joking about things no one could really hear. C didn't know most of them; it was clear this was a Liddell reunion on a grand scale, for both brother and sister. Carol, with the help of Sam, and Woodie, of course, had compiled an amazing invite list, pulling in a bevy of long-lost friends, Belvidereans spread near and far.

Carol had escaped the human tide, riding a crest of humanity, taking up a position away from the Lilly-throng, wedging herself between Earl and Cord.

"Jesus, that was fun! I was all excited rubbing my butt on your crotch Earl, till I realized it was your sister's ass! Her butt wasn't half-bad actually; kick-boxing class certainly helps."

She closed her eyes and tilted her head back, letting out a big breath of relief.

"I haven't gotten into a fight with another girl, with *anyone*, since I was in the fifth grade; my God, my heart is still pounding from the adrenaline....powerful stuff."

Carol let out a second big breath of air, blown up at the ceiling. But she got no answer, no retort at all from either of the boys. She expected some acknowledgment in return, something nice, witty, sarcastic....something. She tilted her head forward, stripped off the shades and opened her eyes; ready to scold the two of them for ignoring her.

Instead, she got an eyeful of *her*.

CHAPTER 369 – LIFE CHANGED
FOREVERMORE

The dance floor was ablaze in bodies, all in chaotic motion, yet a cocoon of quiet somehow surrounded the two women, sequestered in a corner, near a stack of mismatched plastic plates and a tin beer sign, hung crooked on the timber-log wall.

C and Earl had abandoned her, absorbed into the throng of party-goers milling the dance floor; they were nowhere to be found. Carol was all alone, naked; she had no life-line, no support, no help. Her heart raced as Lillian, sans shades, gazed deep into Carol's eyes.

Lilly was close....*too close*.

Slowly, deliberately, without malice, Lillian Liddell raised her right arm horizontal and extended a delicate hand toward Carol Crowe.

The words, the same to the letter that Carol had offered up to her fourteen long years ago, in a booth at the *Palace,* left Lillian's lips in a sweet whisper, followed by a small, sincere smile.

"Carol, so nice to finally meet you….I'm Lillian."

And life changed forevermore.

CHAPTER 370 – THE BEST FRIEND SHE HAD BEEN WAITING FOR ALL HER LIFE

Lillian held her hand, extended in friendship, toward Carol, not really sure what to expect. If she got a verbal assault, a slap, even if she got decked, she wouldn't retaliate; she would simply take whatever she had coming to her. She deserved all of that, and then more, and she knew it. And she was ready to take it, whatever Carol dished out.

But she had told her mom, promised her mom, that she'd be good, and that her mom would be proud of her. And a promise was a promise. Her mom didn't answer, but it didn't matter, Lillian knew she was listening.

Carol stared back at Lillian, without saying a word, then looked down, oddly, at the appendage sticking out at her, Lillian's delicate hand.

Then Carol smiled small and started to cry, walking right through Lillian's hand, hugging hard the best friend she had been waiting for all her life.

CHAPTER 371 – HER BROTHER WAS RIGHT; IT FELT ENTIRELY TOO GOOD

The two were like twins, that liked each other.

Years of pent-up frustration washed down the gullet amidst two-fisted drinking, and on *this* front, Carol was more than holding her own. Lillian was a lightweight, the dizzy in her head already a steady half-spin.

But Lillian was happy, *truly* happy.

Earl was distracted and Cord saw the two girls together first, seated side-by-side at the bar, and shook his head, to chase away the drunk buzz he didn't have. But he *must* be drunk, because there was Lillian and Carol, shoulder-to-shoulder, drinking and laughing. He jabbed Earl in the ribs, who turned, saw the two of them, and simply smiled wide.

And as Earl looked over at Lillian and Carol, it was clear the big man was listening and nodding his head in approval, like he sometimes did, to no one in the room. Then Earl quickly, silently mouthed *thank you* to the ceiling. No one saw it but C.

And C knew exactly what it was: Lillian and Carol; a birthday present from his mom – the best ever. C smiled, shaking his head once again at this unbelievably strange fucking place, surprised at how much he loved it, and the odd people that roamed its range. There clearly was never a place like this. Never.

Cord turned back to Lillian and Carol. Sam was saddled beside them; he kept hugging both his new-found daughters, first one, then the other, then both at once. Non-stop. Frank was on the other side of Sam, sullen again, bent over a beer at the bar, sunk in a typical funk, his dreams of chaos unfulfilled.

C was still speechless. He watched, voyeur, as Lillian kissed and hugged Carol, over and over, half from the alcohol, half from talking to her mother, half for her brother and the last half from absolute, positive relief....drop-kicking a lifelong bag of bricks, to the curb, forever. She had no idea what freedom really felt like, until today, till right now. And you couldn't beat it with a stick.

What a feeling. Lilly committed, right then and there, to get drunk, as often as possible, and then some more.

Her brother was right; it felt entirely too good.

CHAPTER 372 – *HAPPY BIRTHDAY BROTHER*

The two of them had been there the whole time, but had kept to the background.

But now it was time.

Earl was drinking whiskey sours in jumbo root-beer mugs, two lined up on the bar at a time. He had at least four so far, numbers five and six sat before him. The tree was getting a bit weak in the roots; happy, but weak. Earl's eyes were glazed, but there was no mistaking the number ringing his phone.

"Hey C, it's Mac! He's calling me on my birthday! Is it still my birthday?"

"Sure, till the party ends, and this one doesn't seem to be ending anytime soon. Maybe you'll be forty forever!"

C said, as he downed a neat scotch; *Glenlivet*, he thought, but at this point, wasn't really sure. He had finished off the last of the *Cabin's Laphroaig* stash about a half-hour ago.

"I hope so! If this is what forty is, it's the best ever!"

Earl yelled as he flipped open the phone.

"Mac! Mac! You won't believe it! I got so much to tell you! I'm at the *Log Cabin*, and it's my birthday still; C says it'll stay my birthday *forever*! And Lilly and Carol are friends now! Can you believe it?! And I'm drunk! And all my friend are here, and…."

And suddenly, Earl realized all his friend *weren't* there.

"Hey, how come no one invited? Hey, I'm sorry…."

Earl put his head down, ashamed; every day, even the best ever, has its disappointments.

Except this one.

"Hey buddy, that's okay, no worries. But you know what, I think Lucy may have made it; why don't you turn around."

And as Earl spun, he saw Lucy on the far side of the room, smiling and waving tiny. And standing next to her, with the phone to his ear, was Mac.

Earl dropped the phone in the crowd, ran, and in a full sprint, bear-hugged Mac, the only man big enough to get his arms around the biker-girth. Mac kissed Earl on the cheek, the first and only man Mac ever kissed.

"You think we would miss this?! If we did, your sister would be all over me, and trust me, I don't want any part of that, for sure!"

Earl smiled and gave a big hug and kiss to Lucien, who hugged like only Dominicans can. Lillian spied the scene and came over.

"Lucky you came, otherwise, *big trouble*."

Lilly said, in a drunken mock threat.

"See, I told ya! Are you kidding, I just said the same thing to your brother!"

Lillian kissed and hugged both of them, in a waft of alcohol.

"Hey Earl, I saw a *huge* pile of presents for you, over by the pizza ovens."

Mac said, like it was Christmas.

"I know! The most presents ever! But I'm not allowed to open them yet; Carol said so, but I wouldn't mind cheating, just a little."

Earl whispered sneaky-Pete through a whiskey-sour haze.

"Well, I'm impatient, so let's cheat together. Plus, I want you to open mine first; we won't tell Carol....deal?"

Mac half-whispered, seeing that Carol was standing right beside Earl, smiling, hearing every word he said.

Earl looked at Carol, and she nodded once.

"Oh boy, first present!"

Earl yelped.

Mac took Earl's arm, Lucy hooked the other, and to the pizza ovens they went. Atop a mountain of boxes, of every shape and size, laid a small white envelope, simple....plain. A very tiny envelope, as thin as paper. Earl picked it off the pile top gingerly, and very carefully opened the seal; out dropped a small note, written in wobbly script by a man who rarely took up a pen.

IOU

Love,
Mac & Lucy

"Thanks Mac, that's the....best."

Earl really wasn't sure what it meant, but he didn't want to hurt anyone's feelings, especially Mac and Lucy. So he fibbed, just a little.

So C filled in the blank.

"Earl, it's your bike ride, on the *Knucklehead!* You haven't done it yet; you guys never seem to hook up. So now, this makes it *official.* Pick a day, any day, and Mac will take you....no questions."

Earl looked to C, then smiled wide at Mac and Lucien.

"Thank you! You know getting to ride on your bike is the best present ever! Did you bring it? Did you? Maybe we can go on a night ride, right now! I want my IOU *right now!* You haven't been drinking, have you Mac? Remember, no drinking and driving! I can't drive, because I'm drunk! But I can't drive it anyway, even if I'm not drunk, 'cause I don't even know how to, even though I'm gonna beat the dust on the levee rim road, because my mom said so, and if she said so, then you know it's true, and C's gonna lose that bet *big time* and owe me the *Marked Claw* **and** the *Coiled Cobra*, but never mind about that right now, let's go for a ride! You can ride the *Knucklehead*, if your not drunk, right? Mac, are you drunk? No fibbing!"

Mac was standing with a near-empty bottle of light beer in his hand, and his eyes were bloodshot to boot. But it wasn't from the alcohol.

"Thanks C."

Mac said, for his explanation of the IOU; C nodded in acknowledgment.

"But that's not quite it."

Mac said; C looked surprised, feeling a bit the fool.

"Oh, sorry."

C said meek. With that, Mac reached into his pocket, grabbed it, cupping it tightly in his hand.

"The IOU's not for you buddy, it's for *me;* it's a promise from *you* to me."

Earl looked confused.

"Okay, but you know I'd do anything for you, *anytime, ever*, for you or Lucy, all you have to do is ask. I **love** you both; you're my family."

Earl whispered sincere.

Mac choked up, not because he was sad, or in doubt, but because he was so incredibly happy, the happiest he had been in years, happy that he, who had done so much bad, was doing something so good, so selfless, to a man who deserved it more that any man in the world. To a man he truly loved.

Tears started to run down Mac's face.

"I realized I was only ever just a renter, kind of a custodian, waiting for one of the two very best things in my life to knock on my door. Lucien was the first one, and you, Earl….you're the other. You knocked on my door and changed my life, brother, you saved me; just ask Lucy, you did *[Lucy nodded, and was crying too, hugging Mac's arm]*. So, anyway, I just want to ask you a big favor, okay, sorry I'm choking up a bit, but I'm so happy, knowing you and your sister, and I'm not so good at this kind of thing, not much practice. So here's the deal, here it is….I would just like you to promise to take me for a ride, every now and then, on your *Knucklehead*."

And Mac shook Earl's hand, and dropped the keys into his palm.

"Happy birthday brother."

CHAPTER 373 – STICK TO LYING - IT WORKS MUCH, MUCH BETTER

C tapped Earl lightly on the cheek; Earl murmured something, no one was quite sure what, then slowly opened his eyes.

"Hey buddy, wake up."

Cord whispered; Earl blinked his eyes in a flutter, and remembered he was at someone's birthday party. C continued.

"Congratulations, you are becoming quite an accomplished drunk; you fainted and only split half your drink, but you saved the other half and didn't drop the glass, held onto it in a vice grip. Good job, priorities in order….all's good!"

C and Mac each hooked him under an arm and hoisted the big man vertical. He was still a bit wobbly, but stable enough.

Once it became clear the birthday party was his, as was the *Knucklehead*, and he didn't faint a second time, Mac simply couldn't wait to bring Earl outside and go over all the various gauges, gears and doodads, followed by a small entourage of onlookers, including Buck, Marty, Sam, Woodie and Moe. Other than Lucien, Lillian and Carol, it was a gathering of guys, and soon enough, the three girls peeled away; there was only so much talk of carburetors, fuel ratios and horsepower they could take. Boring!

The female trio made their way back to the bar to talk, laugh and drink about important stuff, like guys, and how boring they usually were.

Cord didn't join the boys, or the girls; Margery had snuck up behind him and gently whispered in his ear.

"Hey stranger."

C was genuinely glad to see her; he liked Margery, he really did. She was a girl he could really see himself being with, except for all those hurdles she liked to remind him about.

"So it looks like it finally happened; congratulations."

Margery said, genuine.

"A lot's happened."

C said, only half-joking.

So Margery indulged.

"Lillian....and you?"

"Oh, well, yeah, I think so, but with Lilly, it's always a bit iffy; one never truly knows."

Margery laughed.

"Understood. Just for the record, so far tonight, and the night's not over, Lillian has quit, then she fired me, then she hired me back, and gave me a big raise, and herself an even bigger one....so I guess I know the iffy part."

C nodded and smiled in silent agreement, raising a rocks glass, holding nothing but neat Scotch.

"But I've finally found her Achilles heel; the girl can't hold her liquor; if I don't get lucky tonight, I give up."

C said, in mock triumph.

Margery looked at C, not really sure how to answer that one tactfully, so she left it alone. And C, when he should have just shut-up, didn't. And dug himself deeper.

"I've been dry since, since, you....*the best squatter ever!*"

C pointed his drink at Margery, raised it in salute, and took a hearty shot. It would have been better if he had been sloppy drunk, to excuse the exchange. But alas, he wasn't, not yet, anyway. And he quickly realized that comment sounded as pathetic as it was, as soon as it left his lips. He half-wished he was sloshed; at least then he could blame it on the alcohol, instead of stupidity.

Margery smiled, courteous, which clearly said she hadn't thought of their one-off nearly as much as he had, if at all. A nice ride, quickly forgotten. Which made him feel even smaller, a real punch to the gut, and below.

You would think he would cut it there, stop the bleeding. But no, C babbled on.

"How about you, seeing anyone? Re-hook with what's-his-name?"

"Please! *What's-his-name* - Walter, by the way, is history – not that he doesn't try to get back in, drunk-calling me and asking if he can have just one more, you know, for old-times-sake. But give me more credit than going back to that trough."

"So, you hit a dry spell too; no worries, it happens to the best of us."

C took another gulp of Scotch, happy that they were in the same sorry boat.

But Margery didn't answer, discretely looking away, sipping her Cabernet. Which was not lost on the not-so-drunk Cord. Another body shot; time to throw in the fucking towel.

"Excuse me? You have a new squeeze?"

She smiled demurely.

"Well, we'll see; it's still early yet."

"But he's gotten into your pants?   Sorry, tights?"

That came out a bit snarky.

"Sorry."

C said, not so convincingly.

"Yeah, well, you know I like to fuck."

She snapped back, and C smiled; he deserved that. Then Margery abruptly changed the subject to the real topic at hand, the topic she came to discuss with Cord, which wasn't her or C's sex life.

"Hey, do me favor; as much as I'm truly happy for you - you need to be with Lillian, and her with you - not everyone is quite so thrilled about it. I need you to have a quick talk, or not-so-quick....let her choose, with my mom. She's been watching the display tonight, between the two of you, and is feeling, a *bit down*, to say the least."

"Is she still with *Tool-Box*, the guy next door?"

"Joe? Yeah, and he's really good for her, as I told you, he really is. But you always want what you can't have, even if it's not right, in the end."

Margery kissed C gently on the temple, like an aunt kisses a nephew. That really sucked, he thought. And C wasn't so sure that little speech of Margery's wasn't also meant for him, regarding her. Or maybe it was just him feeling sorry for himself.

As he mulled the meaning, Margery disappeared, slipping seamless into the crowd; C found himself alone and feeling shitty.

He scanned the room, but didn't see Mae. He slowly made his way around the bar, squeezing sardine through a throng of loud, sweaty humanity. It took a full ten minutes to complete the bar loop, and no Mae. The body heat in the *Cabin* was palpable, so he ducked outside and saw the crew of guys still circling the *Knucklehead;* Earl was straddling the hog - it was a big bike, but looked small under his massive frame.

"Looking for me?"

Came a familiar voice, tired, out of the darkness, off to the right. He spied a small red dot; it glowed hot, then went dull, then hot again.

"I didn't know you smoked."

C said, quiet.

"Lots of things you don't know."

She answered blank.

"I smoke when I'm feeling shitty, not that often....sometimes. Usually something to do with you."

C walked over and leaned against the hood of a large pick-up near Mae, but not too close.

"Have to keep a respectable distance?"

"Come on Mae."

C pleaded, already tired of the conversation he knew was coming.

Stiff silence.

"I thought we were gonna be friends without benefits; your rule, remember?"

"When's the last time you called me, *friend*?"

Mae said sarcastic, taking a long drag on her cigarette.

"When's the last time you called me?"

C said, in a snarky retort.

"I don't know, when did you get a phone?"

Shot down with a snarkier retort.

"Margery says you and Joe are together."

She ignored the remark.

Just then, Cord heard her phone ring, muffled in her pocketbook, but still loud enough to plainly hear, to his chagrin. It was a too-familiar jingle, *Romper-Room.* the same *pop-goes-the-weasel* ring-tone that she humped hard on and came to, grinding him into the mattress along the way, when they were fucking that first weekend, when Joe called. Sex, *Romper-Room* and popping weasels, all in the same sentence….that's not easy to do.

It seemed forever ago.

Cord assumed it was the same caller, searching frantic for *his girl*. Please answer the phone, he thought; how ironic, *he* was hoping for a *Tool-Box* rescue.

The weasel pop repeated never-end, a mocking, prepubescent taunt. Neither said a word as the sick jingle sang to them from the confines of her pocketbook. Mae didn't make the slightest effort to acknowledge the ditty; she simply stared at Cord the whole time, an awkward, bitter, sexless gaze, sans a single blink. The phone finally fell silent; the end of an uncomfortable little torture.

She shook her head in the negative, before a word left her lips. Then she spoke.

"So when did it happen? When did you two finally make it *official*? I always knew it was coming, everyone did; just a matter of time."

"Today."

C said, truthfully. He owed her that; he owed Mae the truth, for once.

"You *fucked* her today?! ***Here?!***"

"No, Mae, I didn't fuck her today, or here; I haven't fucked her, *ever*."

And when the words left his lips, which C thought, at first, would be welcomed, the good news she *wanted* to hear, and the truth to boot, he suddenly realized, and should have realized earlier, Mae's question was carnal only. The *Romper-Room fuck* part was all she was asking about Lillian; *Romper-Room* and the weasel-pop was the action in the question. She wasn't asking about, she certainly wasn't expecting, the *relationship* part, since Cord Brin didn't *enter into those sorts of things*, so he had told her, time and again.

And C found himself, once again, neck-deep in the tar pit, after one honest answer. So much for fucking honesty, he thought; he should stick to lying - it works much, much better.

CHAPTER 374 – HE WOULD STRUGGLE TO REMEMBER THEIR NAMES

Margery gently put her hand on C's shoulder, from behind. C was sitting outside, alone, secreted in the dark, where Mae left him. The *Knucklehead* pit crew was revving the engine, with Earl still astride; a whole group mesmerized by the low growl of the hog. They never saw C sitting in the shadows, less than seventy-five feet away.

"What the hell happened?"

Margery asked, incredulous.

"The truth; apparently not a smart thing to tell."

He said, matter-of-fact.

"She's crying in the car; she wishes she never came, she wants to go home, *now*."

"Great."

Was all C spit out.

"Well?"

Margery asked again.

"She asked when it finally *happened,* and I said today. But what she was talking about, asking about, was sex, sex with Lilly, and I told her I never had sex with Lilly. So, what *happened* was apparently way worse than sex with Lillian. I guess she could deal with sex, not happy, but deal. But dealing with a *relationship*, well, not so easy, apparently; that was a game-changer."

"Oh."

Was all Margery said, and it was enough. She patted him lightly on the back.

"Sorry C, but you did the right thing, even though it doesn't feel like it, you really did. She needed to hear it and to let go. It isn't there for her, with you; it's not your fault, or hers, it's just the way it is."

She squeezed C's shoulder.

"Well good for Joe, he finally gets to keep what he wants. He's been calling her all night, non-stop, every fifteen minutes. But she's been ignoring the calls, waiting to talk to you. He's been at her house, pacing, figuring you're gonna put the moves on his gal *[Margery laughed]*. He's out to defend her honor, and he made her some homemade chicken soup *[she laughed again]*; he doesn't like you much."

"I'll lose sleep over that; how do you know all this, by the way?"

Cord asked, annoyed.

"How? Because he's been calling *me* all night, trying to get the scoop since she won't answer her phone! He figured you were banging her in the back of her car, got his dander up, as I said, protecting her honor. Well at least he'll get a taste tonight."

C put up his hand.

"Okay, okay, just because your mom and I are over doesn't mean I want to hear about her riding some skinny, wrinkly old Jew....yuck."

"Well, from what I gather...."

"Enough! *La, la, la; not listening.*"

C covered his ears and closed his eyes.

Margery laughed and spared him the rest.

"Hey, it was good seeing you, good luck with your *girl*. And don't worry about my mom, she'll live. And your drama just keeps bringing mother and daughter closer and closer together....*thanks!*"

And she pecked Cord on the cheek.

"Always happy to help."

C said, cocking his head and smiling sarcastic.

"I better get going before Lilly fires me again, or docks my pay; say Happy Birthday again and goodnight to Earl for me, will ya?"

C shook his head yes, and with that, Margery was gone, and with it, a chapter sadly closed. He had hoped to stay friends with the both of them, he really did, but he knew it likely wouldn't happen.

It was the same old drill, every time. A quick fade, followed by a long forget, followed by gone. And some day in the future, years from now, he would struggle to remember their names.

CHAPTER 375 – HE NEVER MADE IT BACK

The party raged on, the alcohol flowed free, and the jukebox rolled from one favorite to the next, non-stop.

By this time, Earl had dove into the presents head-on, opened a third, thanking gifters, who weren't even there, and went to fetch more drinks for the group, before diving back into the pile of paper and ribbons. Everyone had lost their drink-count by that time; *too many* was probably the right answer.

He never made it back.

CHAPTER 376 - SHE SOFTLY FINGERED THE THREE DIGITS IN

It was closing in on 2:30 am; Earl, whiskey-sour mug in hand, was saddled at the bar; he got everyone's next round of booze, but lined them up on the bar instead, wondering why he got himself so many different kinds of drinks. The jukebox and everyone he left beside the pile of presents were forgotten for now and he found himself talking about Loki and the farm with Marty and his dad, along with Ji-Sue, Buck and Linda.

His head spinning, he saw Carol, actually three of them, approach; Earl stood up and proclaimed tall, to all:

"I'm drunk, and I like it!"

The crowd, still thick but thinned, raised their glasses and cheered the birthday boy, as did Carol. Then she hooked Earl's arm, pushed her face serious-close to his and whispered in a warm, delicate breath.

"Earl, can I talk to you a minute….alone?"

He studied her closely, eyeing her up and down with a spaced, drunken stare. Something was wrong, definitely wrong. He could feel it....smell it.

Like a fillip, it hit him, cold and hard.

"*Hey*, where's Joan Jett?! Where'd she go?"

The red leather jumpsuit was gone, switched into comfortable, worn jeans, flat shoes and a black cotton top.

Carol smiled.

"Joan went home sweetie; she did her thing. Now *I* want to talk to you, *just me,* okay?"

"Sure, I love talking to you, all the time; I could talk to you forever and ever and ever! You know, you smell like flowers, good flowers, not bad stinky ones, like skunk cabbage, and your teeth are very white and straight, and the best part is the space between your two front ones, that's the best! Have you always had that, or did you put it there, on purpose, and, and….um."

Earl finally realized he was rambling; and what he thought, words that had always simply swam harmless in his head, somehow found a hatchway out, slurred but sure. And he wasn't clear who was actually deciding to say those words aloud, because it certainly wasn't him.

He felt his face get red.

Carol got on her tippy toes and kissed him on the cheek. He felt them, warm and wet, and he decided it was about the best feeling in the whole world.

"I want you to come over to the jukebox with me. I know these songs are all your favorites: yours, C's, Lillian's; but there's one I put on there too, just for you, special….from me. Just from me, to you."

She took Earl by the hand and led him across the floor; Marty, his dad, Ji-Sue, Buck, Linda….they all followed, instinctive, in silence.

And somehow, the party took notice.

It wasn't supposed to, but sometimes these things just happen. And by the time Carol got to the slanted glass, and rubbed her fingers ever-so-lightly across the special three-digit code that wasn't listed on the song roster, barely touching them, a warm-up, the room had gone quiet, and the dance floor had cleared.

Cord had found Lillian and they were gently holding hands, looking as if they had been their whole lives, an old, happy couple. Lucy and Mac stood beside them, her head on his shoulder, smiling soft.

Ryan, the gay Episcopal priest, and Tommy, his longtime partner, saddled up alongside Mac; both men looking tiny next to the grizzled biker. Mac smiled and gave Ryan a hearty pat on the back, knocking him forward just a bit. To this day, Carol's two favorite neighbors were still taking their morning, four-lap power-walks around the Square, always asking about her house full of cats.

Carol eyed the ring of faces, friends, all of them. She felt butterflies, her stomach in a nervous churn. Worse than any board presentation, any investor pitch.

"I wasn't expecting a crowd, but since I have one, I'll tell you all what I was going to tell Earl alone. This is my birthday present to him, the start of it, so to speak. Now I can't sing a lick, so I'm just gonna kinda whisper the words to Earl, a quiet sing-along. This song is what Earl means to me, every word of it, as if it was written just for me….to him. Now I know I'm gonna cry when I sing this, so I apologize upfront.

She turned to Earl.

"This is for you sweetie."

And she softly fingered the three digits in.

CHAPTER 377 – I WANT TO BE YOUR WIFE

The song began: *Dreams*, by the *Cranberries*.

Carol welled before the first word left her lips. She had been waiting months for this moment; she had been waiting a lifetime for this day.

So it began:

Oh my life,
Is changing every day,
In every possible way;

And oh my dreams,
It's never quite as it seems,
Never quite as it seems.

Carol loosely put her arms around Earl's waist and rested her head against his washboard stomach, to hide the cry, and sang softly to him, as they slowly swayed together:

I know I've felt like this before,
But now I'm feeling it even more,
Because it came from you;

And then I open up and see,
The person falling here is me,
A different way to be.

The room was silent, and tears fell across the sea of faces. Lillian squeezed C's hand, just like her mother had squeezed his hand once before, on that long, dark walk back in the *Jenny Jump* barn. She leaned over and kissed him gently on the neck. Cord looked down at her, wondering which one was kissing him; either was fine, because he loved them both.

Earl was just about the only one not crying; he was smiling wide.

He was the center of attention, but he wasn't afraid at all, not one bit. Not with Carol's head on his chest; it was the best security blanket ever.

Carol lifted her head and looked up at him, smiling with tears on her cheeks. And she sang the next words a little louder, a serenade to him:

The song ended and the dance floor erupted in cheers.

2532

And Earl said something he had never said before, to anyone, ever, but his mom said it was okay, it was the right thing to do, so he did it, 'cause she was never wrong about important stuff like this.

He looked right at Carol, with innocent saucer eyes, took in a big breath, and half-whispered the words, raising his shoulders a bit as he spoke, a half-hide, nervous as the words left his lips. The room suddenly went quiet, with all eyes, and ears, on Earl.

"That was the best birthday present ever, and ever since I first saw you, I knew you were the prettiest, nicest, smartest lady I ever met, I just *knew* it, and I always wished you could be friends with Bibby, but it never happened, but now it did, and I'm so happy you're friends, I always thought you'd be good friends, best friends, like C and I, and so now I was just wondering, do you think, maybe, someday, you could, but I'm not so smart, you see, about a lot of stuff, and I know you like smart people, but I was thinking, maybe, someday, you could maybe pretend, just for a little while, even just for a couple minutes, to be my girlfriend, maybe, 'cause that would be better than the best birthday present ever, even better than the *Knucklehead,* if you can believe it….sorry Mac, but it's kinda true *[Mac was shaking his head yes, eyes teary red]*."

As Earl finished, he winced, raising his shoulders as high as they would go, ducking his head tortoise to hide, not sure if he should ask, right away, for a take-back.

Carol looked at him sincere, not answering for what seemed liked eternity. And then Earl heard her say the words he was most frightened to ever hear.

"I'm so sorry Earl, but I can't be your girlfriend…."

Earl bowed his head in shame.

And Carol ducked down and looked up at him, tears
streaming down her cheeks.

"….because I want to be your wife."

CHAPTER 378 – SHE WAS A VERY GOOD STUDENT....AND A VERY BAD GIRL

Pandemonium broke loose.

The four closest men, because it took four to lift a three-hundred-sixty-plus pound, six-foot-eight tree, hoisted Earl in the air. The *Cabin* ceilings were low, so the effort was better than the effect, with Earl hunched over, his back pressed against the ceiling timbers, all smiles.

Earl was placed, wobbly, back on his feet and immediately looked across the room to Lillian for approval.

"Can I?"

He asked his big sister.

Lillian's eyes were wet; she was still holding C's hand, which turned to a squeeze.

"Earl, do whatever your heart tells you to do, and it'll be alright. But let me just say one thing; I would be honored to have Carol as my sister, as well as my newest, best friend, and I mean that with all my heart."

Lilly turned to Carol, smiled, and continued.

"I just want you to know, I'm happy you're with my brother and I wish you the best, both of you....forever."

Carol skipped across the room and bear-hugged Lilly, whispering in Lillian's ear words meant just for her, followed by a gentle kiss on the cheek. Carol wiped the tears from her face, cleared her throat and made a small confession to the room.

"Now I don't want to come across as arrogant."

The room let out a collective, good-natured groan, to which Carol smiled.

"But I took a chance, a very *big* chance, on a hopeful yes, and booked two first-class tickets to Vegas tomorrow afternoon, so I can be Mrs. Earl Liddell as soon as possible, before our birthday boy sobers up and has a chance to change his mind.

The Cabin erupted in cheers.

"And it has to be in the afternoon, because Earl's getting the beginning of the *absolute* best birthday present he *ever* got in less than an hour!"

Another eruption, all the guys.

"But, to keep it honest, I asked Ryan for a *big* favor, to which he said a quick yes. I want him to marry us right here, right now, in front of all our friends and family, so you can share it with us, and to make our first night together half-legit!"

The crowd closed in on the them, back-slapping, kissing and hugging. Ryan said a little ditty he had prepared, less than ten lines that no one remembered, declared them, by the powers vested in him, semi-officially, but absolutely officially in all the ways that really matter, as husband and wife.

And, with Carol on the tips of her toes, the newly married couple kissed on the lips for the very first time as husband and wife.

In less than an hour, the lights at the *Log Cabin* had dimmed, the cars dispersed and Earl watched Carol slowly walk into her bedroom, drop her silk robe on the floor, and shared with him her own birthday suit, the one he had fantasized about for years. And it was more perfect to him than he ever imagined.

She slid beside him in her bed, their bed, and not-so-quickly, learned firsthand, *every move* that Earl had memorized in the *Kama Sutra* over the past twenty-five years. And Earl wasn't as big as she had feared, he was bigger. To the point, frankly, where she was a bit nervous.

But he was gentle and sweet; a sage *Kama Sutra* professor, who just happened to be a virgin.

And all morning long, she was a very good student….and a very bad girl.

CHAPTER 379 – YES SHE IS, AND SHE MOST CERTAINLY IS

She was in awe, he was in heaven; they were husband and wife.

Carol finally fell asleep in spoon with Earl, sheer exhaustion. She was breathing lightly; he could feel her warm exhale tickle his back.

"Is it okay we talk, *here*?"

"Sure sweetie, it's okay, I don't mind. I'm so proud of you; she loves you very much, and I know how much you love her."

"I loved watching her brush her teeth; she's *very* thorough, you know."

Carol squeezed Earl's hand and smiled.

"And we're going on a plane later, first-class, and I don't even know what that means, but I bet it's *real* good."

Carol didn't answer.

"Hey mom, thank you for talking to Bibby."

"I didn't sweetie, she talked to me; she was finally ready to talk to me."

"How come C can't talk to his mom?   I think he wants to."

"I don't know sweetie, I don't have answers to questions like that; I think he's gotta figure that one out himself."

"Am I really married to Carol mom, does it count?   I want to be married *right now*!"

"Like Ryan said, your married in all the ways that really matter, and you always will be, no matter what. You two are a good couple; I'm so proud of you....you are, you have been your whole life, and always will be, the best son a mother could ever hope for. Thank you."

As she lay sleeping, Earl lightly ran his finger down Carol's arm, barely touching the hair, the skin.

"Isn't she beautiful mommy?   And she's my wife."

"Yes she is, and she most certainly is."

CHAPTER 380 – A NEW LIFE, SO ANXIOUS TO START

Carol laid in bed, exhausted and happy beyond words.

Earl couldn't sit on the news – too excited, like a little kid. Which is why she loved him.

Carol smiled and kissed him goodbye; a quick peck on the cheek that said *see you soon.*

In a flash Earl rolled out of bed, dressed and was out the door – all in a continuous sprint....a beeline to see his best friend.

Carol was still naked, sprawled across the top of the bed sheets. She didn't want to dress, she didn't want this morning to end. But she also wanted to get on that Vegas plane, to be official, walking in the desert arm-in-arm with Earl, showing him off for all to see, side-by-side with her sister and new best friend, trying to convince Lillian and Cord to tie the knot too, right then, right there, beside her and Earl....a best-in-the-world two-fer. She knew it was a crazy thought, but so was everything else that just happened at the *Cabin* and after, in the last six hours or so. Incredible.

And it *did* happen, all of it. They were on a good roll; she wanted to keep it going.

Carol shook her head and smiled at how everything turned out so perfect; that never happens....something always skunks the works. But this time, it did, just as she planned; not a wrinkle, not a blemish.

Perfect.

So maybe the Cord and Lilly marrying *thing* would work out too. And why not, since she seemed to be on a winning streak.

She chuckled at her good fortune.

Her staff had arranged everything: the hotel suite, transfers, marriage licenses, flowers, food, candles, champagne, witnesses, Earl's tuxedo, right down to his socks – in a size that didn't exist on any rack – it was being custom-made somewhere in Vegas as she laid in her bed, by someone she would never meet. But it would be perfect, because she paid the money necessary for it to be so, and then more, just to be sure.

Money took care of all those problems; money took care of *all* problems, she thought to herself, especially her kind of money. And she smiled at her success, smiled at all her achievements, with Earl the crown. It was all worth it now, since she had Earl to share it with.

A new life, so anxious to start.

CHAPTER 381 - NOTHING, AND NO ONE, CAN EVER TAKE THAT AWAY

Carol breathed deep into the pillow, sucking in the remnants of Earl's aroma, his warmth.

How could someone be so good? How could she be so much in love? How could she have been so blind for so many wasted years, letting Earl come and go with each month's rent check? But none of that mattered now. This was a new beginning; how could life ever get any better than this?

She smiled and ran her long, slim fingers ever so slightly over the soft and tight-trimmed hair covering her crotch. She had more than most; the *fashionable* thing was to be shaved clean, or some minimal patch or line; she thought that was silly and far too much work. So she had more hair than most – not a lot – just more. And she liked it that way. And, apparently, so did Earl.

But she would change it in a moment. She would shave her crotch clean, make it a line, a patch or whatever shape Earl wanted. All he had to do was ask. Because it was Earl's, only his, *forever* his; she gave it to him this morning, and now he owned it - to have as much and as often as he wanted – no limits, no conditions. Full surrender.

And she was sore, but that was her own doing. She simply couldn't get enough of Earl; pent desire, released at last. And boy did he release it. She didn't know whether to thank, or curse, that damn book.

But one thing was for certain; God, she was *so happy*.

She silently thanked Lillian and her mom, Sam, Ji-Sue, anyone and everyone she could think of, including Chicken.

But as she lay content in bed, a teenager making snow angels atop the silk sheets, feeling the coolness on her bare arms and legs, she most of all gave special thanks to the man who made it all happen, brought the two of them together, the man who served up the love of her life.

With her hand on her heart, nestled between her breasts, she said aloud, for Zeke, Big B, the rest of the cats lounging on the bed with her, and for anyone else who cared to listen to hear:

Earl is my husband,
Earl is everything to me,
Thanks to you, Mr. Brin.
You are a pain in the ass, most of the time,
But when you're not....you're really not.
And I now know, thanks to you,
What a kindred spirit means.
We share one, you and I.
He is the greatest, most important gift
Either of us have ever received.

Carol sighed, turned, kissed Earl's pillow and finished:

And nothing, and no one, can ever take that away.

CHAPTER 382 – A BAD DECISION MADE, SEALED WITH A TANKED HANDSHAKE

Sunday, October 8, 2006; day one-hundred seventy-two, and all was quiet.

Marty was still hung over; his head was cloudy, but in heaven. He was running radar on a sleepy Sunday morning, the Town cocooned safe in a blanket of fog.

That meant no speeders to chase, no reason to do anything but relax, listen to soft rock spilling from the cruiser radio and move his hips slightly up and down, as Ji-Sue buried her head in his lap, quietly blowing him.

She was so good, so smooth; he wondered if it was just her, or maybe it was an *Oriental* thing. *She was his first Asian*, he primped to himself, never acknowledging, in his own mind, that he hadn't had any other lips around his cock besides Warren County farm girls, and even that set numbered a grand total of three, with the total blow count amongst them, in aggregate, at less than ten. Marty's cock never got much of a workout, at least by others. His hand and his cock were lifelong friends; other than that, it was pretty lonely down there.

But no matter, with Ji working him, he still felt sophisticated, worldly....*chiefly*. And his cock was lonely no more.

He tried, unsuccessfully, to rub Ji's crotch, through her thick, baggy jeans. But her position was awkward, and his arm, twisted at a klutzy angle, soon began to ache. It wasn't worth the effort, so he gave up the endeavor, and just enjoyed the ride solo.

Ji-Sue couldn't take his entire cock in her mouth; Martin was simply too big. But she always tried, and now and then gave a little involuntary gag, if she went too deep, which always made Marty proud.

No one was allowed in the front seat of the cruiser; departmental policy. But *Acting Chief* had its benefits. And as long as no one pulled alongside to chat, Martin's front seat little helper was safe. He aided that cause by tucking the ass-end of the patrol car deep into the wood-line along the bank of the Pequest, so you could barely see the car, let alone saddle alongside. So there he sat, in his favorite spot, on the unpaved, no-name dead-end stub road that branched off Water Street, just as you entered Town and the Pequest River slowly arched away from the road, meandering into the woods.

Martin was excited, thinking about the conversation he and Ji had with C at the Cabin, just hours ago. He recounted aloud, as Ji-Sue continued to work.

"Can you believe it? I can't wait to go! Right?"

Ji's muffled *uh-huh* came through a full mouth.

"I wish I hadn't drank so much - I can't remember all the details; maybe C was only kidding and will retell us, at least just the pieces I might not remember so well. What'ya think?"

"Uh huh."

Was all Ji said; talking around his cock was a bit of bear.

Marty didn't remember exactly how it happened; last night was a haze. But somehow Cord was at the bar, it was three-deep, talking of trips C had taken here and there all over the world, as he often did when asked. Somehow, the topic turned to a trip Martin and Ji could call their own, just for the two of them. Martin asked for a truly special trip, something *really* different, that *no one* else had seen, or heard-of, ever before.

C sat back, looking at the floor, thinking. Then he looked up at the ceiling. He stared blank and thought, for awhile, as if he was contemplating something. But he didn't say a word.

Silence.

Cord *knew* he shouldn't be telling this tale; not *this* one. To Martin, Ji-Sue or anyone else. Maybe it was a mistake; no, he *knew* it would be a big mistake - this one would certainly have repercussions.

But he did it anyway. He's not sure why, but he did.

Maybe he was just a little too drunk, in too good a mood for his best friend on his birthday and for himself with Lillian; maybe it was just too good a day, about the best day he had in a long time. Maybe ever, likely ever....definitely ever. Maybe he was feeling more than a bit infallible.

He thought to himself: *A man can't be much more than truly content, that's about the best there is, about as good as it gets.* And C was; he *really* was. Maybe for the first time since he was eleven years old, and was in love with a little knobby-kneed girl named Kristine.

He shook his head; it was a sad shake. Then he sighed.

Or maybe he was simply tired; tired of all the rules, tired of the game, tired of trying to figure out the characters that swam in his head, and what the whole fucking point really was. Maybe he was ready to finally throw in the towel, throw away the box, like Lilly said, and just say:

Fuck You!

to whomever was listening between his ears. Maybe he was ready for it all to end, on *his* terms.

Maybe it was a little of both, maybe it was a little of all-the-above.

So with that, C served one up, just for Martin and Ji-Sue, but under strict conditions.

No notes.   He and Ji could go to this special place, a place he had *never* shared with another soul, only if the conte was committed to memory, on the first try.   There would be no seconds; Cord would tell the story but once, and would never repeat the directions again.   And they could repeat them to no one else, ever.   And if they forgot a piece, well then he guessed they weren't ever going to get there.   Those were the rules, Cord's rules, which really weren't his at all.   C figured the risk was low; they were both toasted, and no way could they remember everything he was about to say.   That was his contingency, and he figured it was pretty solid.   Plus, how could they *really* go, really?   Therefore, the slip was safe.

And those were rules to which Martin Brewer, stone drunk, heartily agreed.   And so the conte began.

A bad decision made, sealed with a tanked handshake.

Of course C remembered *all* the details, he always did. Especially this one. A dream he could never shake, with details that would never change.

Hemmed in amongst the boisterous rabble at the bar, Cord leaned into Martin and Ji-Sue; he spoke low, a shade above a whisper, to add to the mystery, the intrigue. Not a soul heard a word of what C was about to say, except Martin and Ji-Sue....and, of course, those listening, most curious, inside his head.

And as the words began to spill, the puppet smiled wide.

"It's a most-remote stretch of beach, uninhabited. To that end, it's not manicured, raked, swept, prettied-up in any way; this is no fake.

It's natural, raw and unkempt, littered with never-ending rolled and knotted lines of seaweed, mixed with driftwood - raw and charred – from tiny twigs to man-sized logs. Thousands of sea grapes, like marbles, tangle in the rock-weed, like flies in a spider's web. The few that escape trundle lazy in the surf, slowly rolled up and down the sand by each succeeding wave.

And mixed amongst it all is a sea of detritus. But there is beauty even in the debris; it simply depends upon how you view it.

Perfect tiny white spheres, baby blue bottles, cream cups, purple flowers, orange blossoms, all plastic - some exposed, some buried - but all stretching forever along the beach, in all shapes and sizes, a veritable rainbow, washed ashore from a thousand points unknown.

And within are mixed a quiddity, different every time. Perhaps it will be a doll leg, dismembered from its parent, or a stretch of nylon rope from a long lost buoy. Surely there will be solo shoes, flip-flops mostly, separated from their mates, mangled by the surf. But the shoes are always solo, and that's a bit sad, isn't it?

If you look close, I'm sure you'll see a plastic tooth, or perhaps a plastic nose, in the shape of a snow cone, or both. Most come in the color gray. Plastic bits of disparate body parts, from where they come, and for what purpose, is a mystery. But come they do, to this special beach.

It is a pumpkin patch of finds, buried in sand so fine, so loose, you'll sink half-foot with each slower step.

Fiddler crabs will skitter through the littered landscape, half-hiding from the sun. Tiny striped lizards, little dinosaurs, will dart in and out of sight.

And pelicans will surely join your jaunt, brown, lazy and flying low over the shallow surf, fishing now and then, when the urge finds them.

You'll walk by all of it, and more, on your way there.

[C paused a bit, leaned back, took a long drain of his drink, and leaned back in]

And amongst the sea of detritus weave and wind the freshest green tendrils, sporting tiny trumpet flowers, in shades of orange and purple, just beyond high tide, at the edge of a tangle of fresh green scrub brush, nearly impenetrable. That is, except for the single, narrow stria, a barely-wide footpath, almost imperceptible, carved inconspicuously in the sand.

[C paused again, and whispered an octave lower]

But we are getting a bit ahead of ourselves. The journey really begins at the dirt road, off the paved path.

I'll get you to the dirt road - I'll get you that far; I'll even give you the coordinates for same *[C leaned in even closer to his audience, and whispered the fateful digits],* but you must understand, those numbers, those latitude and longitude coordinates, they are *extra special* - they simply don't exist on any map you have ever seen, trust me. They lead into, open through, what you might describe as a *special door*, and I'm the *only one* who can get you there; there is no direct path there from here, *none*, except through me. I'm the conduit, the *only* conduit. If that doesn't make sense, then good, it means your listening, because it's not supposed to make sense. Not here, but it will *there*, trust me.

Proceed careful off the paved path, onto that special dirt road, and follow it faithful as it twists and turns through the scrub, getting narrower and narrower, for several miles, maybe a bit more, until it squeezes so small that you have to abandon your vehicle, and make your way, the balance, on foot. Bring your belongings by backpack, and pack light. You won't need much. Follow the footpath as it constricts even further, like a boa-choke, until the understory scrapes and chafes your sides.

But don't stop....keep going. If you pay attention, and believe, the path won't lead you astray.

And in a bit, and you'll have to determine what a *bit* really is - I won't divulge - the foot path will seem to squeeze even further, until it seemingly disappears into nothing. But don't fret, simply push just past the *nothing*. Only when you're there will you know what I mean, for what you think must certainly be the end isn't....there is further to go, to get you to the prize.

Which is the beach I just described, *my* beach, which will now be *your* beach - I'll give it to both of you – to have, *forever*.

And you will be *all alone*; not a soul exists in any direction, as far as you can see, nothing....absolutely nothing but that which I already described.

Trust me, I know.

And once you leave that footpath, and the scrub, and spill onto that beautiful white sand, and all the *tarnish* buried within it, you'll point to the right, due south, and the beach, seemingly endless, will unfold before you.

Start walking slow in the afternoon sun, and just keep going.

I won't tell you how long a jaunt it is; that, my friend, you must figure on your own. Just don't give up.

Eventually, in the distance, you'll spy the beginnings of a single, lonely structure, which, as you approach, will slowly grow, like a phoenix, from the craggy lava-like rock to which it is anchored.

It is the remnants of aluminum truss-work, like some misplaced power pole, rising into the sky, topped by a lone beacon….a single, shining star. A crude lighthouse. Who built it and when, I simply don't know; it was there long before I arrived. But whomever they were, they are long gone; that I do know.

Long, long gone.

Go to the star.

The craggy base upon which the aluminum truss-work is perched is pocked with holes, eroded by the endless pound of the surf. Some are the size of peanuts, others a bowling ball, all on their way to caves, a thousand years forward. But for now, it is a pockmark of shallow surf pools, dots full of tiny shells and soda cans. And set amongst the pools is a second concrete platform, cracked, worn, broken and empty; the footprint of a *former* lighthouse, long gone….forgotten.

Stand on this second concrete platform, on the spot of a lighthouse that once was, but is no more. Here, there is a small circular survey marker, weathered bronze, set in the stone - it marks the middle. Stand directly atop it, and gaze down the shore; spin your head a mere quarter-head turn, but *not a fraction of a turn* more.

Study the scene carefully.

There will be an inlet, then another, followed by a third; this third inlet is at the quarter head mark. Be careful, take your time and absorb the information – study the shoreline; it sounds easy to find, but it's even easier to miss.

At that point, and *only* from that vantage, about thirty feet above the high-tide line, at the edge of the brush-line, look carefully, and closely. If you are lucky, you will barely see the speck of a corner of what looks like a ramshackle hut.

And maybe it is, *just maybe*.

A structure not visible from the lighthouse that *is*, but only from the lighthouse that once *was*. And barely so, just barely.

Make your way to that ramshackle hut.

Be careful, because the walk to get there is a zig-zag through and beyond the craggy inlets. Don't lose your place, your position, trust me, it is very easy to do. Otherwise you will have to retrace and start again at the missing lighthouse. And if you retrace, and try again, you may not see that speck of a corner of what looks like a hut, it doesn't always show itself. *Others* decide when, and if, you see it. And they rarely give second-chances.

My suggestion, get it right the first time, because you may not, may *never*, be afforded a second. And then you're stuck, like you're on *Free Parking*, in *Monopoly*, with no dice to roll, forever. Trust me, *stuck* is not where you want to be.

*[C sat back and let the information absorb like alcohol
into his drunken friends]*

So remember:

*find the lighthouse that is,
then find the lighthouse that was,
then find the inlets – first, second and third,
find the speck of a corner of what looks like a hut,
and then stroll to your prize,
barely buried in the bush.*

CHAPTER 384 – FOR CHRIST'S SAKE, REMEMBER THE GOD-DAMN RULES

You'll know when you're close.

Vines with rubber leaves, the likes you have not seen on your journey, or *anywhere* else, suddenly appear and crawl through the sand, all about you, festooned with a sea of purple *Victrola* flowers. Brilliant orange trumpets mass over a thicket of bushes.

This is where you duck in, but be careful....*very.*

There will be no footprints in the sand, no visitors, except for the occasional tracks of a single feral dog, a bit too skinny, endlessly scavenging this beach, and this beach alone.

He visits, just him. He will not bother you, as long as you observe the rules. Leave him scraps if you like, but don't encourage him, don't engage him, and by no means should you *ever* touch him - let him be....that is a rule.

And that rule simply cannot be broken.

Beyond the first line of scrub, you'll spy a series of concrete fence-posts, each shifted to a staggered slant in the sand, a drunken line. Three parallels of rusted barb wire, mostly there, corral cattle that are long gone. The prior pasture is now wild, overgrown, with standing water puddled here and there; random pools scattered across the former field.

And there it is, to the left, just past the cattle fence.

[C stopped, downed the balance of the Scotch, and ordered another free-pour, a Cabin special]

It's just a decrepit shack; nothing more than a lean-to really, with a crude, three-step ladder, the first and last rungs too high, and too low, to use. The structure is framed with washed-up beach wood, worn sea-boards and scraps of same, helter-skelter, carried by currents from origins unknown, all held together with rusted nails and strands of baling wire.

The roof is thatched with degraded plastic tarps, ripped and torn from beach wind and forgotten storms....so fragile it crumbles to the touch. The tarp is tatooed with *Linea Caballos* - the circular phrase encompasses a sneering stallion head, in colors blue, white and yellow, all faded from the sun; it is stamped here, there and everywhere, all about the plastic burlap - a hole-ridden, stallion-riding babushka.

Black birds, something like a crow, or a raven, but really neither, the likes of which you have never seen, nor will see anywhere else, may adorn the lean-to peak from time to time. They will come and go as they see fit. Never disturb them, never feed them and don't stare at them; just let them be. That is also a rule that cannot be challenged.

And Martin, Ji – be sure to remember the rules; for Christ's sake, remember the God-damn rules.

CHAPTER 385 - *LAY QUIET, AND SLOWLY TAKE IT IN*

The supports for the hut lean heavy to the north, sturdy enough, but just for quiet sitting and listening to the break of the distant surf.

[C stared hard at Martin]

Not sex. This is **not** a fuck-shack Marty, there's no fucking, not on there, not *ever*….understand? I can't stress that enough; you can't ever do that in the hut – *ever*. Or there will be consequences. Understand?"

With a single nod, the *Acting Chief* acknowledged to rule; but to be fair, Marty really didn't understand a thing C was saying, as the bar, C's face, and the rest of the crowd surrounding him blurred into one messy abstract, rotating in a slow, counterclockwise arc.

"Fuck like rabbits on the beach, fuck in the scrub, fuck in the surf - I could care less, but *not* in the hut. The lean-to is for reflection, contemplation; it's meant to be cathartic, therapeutic, redemptive. And we all need a little of that every now and then, don't we *[C shook his head, sad and slow]?* Think of it as a lunch and siesta shanty; s*tay, lay quiet, and slowly take it in.*

CHAPTER 386 – MAKE IT YOURS....*FOREVER*

Beside the hut is an old fire pit, littered with burnt logs and chips, from fires past. There will be no footprints, and there are no visitors, but you may see a fire; it will come and go, every now and then. Don't ask how it starts, or dies, and don't ask why. Do not tend it, do not touch it, but you can watch it; sit by it, but just for a bit. And under no circumstance should you ever attempt to *make* a fire on your own; do not use that pit....*ever.*"

Marty looked through C with glassy eyes. Both he and Ji shook their heads silently and answered a collective yes to a question that wasn't asked.

"To the left of the fire pit, there is a small path that disappears into the scrub-brush; it will be hard to find at first, but trust me....it's there.

Follow it.

You'll wind and weave for a bit, till you come to a small clearing, where you'll have a *feeling* that something is waiting there, just for you, some sort of prize. And it *will* be there, but at first, it will look like....nothing; just a quiet clearing in the middle of endless low scrub. Small puddles of water will sit in the chalky white soil, ugly, yet beautiful.... if you can look *past* the ugly.

Remember, both of you:

You do not take a trip;
a trip takes you.

Always remember that. Steinbeck did.

And this trip certainly does; it will take you places you can't believe exist. You just need to *believe.*

And if you do, believe, if you *truly* do, without doubt, without resolution, then find your way to the center spoke of that special place, that little ugly clearing. Close your eyes and slowly turn three-hundred-sixty degrees, slowly tilting your head down, then just as slow up, you will finally understand why I sent you here. I can't describe what you'll see, or what you'll feel, because it can't be described in words, it can only be felt, it can only be *understood*. And only *you* will ever know what it is.

But I can tell you one thing, for sure….what you find - you'll own it, and it will be yours....forever. And that will be the second-best day of your life."

And Cord abruptly stopped; the story was over, and he had immediate regret at the telling. But, as usually happens in situations like this, he quickly whisked away the worry, knowing the story was nothing but an exercise that would never happen, and the risk he had misgivings about, was no risk at all – it was the trio's little secret, already half-forgotten by the both of them. And with that, he picked up his rocks glass and milked the balance of the neat Scotch refill, long and slow.

Marty and Ji looked at each other, unsure of the abrupt end.

Martin's eyes were glazed; Ji spoke softly to C, her hand gently touching his arm.

"But C, why it *second-best* day? What the *best* day?"

C looked at them both, Marty with slit, bloodshot eyes, raised his empty glass and tilted it slightly in a half-toast to them, and a *half-fuck* to the bastards in his head, and smiled.

"The day you decide to go, and make it yours....*forever*."

CHAPTER 387 – A DECISION WAS MADE; THERE WERE NO TAKE-BACKS

"I remember a lighthouse, right? And don't wear flip-flops, but then you stand on it and spin around three times, and look at the shore, but don't feed the dog or something about birds, that aren't really birds, or something like that, but don't do it anyway, whatever it is you think you should do, for God's sake, don't do it, or you're in big trouble!"

Marty rubbed his head.

"Christ, that doesn't make any sense; I gotta stop drinking. Do you turn left or right? Jesus, what country is it, even? Do you remember?"

By this point, Ji stopped mumbling answers around his cock. Her jaw was sore, her back ached and she just wanted him to finish, so she picked up the pace, *always* a sure thing.

That got Marty's attention.

"Whoa, whoa....too fast! Slow down....stop, *stop **stop**!*"

Marty arched his hips away and tried to grab her hair to stop the Ji-piston. Radio static crackled in the cruiser cab.

"10-0....10-20 Depue - south end....10-91V....the usual suspect; 10-67....the usual complaints. 10-49 to 200 block STAT."

Ah, a reprieve. Ji-Sue quickly seized the opportunity and sat up, her jaw relieved, her sore back straightened. She silently thanked the dispatcher.

Marty, on the other hand, had a different reaction.

"Fuck! Are you kidding me?!"

The radio responded.

"Chief, are you tied up? It's the dog again; he's out, already got two scared calls. Better get over there, STAT."

Marty yanked the mike off the holder.

"Yes I'm tied up! I'm right in the middle of something! Christ, nobody else available?! Where's Lloyd?"

But he already knew the answer; in his drunken stupor earlier this morning, he raised his glass at the *Cabin* and pulled a *King Cole* - drinks all around - and gave the whole force off today, in honor of Earl's fortieth; that much he *did* remember....shit! And he remembered the cheers, and Lloyd giving him a big bear hug and a sloppy kiss on the top of his head. He couldn't remember any of the God-damn details he needed to remember about the best trip ever, about where to turn, what to do, or where to go, but he could remember *that*....Lloyd's sloppy kiss on top of his head. *Christ*!

The radio response was loud and clear....dead-silence, as the dispatcher patiently waited for *Acting Chief* Martin Brewer to process.

Fuck he thought to himself, trying to find someone to blame for this mess; *stupid booze* was all he came up with. He let out a long sigh and depressed the mike button.

"Okay, okay, I'm on my way....10-4."

He slammed the hand-piece down.

"I swear, that fucking dog is dead. This time he's done; this time, he crossed the God-damn line."

Marty spit the words as he shifted back and forth, pulling up his pants, trying not to catch his swollen cock in the zipper. Then he turned to Ji-Sue and put on a puppy-dog face, touching her cheek lightly, as if he were doing her a favor.

"Sorry sweetie, I'll let you finish later, okay?"

Ji, chuckling inside, and thinking exactly what *all* women think about such man-child comments, smiled politely and didn't say a word.

Depue Street was about as far away as you could get from where Marty had planted the cruiser in the weeds, opposite corners of a one-square mile town. He sighed angry, put the car in gear and made his way through the wisps of gray mist hugging the ground along Water Street.

He didn't switch on his lights, sans siren, until he made the dog-leg at South Water Street, where it and Depue Street met. The blue and red beacons cut the fog, but Loki was nowhere to be found. Marty opened the windows full, front and back, cut the radio and slowly crawled up Depue, heading south, downstream. He could hear the loose gravel slowly scratch and claw, pinched between worn black-walls and pavement, like a conveyor.

He was going no faster than five, the speedometer needle barely off the zero pin. He strained his ears, and his eyes....looking, listening for anything.

Nothing.

He could smell the Delaware as he approached the boat ramp; it was earthy, flowing hard and fast. But he couldn't see it; he couldn't see much beyond a car-length in any direction, his ken shrouded in miasma.

He heard nothing, except the endless pluck, hiss and squeeze of gravel bits beneath his wheels. Depue Street felt strange, other-worldly, a malevolent aura. Ji got a bit spooked, and grabbed Marty's arm, to feel safe.

The cruiser passed the entrance to the boat ramp, on the right. And Ji jumped a bit, as she noticed something large, something strange, moving at the fringe of the mist, too far away to really see. But the outline was too big to be anything else; the movement too familiar to be mistaken. And she relaxed, fear swept aside by a comfort rush.

"Hey, there's Earl, it looks like he's carrying something!"

Ji pointed excited, as if it meant something; what, she had no idea.

Marty leaned over her lap and caught a glimpse just as Earl crested the ramp, heading toward the water. Earl never turned; he never saw Marty's cruiser, and quickly disappeared down the ramp, out of sight.

"He's okay, if the dog was nearby, he'd have gone after him."

"Should we warn him? Tell him, you know, to be careful?"

Marty hesitated, as the thoughts boomeranged his head: *What the hell was Earl doing out here, at this time of the morning, in this weather? What was he carrying? Why was he here – shouldn't he be with Carol?*

As he thought, and thought some more, his fingers tucked into the door handle, about to get out of the car, to run down the ramp and warn Earl about Loki, to find out what the hell he was up to. It was strange, why he was out in this early morning fog, and none of it made any sense. But for some reason, and he wasn't sure why, Marty didn't get out of the car, he didn't warn Earl, he didn't do anything he *thought* he would, or should. The questions and concerns in his mind faded without further action, and he withdrew his hand from the door handle, as if it wasn't his own.

And his attention instead turned to Loki: *the dog, I need to find the dog, deal with the fucking dog, then Earl has nothing to worry about, and I'll fetch Earl later.*

All at once, Marty felt anxious, a will-less body assault. He needed to get this dog-killing over with, once and for all, and end this nonsense. A feeling of urgency engulfed him, like a wave.

He'd cruise to the other end of Depue, past Second Street, just before Fourth, to the white-trash dump where Loki lived, and shoot the fucker. He usually rummaged the trash a couple doors down from No. 260A, on the river side; they never covered their garbage cans – Marty had warned them a dozen times, but they were also lazy white-trash, and never gave a shit.

The road at this end of Depue narrowed; it was still two-lane, but barely, just wide enough for two cars to skirt without hitting mirrors. And although you could pass-through this part of Town – it wasn't a dead-end, per se – no one did, not on purpose, anyway. A lost soul every now and then crawled by, on their way somewhere else.

No one came this way, down this road, by choice, except those unfortunate enough to squat here, and Marty or his boys, on their patrol-rounds about Town, or trolling for the dog after yet another complaint to dispatch.

The road was more pot-holes than not, and most of the houses were shit rentals, absentee landlords who had never been to Belvidere, bought sight-unseen and run into the ground. Just about all the tenants parked their cars on the road, a mix of old-model American-made rust-buckets, dented, dingy and faded. Most didn't run; half had flats that stayed flat.

It had the feel of an ulcer....a festering blight.

Martin was getting close, and his pulse quickened. He crawled the cruiser to a quiet stop and cut the strobes, three doors down from 260A, socketed between the curb and a long line of cast-aside cars. The street was still on a sleepy Sunday morning, encased in a thick soup of fog.

He put the car in park, in the middle of the street and listened hard; he was right-as-rain.

The soft, metallic rattle of the overturned trash can came from afar, ahead and to the right....a stone's throw, just out of sight.

He quietly opened the driver's door, stepped onto the street, and unsnapped his holster; he wasn't going to be denied by faulty snaps, not this time. He slid the revolver out and held it tight beside his leg – safety on; he could count the number of times he had ever unholstered on the job.

His heart was hammering hard; beads of sweat dimpled his forehead. Ji sat upright, motionless in the front seat, anxious, afraid to move, her eyes the size of saucers, waiting scared for something, *anything*, to happen.

Somehow she gathered the courage to close the two windows on the river side, leaving the two facing Martin, in the street, open wide.

Marty stood in the road, sheriff-showdown-style, waiting for his foe. He edged closer, half-a-step at a time, homing toward the rattle around the corner. And within ten steps, he saw the bottom of the overturned, dented metal can, still rolling side-to-side, being worked by a forever hungry dog for whatever scraps lay inside.

But the open end, and the enemy in it, were still out of view, hidden by the front left corner of the house, and foundation shrubs, ratty and overgrown.

Loki was close; Loki was just about done on this Earth.

Marty took a deep breath, processing what to do. All his training, all the years of practice for situations just like this, and he was unsure....logic, and decision, escaped him. Should he rush, rapid-firing in motion, or slowly swing to the left, to get a better view for a static long kill-shot, or should he just wait? Maybe he should lie in the street and assume a camouflage stance, legs spread, belly down....prone.

Maybe, maybe, maybe.

By the fourth maybe, he noticed the metal roll stopped; the can had gone quiet. And he heard nothing, nothing at all. An eerie silence swallowed the street, and Marty with it.

The safety unlocked.

Still silence.

Marty was staring hard at the end of the can, it was warped and morphed by the mist, and he couldn't tell if it was still moving, ever-so-slightly, or if his mind was simply dancing, playing tricks. He froze, concentrating on the still end of the rusted can, waiting for Loki to turn the corner, eye-to-eye.

Nothing.

Then Marty heard a low, evil growl behind him, just as Ji screamed his name.

Loki had circled behind behind the house, behind the cruiser, and was less than a car-length, two bounds away at best, from Martin's throat.

The fur on his shoulders and massive back stood straight, strings of saliva fell from his mouth, sharp teeth filled the void. Loki knew this thing standing in front of him was not a friend; nothing that stood on two legs was a friend.

"Kill! Kill!"

Ji screamed as Martin swung and pointed the barrel square at the mass of muscle.

And although it shouldn't have, there was no reason to, Loki seemed to hesitate for a full half-second, more than long enough for Martin to pull the trigger and bury a bullet in the dog's brain, and end it, once for all.

No question.

Loki gave Martin the chance....the easy shot.

But Martin Brewer didn't use it.

That split second was not spent squeezing the trigger; it was spent remembering a promise to a life-long friend. A *cross-your-heart* promise, the most serious promise ever, the kind you can't take back....no matter what.

In that mere half-second, with room to spare, Martin remembered his conversation with Earl, all of it, because a half-second is a lifetime, in times like this.

Martin remembered the promise, *his* promise to Earl; he remembered it all:

"They're gonna hurt him, Marty, I know it. Even though what you told them, they're gonna...."

"I hope not; I'll keep a better eye on them Earl, promise. They're bad people, white trash [Marty shook his head]. But I promise, I'll take him away next time, for good, promise. Maybe we can bring him out to the farm."

*"Really? Really Marty?! He'd **love** the farm, with all the barns and fields and hay and I could run all around with him and roll in the hay and stuff! He's a good dog, I know it!"*

Marty just looked at him, wondering how Earl could see any good in that animal.

"How about we just keep him in the old hay barn, off the far corn field, down by the creek? He'd be happy there, right?"

Earl looked at him, incredulous.

"You can't keep him in there Marty, that's all by itself, by no one; none of the other animals would get to play with him. He's gotta be all over; he's gotta be free, that's the only way he'll be happy, I know, when no one's kicking and whipping him anymore, and ignoring him, and just rubbing and scratching his belly in the sun."

"And how do you know all this, huh; is that what you two were whispering about?"

Marty cocked his head, looking at Earl. But Earl looked down, at his feet, and shrugged his shoulders.

"Nah, I just know; some things you just know. And I was telling him I knew he was a good boy, deep down, and I loved him, and I was gonna take care of him some day, just him and me, friends. We could lay on a blanket together and everything, in the field out by the cows, and even take a nap together; I could use him as a big furry pillow! He's nice and soft, you know, if you hug him. I told him to be patient and don't hurt anybody and maybe we'll get to play together, you know, lots, lots and lots. He knows, he knows; he's just waiting."

Marty smiled at his friend.

"You'll bring him to the farm, and you won't let anyone hurt him anymore? You promise, no matter what....promise?"

"I promise."

And Marty reached out and placed his hand gently on Earl's chest, on his heart, and did a little cross with his pointer.

"I promise."

And Earl exhaled a sigh of relief, a big one, with an even bigger smile, because he knew Marty didn't lie, especially when he talked like that, like he just did, in that tone, and especially when he did the cross! Earl knew that was some serious stuff, the most serious promise ever; that's what his mom always used to say - when you do the cross on your heart - now that was serious stuff, and Marty knew that. There were no take-backs on that kind of promise, no matter what.

And that's when Earl knew, for sure, Loki would be safe someday, and happy. Earl just hoped it would be soon, real soon, so Loki could start playing. Loki had a lot of catching up to do.

And in that half-second, in Martin Brewer's brain, life changed forever.

A decision was made; there were no take-backs.

CHAPTER 388 – HE NEEDED IT FAST - HE NEEDED IT BAD

Loki blitzed Martin.

His mammoth head caved Marty's mid-section, knocking him off clear off his feet, jaws gnashing and ripping his shirt, tearing and ripping the flesh on his chest, like it was butter.

Loki could have easily killed Martin, right then and there, he could have shifted his weight, swung his body to the left and crumpled his skull in one, maybe two bites.

Easy, quick and done. Loki could have, but, for some reason, he didn't.

Instead he swung to the right, toward the river, toward his feet, and Shanghaied Martin's right leg, like a bone, tossing him rag-doll, left and right, his pants shredded and red with the beginnings of blood and bone, which soon flowed free, which only enraged Loki further, stoking his instinct to kill.

Somehow, amidst the fury of the attack, still holding his revolver in a death grip, Martin got off a single shot.

It was the first, the only, time he had ever fired a bullet on the job, for real. Not at the shooting range, tagging paper targets out by the Town dump, behind the municipal pool, but on the streets, for real, in the line of duty.

And in that one, first and only shot, Marty saved a life.

His own.

Despite the mauling, not realizing how badly he was gnashed, Martin really just wanted to scare Loki, to get him to stop the break-face, the thrashing. He didn't mean to shoot him.

On his life to Earl, he really didn't.

The bullet rang out, grazing Loki's rear quarter, who immediately released his grapnel on Martin's leg. Without hesitation, the assault ended; Loki turned and bolted, running as fast and hard as he could away from the crack of the revolver, a bee-line down the center of Depue Street, upstream, due north.

In a moment, he disappeared into the gray of the mist, and the scene was again deathly quiet.

Martin was in a daze, prone on the cold, shrouded street; his hearing oddly muffled. Shock had set in.

He looked down and saw his midsection stained red, quickly fanning capillary, a rapid soak spreading spider across his shredded white shirt. The sight of blood nauseated him; he couldn't help it, never could. His stomach felt queasy, and his head light. He wanted to touch his stomach, but was afraid of what he might feel, so he didn't.

His right leg was weightless, like it wasn't there; he thought it strange. There was no pain, just a sense of numbness, but that really didn't describe it. Maybe it was like an amputee feeling a limb long gone; he didn't know that feeling, but had read about it; maybe that was this feeling.

His mind was wandering for what seemed like hours, but was really only seconds.

He struggled to sit up, then stand, to see if he could put any weight on his leg. To his surprise, he could, just barely....it felt tingly, like he had little control. He looked down and saw his pant leg was ripped and splayed; he couldn't see the blood, but he knew it was there, lots of it; the navy fabric was soaked, sticking to his leg like wet *Elmer's*. His lower leg looked a bit odd beneath the pant fabric; he couldn't describe it, but it didn't look quite like a leg should look. Maybe it was swelling.

He looked over at the squad car; Ji was ducked down, hiding in the front seat. He couldn't see her, so he yelled.

"Call dispatch! Tell them to send help! Tell them I'm after Loki on foot – heading for the boat ramp….hurry!"

Martin should have gotten into the car, put it in reverse, and barreled down Depue backwards, since the road was too narrow, and littered with junker cars, to turn around.

It would have been quicker, and he could have called dispatch himself.

That's what he should have done.   But he didn't. He wasn't thinking clearly, he was operating on adrenaline, and his instincts told him to run, to hop, to walk, to fucking crawl, as fast as he could, into the fog, to find the damn dog.

And at that moment, he realized, somehow, that Ji-Sue might not know how to use the dispatch mike, so he screamed behind him, as he hobbled down the street, into the mist.

"Push the button! Just push the button on top!"

He hoped she heard him, that the instructions made sense, and that she made the call. Because he needed help; he needed it fast - he needed it bad.

CHAPTER 389 –
HUNGRY….THIRSTY….SCARED

He was just hungry and thirsty and scared. That was all he ever felt.

Hungry....thirsty....scared.

Every minute of every day. Always the same. No end.

And he was usually cold, or he was hot, because he was kept outside twelve months a year, in all weather. On a short leash, in a round dirt circle-rut, that he scribed over and over. No grass, no trees, no shelter.

Nothing.

Always the same.

And if he wasn't getting whipped with a stick across his head, or shot at in a drunken rage, or kicked in the stomach or his back legs, by the people inside the fence, he was being taunted from outside the fence; white-trash kids, who threw rocks at him and rattled the chain-link, ran away, and came back to shake it some more. Forcing him to defend a dirt-patch territory he didn't want, but had no choice but for instinct.

He wasn't safe, in or out. He wasn't safe anywhere.

But sometimes, now and again, he would get himself off that chain.

He didn't know how, but running in circles endlessly, tugging and barking, somehow, sometimes, it would let go, and he could magically run outside the dirt circle.

So he ran as much as he could, in circles, and barked, until it would magically happen.

And when it did happen, he would beeline the fence, hurdle it, and run two doors down, where he could eat, drink and be safe from a beating. And then he would run further, and further still, looking for more food, more water.

More and more, as much as he could.

And he would attack anything he thought would stop him, anything that would bring him back to the dirt circle, to hurt him all over again.

He would attack anything that looked like what starved and beat and scared him his whole life. Anything that walked upright; anything that looked like a person.

This Sunday morning he wasn't even running, or barking. It was quiet, and he was just walking in a slow endless circle, boredom and hunger engulfed him as he half-tugged on the forever chain. He was about to lie down in the cold mud and just quietly shiver for awhile, because there was nothing else to do.

And then he heard a single *clink*, the kind of sound that only happened after he ran hard and endless in circles, barking. It never happened unless he did that.

But somehow, without doing any of that, it just happened, as he walked slow; the chain collared to his neck simply fell, harmless, into the mud.

And he knew what that meant; it meant he was free.

So he ran, jumped the fence and, like always, hoped to never go back. Ever again.

So he wouldn't ever again be hungry....thirsty....scared.

CHAPTER 390 – A BAD LITTLE GIRL; AND
THAT SHE WAS

Ji-Sue hadn't told Martin; it was going to be a surprise.

She was hoping he'd finish, that he'd come in her mouth, so she could stop sucking his cock, sit up, rest her jaw, and tell him the good news.

She had been drinking too, at the *Cabin*, for sure. But she *wasn't* drunk, not like Marty, not even close. And she was paying attention to what Cord said, unlike Marty. And Ji-Sue had a *very good* memory.

So she recalled every detail of what Cord said. Every last step, every forbidden coordinate….all of it.

And she secretly wrote it all down, in the ladies room, right after Cord toasted his empty glass at the end of the telling-of-the-tale. She had excused herself, sat on the toilet and wrote every last word, shoving the illicit paper in her purse. She was sure she hadn't forgotten a single important fact. She knew she wasn't supposed to do that, it broke C's rules, but she wouldn't tell anyone; she would just memorize it, rote, practicing until it was as easy as reciting her address, then she would toss the notes, the incriminating evidence, and no one would be the wiser.

That part of it felt bad, but more of it felt kind of good, *pretty good*, in fact.

She wanted to be, for once in her life, a bad little girl; and that she was.

CHAPTER 391 - DEAD

Ji would talk to C and book the flight later today; she and Martin would be on the plane tomorrow.

She couldn't wait to tell him, she couldn't wait to pack, to get on that plane, to find the beach, find their paradise, the best day of their lives was today, because they had decided to go….just like C had said.

Today was the best day of her life.

And this whole stupid dog thing put a big damper on her plans, delaying the surprise. That's what she was thinking when the dispatch call came in on the radio, when they crossed Town in the early morning mist, even when they saw Earl at the boat ramp and slowly crept down Depue Street in the cruiser, like stalkers in the night.

She had been thinking it right up to Marty getting out of the car. Then she stopped thinking about it. Because it had been replaced by fear: fear of the unknown, fear of Loki; fear because she knew Martin was scared too.

She remembered seeing Loki, and yelling: **Kill! Kill!**

Right before the dog attacked.

She was frozen in utter fright, saddled upright in the driver's seat, watching as Loki mauled Marty, tossing him back and forth like a doll on his back in the middle of the darkened road. She wanted to scream, but she too afraid to make a noise, her eyes glued to the action....immobilized.

Then she remembered hearing a tiny crack, like the snap of a little twig. That she remembered; that's all she remembered.

But she didn't hear Marty yell to her to push the button on the mike, to call dispatch, to call for help. And she had forgotten all the notes of their special trip....every last detail.

Ji-Sue was simply lying quiet, face up on the front seat of the cruiser, her eyes wide open and white, the size of saucers.

The single shot that saved Martin's life, that clipped Loki's rear quarter, had continued onward, through the cruiser window and slipped quietly into the middle of Ji-Sue's brain, where it finally stopped to rest, forever.

She was dead.

CHAPTER 392 - NEVER WOKE UP

He didn't know where he was; he didn't know how long he'd been there.

He was face down on a soft, thick mattress of wet, dead leaves. Something was poking his right cheek; another pricked his neck. He came to realize, without seeing them, that they must be twigs; he was somehow proud of himself for figuring that out.

He was a good cop.

Martin laid still, unmoved, as the fog in his head tried to clear.

He could hear the constant rush of water in the distance and recognized it like one recognizes a particular smell, that takes you, non-stop, to some immediate place, some memory. That sound was the *Rift,* or more particularly, the water queuing above *Foul Rift,* before the big bend in the river, just downstream of the boat ramp.

He had played in these woods countless times as a kid, running up and down the shoreline, in and out of the woods, weaving along narrow paths, dodging gnarled tree roots, traipsing through the poison ivy without a care, like kids do, and smelling the honeysuckle in the early summer. God, the smell of honeysuckle always brought him right here, to this place. He figured he must be close to the old stone drainage tunnel, just downstream of the boat ramp; it was probably right near where he now lay. It, the tunnel, was huge, to a kid anyway, built of oversized river stone in a wide graceful arch. It was their medieval fort, with one group of kids or another always trying to capture and hold the tunnel from the enemy, when they played *War* in the woods.

The tunnel was home base; the tunnel was safe.

That's what you all yelled at the top of your lungs when your team captured the tunnel. No one remembered who said it first, and why that meant the tunnel was yours, but some kid, at some point, said it....and it stuck.

It meant you were golden.

And no matter what type of *war game* they were playing: cops and robbers, cowboys and Indians, good guys and bad guys, you always wanted to capture the tunnel, to hold the tunnel, to yell that *easy peasy* chant into the roar of the river beside the boat ramp.

And regardless the set-up, no matter how big the crew of kids, Marty always played the good guy, on the good side....a lifetime of wearing white, which morphed to Belvidere blue.

Boring, but good; it seemed his lot in life.

With his face down, Martin couldn't see the tunnel, but he could somehow *sense* it; it was *that* close, and that made him feel better. God, he hadn't been here, in these woods, since he probably twelve years old, more than a quarter-century had passed since he last saw that magical tunnel.

He wished he could see it now; for some reason it mattered. But Marty couldn't seem to get himself to lift his head. He was simply too tired.

He heard the lilting call of a downy woodpecker, hiding somewhere in the woods, followed by the lonely caw of a single crow. A blue-jay jumped in, and repeated an angry bark, over and again, annoyed at something; blue jays were always annoyed at something.

His mind wandered and he began to remember a stumble-run in the fog, following the distant bark of the dog, too far ahead to see. His right leg was throbbing, and he left a trail of blood-crumbs down the center-line of Depue. That much he remembered.

But how he ended up here, in the woods, by the tunnel, was a mystery.

At some point, he must have run off the road, into the woods, toward the river, toward the sound; he must have thought Loki was this way. But he didn't remember that part, or falling down the steep ravine, to the bottom, where he now laid, cut up and pinned amidst a large bramble of angry wild rose and that same patch of poison ivy, that grew there year after year, that never left, for decades, as if it was waiting for him to come back and play.

There was no sign of Loki, not a sound, just the constant dull roar of the distant Delaware. It sounded angry.

Martin Brewer needed to get up, to find the damn dog. He had so much to do, if he could only dislodge himself from the tangle of pickers. Ji-Sue had called for help from dispatch, it was surely on the way.

She was a good girl.

Martin knew he had to get up, to get going, but it was overridden by the urge to simply close his eyes, to rest just a bit more, to go to sleep. The Delaware rolled on by, like a lullaby:

Easy Peasy Lemon Squeezy

lazily circled his head; it made him feel good, golden, like a kid, all over again, defending the tunnel....home base.

Martin thought about that beautiful tunnel and closed his eyes; he went to sleep.

He never woke up.

CHAPTER 393 – SMILED AND PULLED THE TRIGGER

Lloyd got the word from dispatch. The call came in from someone on Fisk Street; anonymous.

Always anonymous.

That dog was hung up somewhere on the Georgia-Pacific property, along the river; they could hear it howling.

The Chief's radio was silent; no word from Martin....dispatch was worried.

Lloyd was still hung over, and struggled to get dressed. He didn't get lucky at the *Cabin*, despite valiant efforts, that became more desperate as early morning came, the clock was winding down, and last call was barking at the *Cabin* door.

He was embarrassed for himself at the lines he threw in the water down the stretch, at the blow-pigs he propositioned, but even they turned him down. So he ended up home alone, with his dick in his hand.

So he was angry, and hung over, and mad at Martin for getting him out of bed after promising him the day off. Lloyd had anger management issues, and now they were on steroids.

Half-dressed in his uniform, disheveled, he barreled through Town and soon found himself near the bridge, on Fisk Street, crawling toward the dead-end at the old Georgia-Pacific parking lot, abandoned and overgrown. He rolled open his window and the fog seeped in as he made his way across a quilt of grass growing in alligator cracks that spread across the forgotten macadam.

And when he got to the far end of the lot, nearest the river, a hundred yards upstream of the bridge, he heard it.

A whimper, a low whine, a dog in trouble….a dog that was hurt. A dog that needed help.

He exited the cruiser and walked slow, gun drawn, toward a grassy knoll, that quickly sloped down to an overgrown freight rail, before the ridge dropped steep and ended fast and hard at the river.

Lloyd stood quiet, and triangulated the faint whimper of the dog. Two steps, wait, two steps more.

He saw Loki.

He was beside a fallen sycamore tree. Loki must have slipped into the immense divot created when the majestic, speckled white and tan tree toppled; the root mass had pulled a cleft of soil the size of a small car. The mud was slick, and the hole full of tangled roots, leaves and rock. The dog lay shivering in the bottom, in a puddle of stagnant water, his leg bloodied and twisted in a way that meant it was broken.

Broken bad.

He was just trying to get away, as far away as possible. To never go back again.

Lloyd knew the dog; everyone in Town did. And he hated it.

But it was hard to hate this dog, hurt, vulnerable, with sad eyes, wanting nothing more than to be helped. To stop the pain in his leg.

To feel safe.

Lloyd slowly, carefully made his way into the cleft; the sides were clay; wet and slick. If he wasn't careful, he would end up in the bottom, lying beside the dog.

He got about ten feet away, and Loki lowered his head onto his front paw, eyes half-closed. He had never done that before, and he was afraid of this person, because he looked like all the other people that hurt him....over and over again.

But this one was different. He felt it.

So Loki submitted, and waited to be saved.

Right up until Lloyd smiled and pulled the trigger.

CHAPTER 394 – HE WASN'T SURE WHY THAT WAS SO, BUT IT WAS

He remembered everything, every last detail.

He wasn't sure how that suddenly happened, how his head cleared and his mind was sharp, but was happy it did; he'd take it.

He was barefoot, in his favorite shorts and navy muscle-tee; both were loose and comfortable. His bare feet sank softly in the warm fine-grained sand as he left the narrow scrub-trail. It must have been noon as he stepped off the path; the sun was directly overhead.

The beach seemed to stretch forever; the surf was gentle, waves quietly lapping in the distance.

His eyes followed the never-ending rolled and knotted lines of seaweed, mixed with driftwood and sea grapes the size of marbles, all set amongst the detritus - a veritable rainbow of plastic, bits and pieces washed ashore from a thousand points unknown. It ribboned in both directions, as far as the eye could see.

Cord was right; it was beautiful.

He stared at his feet, half buried in sand; he saw a plastic tooth....he saw a plastic nose.

Fiddler crabs skittered through the littered landscape, half-hiding from the mid-day sun. Tiny striped lizards, little dinosaurs, darted in and out of his ken. He saw a half-dozen, without really trying.

A brown pelican, solo, flew low and lazy over the shallow surf. It didn't fish, not this time. He watched it till it disappeared into the haze of the horizon.

There wasn't a soul in sight, in either direction.

He turned to the right, started walking, and kept going. That is, until he saw it; it seemed like hours, but then again, it seemed like minutes, because both felt the same here, in this wonderful place. He couldn't describe that feeling; he had never felt it before. It was strange, yet comforting.

Seemingly from nowhere, far on the horizon, a single lonely structure emerged from the craggy pocked rock to which it was anchored. It looked like aluminum truss-work, like some misplaced power pole where none should be, topped by a lone beacon.

Just as he expected.

He soon found himself there, amidst the pockmark of shallow surface pools, filled with tiny shells and soda cans. He stood quietly where he needed to stand, where he was told to stand, on the second platform, the footprint of the former lighthouse; it was cracked, worn and empty.

Just as he knew it would be.

He straddled the small bronze survey marker and gazed a quarter head-turn down the shoreline, not a fraction more.

And he saw the first inlet, then another, followed by a third. Thirty feet above the high-tide line, at the edge of the brush-line, he saw the speck, which he knew to be the corner of what was a hut.

A very special hut.

He carefully walked, zig-zag, knowing he had but one chance to get it right; knowing there would be no second chance to find the pot of gold.

But he was confident he wouldn't fail, more confident than he had ever been in his life, about anything. He wasn't sure why that was so, but it was.

CHAPTER 395 – LAY QUIET AND SLOWLY TAKE IT IN

He was close.

The vines, with rubber leaves, the likes he had never seen, suddenly appeared and crawled through the sand, all about him, awash in a sea of purple *Victrola*. Brilliant orange trumpets massed over a thicket of bushes.

Just as he remembered.

There were no footprints in the sand, except a single set of tracks from a dog. They seemed to appear from nowhere, originating in the vines, near a small bleached tree, and wended their way toward the hut.

And he remembered the rules:

leave him scraps if you like,
but don't encourage him,
don't engage him,
and by no means should you ever touch him;
let him be -
that is a rule that simply cannot be broken.

He quickly ducked into the first line of scrub and saw the drunken line of concrete fence posts, the rusted barb wire, the overgrown pasture. And just past the cattle fence, to the left, there it was. It was just as C described.

There stood the lean-to shack, with a crude three-step ladder, the first and last rungs too high, and too low, to use, framed in washed-up beach wood, held together with rusted nails and strands of baling wire. The roof was thatched with ripped, storm-worn plastic tarps; *Linea Caballos* was stamped here, there and everywhere, just as he knew it would.

A single black bird perched the peak, something like a crow, or a raven, but he knew it was neither. He quickly turned from the bird and lowered his eyes, because that was a rule that could not be challenged.

He thought to take a respite, his legs were tired and the sun was warm; the hut was inviting and a siesta felt right, to stay, lay quiet and slowly take it in.

CHAPTER 396 – THE BEST DAY, WHICH BECAME EVERY DAY, FOR EVER MORE

But he didn't; something told him no.

It was a voice in his head, one he didn't recognize; actually it wasn't a voice as much as it was a *feeling,* there was no other way to describe it. But he knew it was a feeling he had no choice but to heed.

He saw the old fire pit, littered with burnt logs and chips, from countless fires past. There were no footprints, but the logs glowed a dull red, from a prior fire, on its way out.

To the left of the pit he saw the small path that disappeared into the scrub; it was hard to see at first, but he found it. And he followed it.

He wound and wove for a bit, the scrub-brush scratching his arms and picking his sides as he walked along. In short order, he found himself in a clearing, *the clearing,* expecting to find his prize.

But what he found….was nothing.

Nothing at all, just a clearing in the middle of endless, quiet scrub, with puddles of water dotted in chalky white soil; ugly, yet beautiful, once he looked past the ugly.

He could hear the muffled lap of the ocean surf beyond the scrub, beyond his eyesight. The black bird lit from the hut, flew over his head, letting out a single throaty call, unlike anything he had heard from a bird before. Then it was gone, and he was alone, in the middle of the clearing. The air was thick and humid; he began to sweat more than he already was.

And then he remembered Steinbeck's words, as C described them:

And at that point, he believed....without doubt, without reservation.

Martin slowly closed his eyes and began to spin, three-hundred-sixty degrees, arms extended outward, as he tilted his head down, then up.

And as he slowly spun, he thought of *Easy Peasy, Lemon Squeezy* and cross-your-heart promises, the kind you keep forever, and Marty began to smile. For it was then that he felt it, that he understood it.

Martin was finally, truly happy.

He opened his eyes and smiled at Ji-Sue, lying in the sand, her head buried in the plush of Loki's thick belly-fur. He was asleep, content, his paw lying gently atop Ji-Sue's arm. He had a full belly of food, he was warm in the afternoon sun, and most important, he was free, and safe, with best friends who would love him....forever.

Martin walked over and kissed Ji lightly on the cheek and laid quietly beside her, his hand rubbing and scratching Loki's belly. Loki opened his eyes, yawned, stretched long and lazy like a happy dog does, and closed them again to nap untroubled; he had a lot of catching up to do, and forever to do it.

The three of them slept together under the tropical sun, with the roll of the surf a distant lullaby, for the rest of the day, which would last forever.

It was their second-best day, which was also the best day, which became every day, for ever more.

CHAPTER 397 – WHAT HAPPENED, HAPPENED
- THAT'S ALL THAT MATTERED

It happened *there*, sixty-three days ago.

But time is different *here*.

In fact, there is no time; it's not called that, nor measured in that way. Or any way, come to think of it. So in a sense, you could say that it had just happened here.

Or maybe it happened sixty-three days ago, early in the morning, on August 6th.

But that made little difference here, because there was no such thing as August 6th; there never was, nor would there ever be, an August 6th here. Here, the game simply played, on and on, with no such thing as a beginning, and no such concept as an end.

So what happened, happened – that's all that mattered.

CHAPTER 398 – HE JUST SAT AND WAITED....SCARED SHITLESS

Button found himself sitting quietly in the dark, naked, on the edge of a slight, single bed, covered with a worn, brown bedspread. The pillow and sheets were disheveled and held just a tinge of what remained of body heat, as if someone had slept in them, had gotten up, and had just left, moments before. And it was somehow clear to him that whoever that was, wasn't coming back. *Ever*.

It was a bed he didn't know, in a room he'd never seen. He wasn't sure how he got here, or where he even was.

But he knew, instinctively, that he didn't like this room; it had a *bad* feel.

He looked down and noticed his skin was unblemished, like a baby, not a single mark marred his hide, nary a mole, scar, smudge or stain remained....wiped clean. Every freckle, flaw and bruise, every defect of any sort accumulated in life, and all the stigma, disgrace and dishonor they held were seemingly washed away....gone from the surface, forever.

His tattoos had all disappeared, not a trace remained. The arrowhead-shaped birthmark on the underside of his cock, his signature....gone.

He was a pale virgin canvas....*perfection*.

He sat still, simply absorbing the scene, and himself.

Beside the bed was a single window, which faced the street. He was apparently on the second floor. The window was open, the wire screen down, letting in the fragrant night air. His instinct was to run, but he didn't bother; he somehow knew the screen would stay shut, and he knew he couldn't leave the room via the hallway.

He somehow knew that too.

He was all alone. So he just sat and waited....scared shitless.

CHAPTER 399 – AND THEN THERE WAS NOTHING

It felt like an Indian summer night; a slight night breeze wafted the room. A steady drone of crickets hummed outside the window, hiding out there, somewhere, unseen in the dark.

It was a beautiful summer night, but it had a decidedly different feel.

That's when Button heard, distinct from the blackness beyond his window screen, a lone cricket, hiding somewhere, unseen, *in* the room....the room he now found himself in.

It chirped quietly, irregularly, almost hesitantly, a genetic need to mate apparently tempered, conflicted, by caution. He found himself straining, arching his head to trace its origin, to try and separate the chirp inside from the medley of calls outside.

It was *so* close; the cricket must be under the bed, he thought, maybe even in the bed, under the covers....it seemed *that close*.

And then it stopped. As if it knew what was to happen next, it just stopped.

The long side of the bed lay directly against the outside wall, the top tucked just beneath the windowsill. He turned his head to the left, and gazed between the upturned slats of the Venetian blinds; the warm summer air gently kissed his cheek.

Billy Bones blinked his eyes hard, several times; he rubbed them with his thumb and forefinger, and blinked some more. Then he slowly grabbed the blind rod, turned it clockwise, and rotated the blinds, just a bit, to open his ken to the quiet street below.

He scanned the scene; the crowned asphalt tar road looked to have been recently chipped. The new layer of white and gray quartz gravel hadn't yet been driven into the base tar by passing traffic - it lay thick on the road in front of this strange house he found himself in. He saw a simple black lamppost adjacent to the driveway and a curved concrete walk, which led to a three-stepped field stone and mortar front stoop, covered with a portico, sporting a weathered Dutch hex sign. The heavy, six-panel wood entry door was painted a dulled yellow; the brass knocker in the shape of a lion's head.

The lamppost was dimly lit with an amber bulb, which cast a soft yellow halo around its base, barely extending into the shoulder of the road, the driveway, and the walk.

He turned his head slowly to the left, and gazed down an empty street, to a lonely intersection, about hundred feet away. There wasn't a car on the road, nor a soul to be seen.

A lone streetlight illuminated the intersection; a large, thick pine, over a hundred feet tall, stood abreast the street post, which was too far to read. There were three houses across the street within his view, all cloaked in darkness, all seemingly asleep.

The lamppost and streetlight lumens were the only glow to pierce the night; the crickets the only sound to reach his ears. The warm night air continued to blow silent through the tiny holes in the screen; he felt it gently kiss his cheek.

It was a serene setting, a perfect night. But Billy had already decided he didn't like this place, or this dream. Not one bit.

Button ran his hand up and down his arm, he felt his own touch; it felt real, it felt conscious. Nightmares don't feel like this.

He turned and inched closer to the screen, raising the Venetian blinds slowly, as quietly as he could, so he could put his face against the metal meshing, to get a better view of what lay below.

Nothing.

He saw nothing but the quiet street scene, just as before. He kept his face there, pressed lightly against the mesh, looking left and right, up and down, for any evidence of *anything*. Any reason to explain why he was here.

Nothing.

Until he heard it. A slight, ever so faint, whisper, in a deep baritone.

It was as if someone had pressed their lips against his head; the moist hot breath tickled the tiny hairs inside his ear, the tongue lightly flicking his skin as each word was spoken, like a lizard, a snake. It was a simple phrase, presented in a maniacal tone.

"I'm going to get you."

He instinctively pulled his cheek from the screen, to get away from something he couldn't see, that wasn't there. And once again it was silent, and stayed that way, for ten seconds, maybe a bit more.

Then a second whisper followed; this one the high-pitched shrill of a malevolent child.

"I'm going to get you!"

Billy felt himself slowly pulled, involuntarily, back to the screen. He couldn't stop - iron filings to a magnet.

Again he canvassed the road below. But nothing was to be seen, just the glow of the lights and the tickle of the night breeze.

Nothing.

Except for a single cricket chirp, the one that must be right beside him in the bed; *it was very, very close.*

But still, out of sight. A single chirp, then again, silence.

He peered out the window, straining his eyes, first to the right, up the street; nothing but ink. He looked to the left, down to the majestic pine by the street post, at the intersection.

And that's when he saw it first move into the open, from behind the conifer.

It was a neatly dressed little man, with a bow-tie, jacket and matching pants, but he looked too small to be an adult, and it wasn't a child. It didn't even look human. It looked like an oversized doll, some sort of man-puppet.

He squeezed his eyes shut and open again. It **was** a puppet.

It had exaggerated facial features, painted in once-bright colors, with a hinged lower jaw. It wore an overall dinge, dirty, unkempt, neglected….forgotten. It stood motionless under the dim glow of the streetlight, slightly hunched, head bowed, as if a battery switch was toggled to the *off*.

It had the disturbing look of an old *Danny O'Day* ventriloquist doll.   The creep-face was frozen in an expression that wasn't happy, nor was it forgiving, nor was it kind. It was somehow *off;* it somehow didn't *look* right.

And this puppet stood upright, alone; there was no puppet-master to guide it.

Then suddenly, as if it came to life consequent to Billy's gaze, the puppet slowly raised its dirty, dimpled chin off its chest and looked up, with round eyes, yellowed and bloodshot. It swiveled its head and gazed right toward him, right into the second-story bedroom window, eighty feet away. Its mouth was closed, its eyes dead.

And then he heard the frightening whisper, the same whisper he heard twice before. Its high pitch cut through him.

Now he *knew* from where it came, and the words were so crisp, so close, it sounded as if the puppet was sitting right beside him.

"I'm going to get you!"

With that, its over-sized eyes opened extra wide and rolled back in its head.

It had real eyes!

It sprung open its jaw, like the ugly snap of a bear-trap, exposing a wide-open mouth, with a full set of brilliant white teeth. It slowly swiveled its head left to right and quickly snapped its mouth open and shut, over and over, its teeth making an awful gnashing sound, all while it laughed in a demonic, shrill howl.

The mannequin slowly started to walk up the street, toward the house, in a herky-jerk, stop-motion manner, like a marionette without strings. Every ten steps or so it would stop, slowly swivel its head and look up at the window, drop open his mouth and rapidly gnash its teeth together. He could hear the loose, road gravel crunch under foot as it ever-approached.

The doll left the dull orb of light at the far street corner; he could still hear it kick the gravel with each footstep, but it was hidden in the shadows of the night. Out of sight, but getting closer….and closer.

In the darkness, he would hear it stop and click its teeth, followed by a demonic, high-pitched laugh…he knew it had swiveled its head and was looking at him.

He just knew it.

Billy quickly closed the blinds, turned his head and squeezed his eyes shut. It *must* be just a dream, just a bad dream. He rolled the thought over and again in his head, trying to convince himself it simply can't be real. Gulping the suddenly-stale bedroom air, his chest heaving, his mind racing, he struggled to devise a plan, wondering what to do.

That is, until he noticed everything had become quiet once again.

Button didn't hear the gravel kick, or the whisper in his ear, or the sickening laugh. He waited, frozen, straining to hear something….anything.

But he heard nothing.

He exhaled a long sigh and again looked at the window. The blinds were again turned slightly downward and the window was open, just as it was when he first found himself in this strange place. The crickets were lightly chirping again and the warm night breeze licked his face.

He *did* dream the whole thing, thank God. He let out a long breath. And for a moment, he felt foolish. But the feeling turned to apprehension; he wondered if it would all happen again.

And with that, he sat frozen, breathing quietly, waiting for the cricket hidden in the room to announce itself, a single chirp, like it had done before, before the bad things began.

But nothing happened; no chirp….nothing.

2599

He stared at the ceiling, blinked, and felt his heart beating normally. He smiled in relief, like one does when awakened to realize it had all been just a bad dream.

Just a bad dream.

But then his mind began to wander; why does it always have to wander? He tried to reason, to make sense of all that had happened, or hadn't happened, that night. To reason where he was, how he got here....and why.

And the wandering led him to this; he just had to be sure.

He leaned over to the window, turned the wooden rod clockwise and slowly opened the blinds to see. His heart raced just a bit as the blinds rotated away and the leitmotif unfolded before him.

The street was quiet; he looked down to the left – down to the towering pine at the intersection, and the road was empty and safe. He smiled and an uplift of calm washed over him.

As he smiled, Billy's gaze casually fell toward the amber glow of the lamppost, below his second floor window, to the light that was never on; but now, it was.

And that's when he saw it. It was in the front yard, adjacent the mountain laurel, just below the window by which he sat.

Its oversized head slightly askew, there stood the man-puppet, with yellow, bloodshot eyes. It was so close he could see the gray lint lay in the wrinkles of its jacket and pants, along with a smudge of grime across the peel of its painted face. It was as if it had laid in wait, in a dirty, forgotten place, for this night to finally arrive. To finally meet Billy Bones.

When it knew he was looking, it deliberately swiveled its head in a quick-jerk and snapped open its mouth, showing him a full set of corrupt, malignant teeth.

But now, somehow, there seemed to be many more of them filling the widened gape of its mouth; they massed angular, sharper....dangerous. The once brilliant-white had morphed to yellow and stained, with the earthen-brown tinge of rot spidering the roots, coated opaque with a thick film of saliva.

He didn't hear the crickets anymore; all he heard was a low, deep whisper in his ear.

"No more silly games; now I'm going to get you."

Followed by the sickening click of its teeth, and the shrill laugh of a child possessed. Long stria of drool spilled from its mouth, dangling as they made their way to the ground, pooling at its feet.

Button's blood chilled as he again froze in fear; he couldn't move his arms or legs.

He watched helpless as the doll advanced in a jerk-motion up the concrete walk, mumbling and laughing quietly to itself as it climbed the three steps on the porch. He heard it grab the doorknob and jiggle it; he could hear it out the window - at the same time, he heard the noise down the hall, from within the house.

The door was locked; someone must have locked the door!

He heard the faint sound of whispering and a sickening snicker, like one who talks to himself in demented amusement, while assessing the task at hand.

He strained to put his head against the window screen, to see if it got in....to see where it went, what it was doing.

Then he heard faint scratching on the wood shingle siding, and he knew it must be crawling up the side of the house.

He jumped back and tried to shut the window, but as much as he leaned on it, it wouldn't budge. He didn't try to call for help; he knew that was useless.

He was utterly alone.

The scratching on the wood shakes was getting closer; it must be just below the window, barely out of sight. The closer the puppet got, the more he felt himself pulled toward the screen. He couldn't stop himself, his face was pinned fast against the mesh, the metal pressing into his cheeks, checkering his skin.

The scratching was close now, it was *right* below the sill, inches from his face. His eyes were wedged wide open, he couldn't shut them. He heard a *click-click…click-click* of its teeth and a sickening light laugh, followed by its deliberate, slow, breathing, labored breathing, followed by a slight giggle and a mumble of incoherent words that made no sense:

Kitty Cow Go Moo

The puppet was *so close*, inches below the sill, but still out of view. He could smell its disease….a putrid mixture of mold, canker and rancid meat. In a moment, it would be less than an inch from his face, separated by the wafer thickness of the wire mesh screen.

Why was it waiting?

Billy tried to scream, but no sound emerged.

He heard it chuckle, just once, right as he saw the slight curve of the top of its head, the oily mat of filthy brown hair, just below the sill.

He knew it was ready to come right through the screen, and he was helpless to stop it. His heart pounded, waiting for it to attack, to sink its razor teeth through the screen, into his face, and tear him apart.

He was immobile, stuck to the screen, eyes glued open, staring straight ahead, waiting for the reaper to slowly raise its head above the sill, its dead eyes to meet his.

Then he heard nothing.

The top of its head had disappeared; he heard not a single breath, nor trace of a chuckle....the smell of death faded away.

There was simply nothing.

And it remained so for what seemed forever, but really was simply seconds. Because where he was, where Billy Bones found himself, time worked like that, because it wasn't really time at all, it was something else. Something entirely different, which didn't have a name.

And then the nothingness ended.

Outside the window, he heard a distant click of teeth as the big wooden front door creaked open and slowly click shut.

The puppet was *in* the house!

His face peeled from the screen, like a magnet switched to *off*; he collapsed into the bed, and immediately craned his neck to listen. There must have been some sort of swinging, wooden door to the second floor, on an old metal spring, somewhere near the entry foyer.

That door must have been closed, because he heard the spring slowly creak, strain and stretch as the door was carefully swung open, followed by the same sequence as the spring relaxed into itself and quietly tapped shut, tempered by an unseen hand. A second of silence was soon followed by the dull thud of shoes on a stairway carpet runner, accompanied by the creak and moan of old, wooden treads, as the puppet began its ascent to the second floor.

One step, two steps, three, then stop. Billy had no idea how many steps lay between it, and him, but he knew it had stopped on step three.

He thought to run, but his legs were again leaden....useless.

It began moving again, climbing steps four, five, six, followed by a childish giggle and a triple-snap of it's teeth.

Followed by nothing.

A cat meowed – a single call. It was followed by a short giggle and a mumbled whisper. Another faint meow followed, cut short by snapping teeth, then silence. Billy never heard the cat again.

He peered out the bedroom door, down the short length of hall. A small nightlight in a baseboard outlet provided thin illumination, nothing more than a dim orange haze, which barely washed the far corner of the hall, where it turned ninety degrees and extended to points unknown, and ultimately, he suspected, to the stairwell the puppet climbed.

He looked for a weapon, something, anything, but there was nothing, just a pillow and blankets. Billy heard the distinct tap of its shoe on the hardwood landing; it somehow got to the top of the stairs, but he didn't hear a step beyond number six. Maybe there *were* only six; he simply didn't know.

It sounded close to the blind corner; once it reached the bend, it was a straight shot, down the short hall to the bedroom, with its open door, to where Billy sat.....waiting. His heart was pounding; there was nowhere to hide.

He heard it for the last time, a snicker, with the clicking of its teeth.

"I'm going to get you."

The puppet finished the words just as its leg came from around the corner. Billy Bones closed his eyes hard and imagined dying.

Everything went black, and it was quiet once again; no more footsteps.

Button slowly opened his lids and spied the hallway; there was no laughing, no sickening click of its teeth....just silence.

No puppet.

From the corner of his eye, at the bottom of the bed, to the left, he saw a small lump in the comforter; it might have just been a fold in the blankets.

That fold wasn't there before.

He stared at it, intently, mixing in the murk of the room. It seemed to rock a bit, back and forth, but he couldn't tell, since it was swaddled in the shadows. Did it really move?

He felt control of his legs, but was afraid to sweep his limb toward it, or away from it; he just sat there frozen, for what seemed forever, not moving a muscle, waiting

for something to happen. His legs started to tingle; they
had fallen asleep.

He stared at the fold till his eyes saw double;
staring....staring hard at the folds in the dark, his heart
racing.

And then the fold in the comforter started to move; it
was *clearly* moving. And it **wasn't** a fold; something
was in the bed, hiding under the blanket. And it was
slowly moving toward him. It looked to be the size of a
cat, a *large* cat.

Involuntary, he slowly found himself going prone on the
bed; he could do nothing to stop himself, nothing to halt
his movement. His head turned toward the end of the
bed, eyes locked on the moving fold.   It had stopped,
and was now lilting left to right, as if waiting for Billy.

Then, without warning, like the scurry of a roach, it tore
right at him, scratching and clawing the sheets beneath
the blanket as if it had talons. He squeezed his eyes shut,
held his breath and tried to scream.   Not a sound
emerged from his lips.

Nothing happened.

Billy Bones chest heaved in fear, but the room was again
eerie silent. He slowly cracked open his left eye, barely,
peering through his eyelashes.

The lump under the blanket had grown in size, and was
now *inches* from his face, separated only by the
thickness of the fabric. He could hear it breathing; light
fast breathing, as the blanket moved in and out. A small
wet circle of saliva emerged in the fabric, which slowly
started to grow. The room smelled rancid....the smell of
death.

Whatever hid below the blanket began to rise beside him, the blanket falling away, revealing utter blackness in the void.

A shape emerged, and he saw it, followed by the same four words, in the shrill of a tortured child:

Kitty Cow Go Moo

The hair on his neck rose and he screamed silent.

The last thing he heard, before it went black, was a *click-click;* the last thing he saw was yellow, red and white….infinite white.

A lone cricket, hiding in the room, lit; its single chirp came and went. And then there was nothing.

CHAPTER 400 – AND THE GAME PLAYED ON

Where was he?

He could see, but the eyes he used weren't his. They were bloodshot….and dead.

His skin crawled, even though he had none, a sort of quivering flesh-creep that he couldn't shake; there was no other way to describe it.

And he wasn't alone. He could feel that there were others with him, faceless, countless others, thousands - too many to count. They weren't beside him, they were somehow *in* him, and at the same time, he was *in* them, and they were *all* inside one another, inside here, within this thing, whatever *it* was. An ulcerous nest.

And he, and all those with him, were looking out through the same pair of large, lifeless eyes.

And then he heard the gnash, snap and click of teeth, followed by a demonic, shrill howl, a laugh he knew. And the gnash and the laugh, they weren't directed at him, they came *from* him.

And all the hatred, taint, tarnish and perversion that Billy Bones had accumulated and absorbed his whole life had seeped and soaked inward, absorbed into this *thing*; every vice rolled and morphed into a festering, malignant rot. Compounded by the thousands of corrupt souls beside him, that came before him, he swam in an endless sea of evil.

Evil incarnate.

And, like a light, he suddenly realized where he was, and what he had become. And he finally understood. He, along with the rest, directed their attention, focused their energy forevermore, on a single source, as they danced and hid in the folds of their prey's brain. Someone he knew well.

Someone whom of late called himself *Cord Brin.*

Billy Bones smiled wry, spying through spidered eyes; and with it, the puppet snickered as its head swiveled back and forth and its razor teeth slowly clicked, one, two, three times.

And the game played on.

CHAPTER 401 – I LOVE YOU TOO

"Hey C, *wake up!* *Wake up!*"

Earl yelled, barely inside the apartment door and out of breath from a crosstown sprint.

C rolled off the couch and hit the floor in Earl's apartment, half-wrapped in a blanket, naked, save his boxer briefs.

"I went up to your apartment, but you weren't there, because you're here! Hey, where's Lilly?"

C rubbed his eyes, yawned, then raised his arms above his head in a long cat stretch, as he answered.

"Passed out. I put her to bed; struck out again. I swear I'm cursed with that girl. How did *you* do?"

Earl just smiled through a blush. C smirked through a second yawn.

"You lucky, lucky dog; was it as good as you hoped?"

"It was **hard work**! All those moves, doing it for real, you gotta be in shape! Sorry C, but I don't think you could really...."

"Okay, enough! Jesus *[C shook his head]*! I would settle for a quick poke, in and done, at this point."

"Hey, I talked to *[Earl smiled wide]*, my wife, and she wants you and Lilly to come with us this afternoon, on the plane and everything! She got the tickets already, yours too! Wanna come, *wanna, wanna, wanna*? Maybe you and Bibby could get married right next to us! What'ya think? Wanna, wanna, wanna get married too?! I was so excited that I couldn't wait, so I ran over to tell you; wanna come? Huh? Huh? Huh?"

[Earl poked C in the chest, one for each huh]

"I haven't even tagged your sister yet; not sure if she's quite ready for marriage, but thanks for the invite. Why didn't you just call? And stop poking!"

"***You don't have a phone!*** And if you were down here *[Earl smiled sly]* I didn't want to bother you, 'cause you might be *doing-it!*"

C just looked at him and frowned sarcastic, the kind that says *no such luck*.

"Plus, I wanted to tell Chick all the news! She missed out on the party and everything and I didn't think that was very fair, so I wanted to tell her myself, first thing, but Carol wanted to redo some of the moves I taught her all over again this morning; boy am I tired! I barely got out of the bed alive! I think she's a crazy sex-addict! Just like the people in the book! I've read about girls like her, guys can *die* that way you know, just saying."

"Really, I wouldn't know."

C said, deadpan.

"And boy can she moan! Loud and long! Over and over and over, like a fire engine siren or something; the cats all went running, and I don't blame 'em! And the best part, I can't believe I forgot to tell you what she can do; it's amazing, upside down and backwards, she can *actually....*"

C put his hand up.

"Earl! You gotta stop talking about that; I don't wanna hear it! Jesus, I gotta get laid, I seriously gotta get laid; your sister better wake up, sober up and put out....*fast!*"

"You know, I think Bibby's read my *how-to* book too, all sneaky and stuff, and if she did, boy you're in big trouble!"

"I'm okay with a little trouble like that, trust me."

C said, shaking his head.

"Anyway, I wanted to tell Aloysius the news; he's gonna be so happy! My mom said he's down at the ramp, waiting just for me, **right now**! She said she'd come down to the ramp too, like old times, when we used to feed the ducks together. She hardly ever comes to the ramp with me anymore; this must be *really* special! I wanna bring Chick down in the Sherpa, so she can finally meet Al before he leaves, and the ducks, and my mom too! I know it's early and everything, but we don't have much time before we hafta pack and leave on the plane. So can I? Can I bring Chick? Can I *[three more chest pokes]?* I won't be long; my mom said it could be a quick trip, then I'll run and tell Carol you guys are coming with us to Las Vegas, right? And maybe getting married too?! I hope she finally has her clothes on! I can't go through *Part 3* again; she *loves Part 3, Chapter 4!*"

C put his hand up, another stop signal on the blow-by-blow.

"Sure, right, we'll come; just stop talking about sex, please....you're killing me."

Earl kept his mouth shut, but his cheeks swelled like a chipmunk with a mouth full of nuts, about to burst.

C shook his head and smiled.

"Okay, what?"

"You never answered; can I take Chick? To the boat ramp? My mom won't say yes or no, she says *you* have to decide, she says it's up to *you* whether Chick goes or not."

C looked at Earl strange; why would his mother have an opinion about Chick, and whether she could go to the boat ramp or not?

"*Up to me?* Okay, sure, you can take Chick, but **don't** let her out of the Sherpa Earl, she'll get scared; promise me you'll leave her in the Sherpa."

"I *never* take her out of the Sherpa....*never!* **You know that!** And you can come too, if you want; my mom said you can come to the ramp too – she *specifically* invited you, if you want to come, you know, with me and Chick. She thought you might want to come with me."

C looked direct at Earl.

"I know you never take Chick out of the Sherpa, sorry about that. Hey, tell your mom thanks for the invite, but I'm gonna pass on the boat ramp, and don't hurry back, I *gotta* tag your sister first - tired of being the only one not getting any, and you don't have to tell your mom the *last* part, by the way."

Earl smiled and whispered.

"I bet it'll be worth the long wait; *mine* was. Bibby has been waiting her whole life for you C, she just didn't know it."

Earl then smiled sly.

"And if she read the sex book, you're a goner for sure."

"One can only hope."

C deadpanned.

Earl turned to leave, then stopped and looked back at Cord.

"I'm married you know; not really, but really."

C smiled.

"And I'll really be, really, later today; I can't wait."

"Really?"

C said, in a sarcastic smirk.

"Really!"

Earl parroted.

"You know Earl, you really are a smiling snapper-head."

"*Ford Fairlane!*"

Earl yelled, arms extended overhead.

"And I bet you could eat a baby's butt through a park bench."

"*Neighbors!*"

Earl yelled again, hands still extended touchdown. Guys yelling and laughing about stupid movie quotes; only guys get it, and only guys know it doesn't get better than that.

Then Earl got serious, his voice lowered to a whisper.

"Hey C, we're best friends and brothers, right?"

"Right."

C answered.

"And even though I'm married, were still kindred spirits, right?"

"You bet, more than ever."

"You got any others, you know, kindred spirits?"

Earl asked, sheepish.

"Nope, just need one."

C whispered through a pirate smile.

Earl looked relieved.

"Hey C, can I tell you just one more thing before I go, something *really, really* important?"

C looked at Earl, and nodded a small yes.

Earl got real close.

"I love you."

He whispered, as he kissed the tip of C's nose.

And as he spoke to his brother and best friend, C smiled wide and held Earl's face gently in his hands.

"I love you too."

CHAPTER 402 – A PERFECT THREESOME....A PERFECT DATE

Earl tip-toed past Lillian's room; she was sprawled, face-down, clothes on, across the bed – sideways, half-mixed in a mess of sheets. He stared for a bit; all he saw was her back barely rise and fall, with each small breath. He smiled at the scene; he's wasn't sure why.

He hoped C would soon be lying next to her.

And with that, he scooted out the door, up the stairs, and played with Chicken a bit, like he always did, calling her pet names: *Chimichanga, Teriyaki, Cacciatore,* and more, lightly running his hand from the top of her head, down her back, to the end of her crooked tail. She purred for Earl, like she always did. She purred for him like no one else.

He scooted her in the Sherpa and was down and out on the street, trotting to the boat ramp.

The early morning sky was a cold, steel gray; a solid sheet of drab, ashen clouds. Fog hung low and shrouded the road, enough that the way before him disappeared into a powdered white no more than fifty yards ahead.

But the look didn't dampen his mood; Earl was going to spend his first morning as a married man with Al, Chick and his mom, for him, a perfect threesome....a perfect date.

CHAPTER 403 – NO POKE JUST YET, NOT LIKE THAT....NO WAY

C was smiling, still half-asleep, watching from the second story window as Earl, Sherpa in hand, scampered across Water Street, heading down Greenwich Street. His brother dissolved into the mist before he made the turn at the hardware store onto South Water Street, on his way to the ramp, two blocks further.

From nowhere, Cord got a cold, hollow feeling - a quick swipe, like he somehow wasn't going to see Earl again. But it passed as quick as it came. Dark thoughts like that clouded his mind workaday; there and gone....they were commonplace, pedestrian. And to that end, he gave this swipe what he gave them all....no heed.

C tip-toed down the hall and peeked in at Lilly; he saw the same scene as Earl moments earlier. He smiled and turned away. He wasn't going to force the issue, grope some cheap passed-out drunken sex, not after a long, six month hunt.

No poke just yet, not like that....no way.

CHAPTER 404 - *AND THERE WILL BE TROUBLE*

He didn't remember stumbling back over to the couch, but he must have, because that's where he found himself, in a semi-daze, when he felt her, in the folds of his brain, standing over him, breathing heavy. The air was bitter cold, raw around her, and it enveloped him, a heavy feeling of dread….a smothering of pure white deadness.

And his skin began to crawl.

He couldn't see her, she was off to the side, but he knew the look, and he knew she was smiling; he felt it. An evil, dead smile, parting parched lips. He was more afraid of that smile than anything else; lifeless, behind blue, cracked and cratered lips.

And he remembered all her horrible details, a surge of the tide, flooding back into his brain: ice-white pants, thin black fabric cloaking bony, decrepit shoulders; transparent, wrinkled skin, its pallor the color of death; hair the consistency of straw, which had no color at all, not even white described it, it was beyond white, simply blankness. But worst of all, he remembered her horrid, succubus eyes, and he knew they were drilling into him, opaque orbs in sockets where eyes should set.

C froze as her bony hand grabbed his shoulder and cinched him tight, much too tight for such a frail corpse; a grip he couldn't wrest.

And at that very moment, for the first time, he heard the hag's voice. And it was by far the worst of it, a sound so hideous, so unholy, it could not be described. C's heart pulsed violent; he wanted to escape, to break free and run, but knew he couldn't move, not an inch.

He had to listen, he had no choice.

And the hag's words, Jenny's words, were clear, the message succinct and the dilemma loomed large.

Her last line of the fateful four-line stanza lay like a lead slug, waiting for him patiently in a box in the closet on the third floor.

....and there will be trouble.

CHAPTER 405 – LAST SWEET WHISPER TO LEAVE HIS LIPS: KRISTINE

As quick as it took to recite Jenny's words, the hag simply disappeared, dissolving into his brain, back between the folds, leaving nothing behind but silence.

And C found himself prone and alone on the couch; he was scared shitless.

For he realized, when looking out the front window at his friend earlier, that cold hollow feeling, that quick swipe of dread, was not commonplace, nor pedestrian. Not this one, not this time. And he then knew, for certain, that he wouldn't see his best friend, his kindred spirit, ever again. And for that, he was sad.

But he was also happy.

Happy for Earl, and for Carol, and for Lilly. The three of them would be fine, along with Chicken. They would all have a long, full, robust life together, a life that wouldn't include him. He would miss them all; he missed them already. That wasn't supposed to happen; he wasn't supposed to miss anybody, anywhere he went.

But Belvidere wasn't just anywhere, and now the whole thing, the whole conte, the meaning behind it all, became crystal.

The blood in the bowl yesterday morning was a harbinger, letting him know that Jenny was coming, one last time. For him, Belvidere truly was the last stop on a long journey, the last station at the end of the line. The cannonball was *finally* rolling to a rest. He sighed long in relief, hanging his head.

And he had a date he was late for, waiting patiently in a box, on the top shelf, in the closet on the third floor. And this time, he *knew* it would be successful. He would score that seventeen percent, the bullet would finally enter his brain. He would leave this world, or whatever this place really was, and exit with his last thought being of his best girl, the one who stuck with him, in his mind, through thick and thin, one mess after another, for the past three decades, with no complaints.

That last sweet whisper to leave his lips:

Kristine

CHAPTER 406 – ON THAT SCORE, HE WAS PERFECT

Cord stood quietly, his right cheek pressed against the wood jam of Lillian's bedroom door.

For the second time, he saw what Earl saw; the slow rise and fall of Lillian's back, as she lay belly-down on the bed, her arms and hands buried under the bedding folds. But she had since burrowed clear under the covers; he didn't see her so much as he saw a lump, her amorphous outline under a rumpled chaos of sheet and blanket.

Even though he couldn't see her, he smiled at how beautiful she was. And how she was, finally, happy, and hopeful. In a small way, he felt he had a bit to do with that.

And the same held true for Earl and Carol and even Marty and Ji-Sue.

All healthy, happy....safe.

And it felt good.

For once, maybe just once, he would do some real good; he would leave a place a little better than he found it. That had never happened before. He always left a mess; any place he landed was a place worse off than it was before he arrived, most times immeasurably, unspeakably, so. That was the drill; those were the rules.

For decades, on that score, he was perfect.

CHAPTER 407 – MAYBE HE WAS FINALLY READY. MAYBE

Cord's cheek was still pressed light against Lillian's bedroom door frame. Looking at her, his mind raced.

This was a foreign feeling.

Jenny's words were spoken, day one-hundred seventy-two finally marked the occasion, and when that happened, he didn't have a choice, he *never* had a choice. The box opened and the game was played.

Always.

But now, he was unsure what to do.

He'd never had indecision before, not like this. Oh, the fucking irony; best day ever….worst day ever.   One and the same.

He rubbed the stubble on his head, back and forth, back and forth; what to do? The indecision made it worse, which made the voices in his head that much more delighted. The puppet reveled in the drama….C's little dilemma.

Lillian lay drunk and asleep before him; Earl and Chicken were already at the boat ramp; happy and unaware. His friends, Carol, Marty, Ji, Buck, Linda and the rest of the crew were likely all still in bed, sleeping off the revelry at the *Cabin*.

So there would be no witnesses, no mess, nice and neat, with Selena nearby to tidy the mess, and skip out before anyone was the wiser. That was important.

That is, *if* he proceeded, *if* the game was played. Then Cord smiled at the epiphany.

This was where the *whole* odyssey for Earl and Lillian started twenty-five years earlier; Earl and Al at the ramp, while Carol died in Lillian's lap. And here he was, about to die, with Lillian, and there they were, Earl and Al, and his mom. So had he stepped into Carol shoes?

Kind of?

Maybe this was the whole plan to begin with, quietly set in motion decades before – a slow spin of the revolver chamber that took twenty-five long years to come to a standstill. He wasn't sure how he tied into them, to 1981, to Carol. But just because he didn't understand, didn't mean the plan didn't exist. Maybe, like the game itself, it was simply beyond him; it was on a need-to-know basis, and someone decided he simply didn't need to know. The theory sounded good, anyway. At least to him, standing in the doorway, looking at Lillian.

Maybe *Open When You're Ready* was finally now, and maybe he was finally ready.

Maybe.

CHAPTER 408 – DRIVE CAREFULLY....SOMEBODY LOVES YOU

The puppet was playing with him.

It's only seventeen percent; the statistic ricocheted between his ears. But C knew if you ever allowed yourself to think that way, you were done. And he *was* thinking that way, so he *was* done, as he quietly looked at the girl who stole him like no other.

No girl had done that to him, not since he was twelve, which was before the angry fence spikes, before everything that was now.

But what of Lillian? Was she the ace to finally make him stop playing the game, knowing he really can't, and finally not wanting to die, which meant he most certainly would?

He promised Lilly; he promised her lot of things, but was she just another part of Jenny's game? The puppet's game? The hag's game? The game set up by whomever ultimately pulled the strings? Were they really, in the end, all the same?

His mind raced and he stood frozen, unsure what to do.

He walked through the threshold, lifted the tangle of blankets and laid quietly, spooning gently next to Lillian, feeling her heat. It felt so good. He kissed her quietly, but long, on the nape of her neck. She rustled ever so slightly, exhaled, then was still once again.

"I love you."

He whispered, aloud, so he alone could hear the words he rarely uttered.

And his thoughts drifted to Sam's bus that he would surely step in front of, to save Lillian's life, and to that neon sign on the bridge crossing the St. Lawrence River, in Montreal, that quietly preaches:

Drive Carefully....Somebody Loves You

His head had somehow calmed; he thanked Lillian for that. And he now knew what he had to do.

He smiled, slipped out of the bed and soft-stepped the steep hallway rise to the third floor. As he slowly clicked the latch shut on his apartment door, he began the ritual yet again, this time, for the very last time.

But one last thought wormed its way in, and it made him melancholy for the love he left on the floor below:

Drive Carefully....Somebody Loves You

CHAPTER 409 – THE HIDEOUS HISS OF LAUGHTER

C had begun to carefully, deliberately unpack the box. It was open, the contents partially exposed....the envelope, the revolver, his outfit. Funny, he knew they wouldn't fit so well anymore, like a kid wearing his father's oversized clothes.

To die like that, in baggy clothes, seemed a bit goofy.

He was still in his boxer briefs and tee-shirt, and he hadn't yet made the call. He found himself moving slower than usual, not due to fear, because he already decided the game needed to be played, but to spend a bit more time breathing the same inside air as Lillian. And he had already decided, in the off-chance, the fluke that he might live, then he would throw away the darts, there would be no *next place* to go; he would let Lilly throw away the box. For good....forever.

The game ends today, one way or the other. He decided it was *over*. He smiled; it felt good to finally be in charge.

Door number one: to die, and leave behind good friends, safe friends, kindred spirits; door number two: to live, and live with those same friends forever....happy.

Either door worked, because he would *finally* leave a place better, safer, than it was when he arrived.

But Jenny, the puppet, the crickets, the rest, they all deserved one last turn at bat....it was only fair. They showed up this morning expecting to play; he couldn't unilaterally take the ball and go home. That simply wasn't fair. *He* decided it wasn't fair, because Cord was finally in charge.

If it turned bad, he hoped Lillian would understand; in the end, someday, he hoped she would. Button was finally gone, and she had Carol as a new-found friend; she would turn out alright in the end.

But still, something didn't feel right.

The game, as it was played by the parties at hand, had a certain feel. It always did, and it always felt the same. But this one, the *feel*, was decidedly off, and it was gnawing at him.

He slipped in the battery, flipped open the phone and began to depress *Speed Dial No. 2*, like he always did at the beginning of every box opening, at the start of every game.

Then it hit him like a shot; a flesh-creep, followed, like a wave, by something much worse. Something cruel, nothing human.

It was the puppet, and the hideous hiss of laughter.

CHAPTER 410 – THE DOOM WASN'T FOR HIM; IT WAS *NEVER* MEANT FOR *HIM*

The puppet's laughter spread, dissipated, then quietly disappeared, like ripples in a pond.

It was replaced by some vast cloak of quiet. A boundless, timeless vacuum. And from within it, *It* came.

It wasn't so much a voice, as it was a thought, conjured, rooted, *deep* in his brain, from a place he'd never been, a seemingly barren region from which no other thoughts had ever sprung. It seemed cold, remote. And it clearly wasn't C's voice, or his thought; it was someone else; someone he had never met. It was not even someone else; it was a *something* else. Something he didn't know or understand; something he was afraid of more than anything else, more than the puppet, even more than the hag.

This *something*, this *It*, was *much* worse.

It was neither benevolent, nor malevolent, and it certainly wasn't human; it didn't operate in that arena, nor recognize or acknowledge that sphere in the slightest. And C immediately knew, instantly felt, that *Its* role was simply to ensure the game is played, rules are followed and each part provides its function, much like the origin and orbit of celestial bodies, the travel of light, the workings of dark energy and dark matter. *It* was seemingly on, or from, that higher plane, which was well beyond anything C could even begin to understand.

And *It* made clear the origin, nature and rules of the game, for those chosen to play, are never questioned, explained nor rationalized; the game simply exists – it always has, and always will. And the concept of time, as interpreted by humans, doesn't work in this arena; there is no before, no now, no later; it all just *is,* forever, whatever *forever* means in this place.

But more to the matter at hand, and as to why *It* surfaced now, and provided the message in the thought above, from deep within the folds in C's brain, the reason was simple, and direct:

Fuck you?
Did C really mean to say that?
Was that really his message to the others he played with?
How dare he decide to think that, to think he was actually in charge.
How dare he decide to tell tales to others, outside the game.
Tales of forbidden trips, of quarters off-bounds....places off-grid.
How dare he decide to no longer play the game.
How dare he even contemplate the possibility.
All the parties have a role, and the game exists simply to be played.
If it isn't played, then there is no game.
And that is simply not allowed.
It was time for a few repairs.

It was then that Cord suddenly understood the hideous laughter in the recesses of his head; it was directed *at* him, acknowledging the fool that he was, to think he could simply stop playing, to skip off the carousel, to walk away, on his own. With no repercussions.

C's *Log Cabin* **Fuck You** to the inhabitants in his head had been twisted, turned and morphed into a new message, and that message was crystal clear:

Fuck C....but good.

So the worm turned, and the game continued.

2630

And Cord suddenly realized the doom he had felt earlier
was simply a lesson; a lesson never to question the rules,
never to stray from the game, *ever* again. A lesson that
would hurt C the only way they *really* could, the only
way that really mattered to him, and to hurt him *bad*. It
was to be punishment topped with a too-cruel twist.

So C began to run.

Because he realized the doom wasn't for him; it was
never meant for *him*.

CHAPTER 411 – THAT ONE BIG QUESTION WAS FINALLY ANSWERED

Cord reached the crest of the boat ramp in boxer briefs and tee-shirt, barefoot and gasping for air. His feet were raw and bloodied from sharp street-rocks and shards of glass in the sand.

The ramp was deserted; the river beyond was shrouded in a thick fog soup. The October air was chilled by a coarse breeze that cut hard across the river.

C felt a presence in the woods to his left; he didn't know what it was, but there was something in there, buried in the brush; he was sure of it. He looked and listened hard, but heard nothing, save the constant rush of the river. He thought to go look, then decided against it, for something diverted his attention, something to the rear.

He turned around; far behind him, standing beside the broken macadam edge of Depue Street, about fifty yards away, was a silent figure staring stone at him, cloaked in the ethereal mist. It looked to be a large animal, the size of a wolf….bigger even. And C immediately knew *what* it was, *who* it was.

But as quickly as Loki appeared, he was gone, a limping run to the left, swallowed whole by the fog. Was he hurt? How? Why didn't he attack? It made no sense.

C turned back to the river. In the distance, beside the water's edge, he saw the faint outline of the Sherpa bag, ripped in half, shredded. It looked empty, and C panicked.

"Earl!"

C screamed into the void.

Although barely audible, he heard something cut the mist; it was Chicken - a single frantic meow.

He sprinted to the edge of the water, his feet a hot sting –
cold water on bloodied, open wounds. He barely saw
her, in and out of the brume, huddled and shivering,
clinging to the tip of a large submerged river-rock, about
twenty yards from shore, thirty yards downstream.

The current was running swift, but it shouldn't have
been. Last week's rains had long passed and the river
should have been calm. But it wasn't; it was roiling.
The waves were cresting the tiny tip of rock to which
she clung, threatening to wash her downstream.

The water was the color of molten lead; the current
foreboding, threatening, with waves, swells and surges
colliding as they raced angry downstream. Chicken, if
she went in and tried to swim would be swept away,
quickly drowned.

"Earl!"

C screamed at the top of his lungs, frantically scoping
the river, but he saw nothing, heard nothing, but
Chicken, clinging to the slippery rock, crying for help.

"EARL!!"

C screamed hysterical a third time.

And then he saw, or thought he saw, a hand in the water,
a hand and an arm, waving, but no sound. It looked like
a hand, but he couldn't be sure; it was too far
downstream for him to really see, yet see it, or
something, he somehow did.

Or so it seemed.

Cord ran along the water's edge, shredding his feet
further on shards of broken beer glass, pitched long ago
by bored fishers; now spiked vertical, hard in the sand, a
continuous, cruel, morning-star punching and shredding
the raw soles of his feet.

He paid it no heed, and ran wild into the cold drink, diving thirty yards upstream of the rock. He fought against the current and somehow, miraculously, clawed his way to Chicken. The rock was smooth and slippery, primordial, covered in a mucous of green-brown algal slime. He hugged the stone, face-to-face with Chick. She was soaked, shaking uncontrollably, eyes saucer-wide in fright. She cried non-stop, louder and louder still.

Just then, seemingly from nowhere, a young boy, thin and pale, appeared at the base of the ramp. He looked lonely, lost....out of place.

It was someone C didn't know, and had never seen before. At least that's what he first thought. But then he thought some more. And he realized the young boy *felt* familiar.

Much too familiar.

He looked preteen: thin, wiry, with arrow-straight straw-blonde hair, in a Dutch-boy cut, the kind people wore in the '70's, but don't anymore. He was a bit hunched in his walk and looked cold....hungry. His gaunt body, his sunken eyes, both seemed much too tired for such a young boy. His baggy jeans were worn and scuffed, cuffed at the shoe; his tan tee-shirt was wet, and clung tight to his chest...his stomach. His shirt was ripped, and a bit bloody, and C first figured he had a run-in with Loki.

But then he didn't.

Because C realized he recognized the young boy; how could he not? But the young boy didn't recognize him; but then again, how could he?

And his lifelong doubt about that one big question was finally answered.

"**Hey!** Grab that bag! Over there!"

Cord screamed. The boy momentarily froze; he hadn't noticed C in the river.

"Come on! Come on!"

Cord yelled hysterical. The young boy instinctively grabbed the shredded Sherpa, running along the shore, downstream, to the point opposite C. He could see the boy was cold, shivering; he could see he wasn't sure what to do, or why he was doing it.

"I'm gonna grab her and drift to shore; follow me, downstream, and meet me....***meet me!***"

C grabbed Chick by the scruff of the neck and held her high, rolling partially on his side, partially on his back, as the current grabbed, sucked and shoved him rough down river. Surprisingly, Chicken didn't scratch or fight, she just instinctively hung limp, meowing....cold and scared.

It was then that C heard a faint voice, from somewhere far away, downstream, in the raging river.

It floated on the mist, like a kiss. It was Earl.

And they were the only words, the last words he ever heard:

Save her!

"I wish I knew how to swim."

Earl said to his mom, his head barely bobbing above the water. She was holding his hand.

"It's okay sweetie, just relax."

"The water is really cold."

"It won't be for long."

"I'm kinda scared; should I be scared mom?"

She hung her head.

"I saved Chicken mommy, all by myself!   She jumped in the water; she was really scared of Loki. I know I'm not supposed to go in past my knees, but she wouldn't have made it without me, would she?"

"No sweetie, she wouldn't have; she surely would have drowned. Because of you, she didn't. Because of you, she was saved."

"I should have never put her down, but I didn't see him; I didn't know he was hiding in the fog. I think he was hurt mommy, I think he was scared too."

Carol didn't answer, she just squeezed Earl's hand.

"I'm worried about Loki mom. He didn't mean it, to scare Chick; he's gonna get in *big* trouble now. Do you think Marty will take him to the farm, and take care of him, like he promised? He crossed his heart you know, and that's pretty serious stuff!"

"Loki will be fine sweetie; Marty will do exactly what he promised to do. A cross-your- heart promise matters, it sticks, no matter where you are, no matter where you end up. Marty knows that. So don't worry sweetie, Loki will be happy and safe....forever.

"Hey, I see Cord! He's at the ramp! He sees Chick on the rock!"

Earl waved frantic, expending precious energy. He got two words out, before he slowly slipped below the surface.

And C heard him:

"Save her!"

"Do you think he heard me?"

Earl asked quiet.

"He heard you sweetie; Chicken will be fine, don't worry about Chicken, okay?"

"Hey! C's coming downstream mommy, he's getting closer, maybe he can save *me* too, like Chick! What do you think?"

Carol looked at Earl and didn't say a word; she was crying.

"Look! He's right over me, but he can't stop, the water's too fast! He can't see me! Hey C, I'm down here!"

Earl was waving his arms wild.

"I didn't know you could breathe underwater. Hey mommy, I can *see you*! *I can really see you!* You look the same as you always did! You're so pretty; I wish C could see how pretty you are. Can you see me?"

Tears streamed down Carol's cheeks, as she smiled sad at her son.

"Yes sweetie, I can. I'm so sorry, I can."

He smiled back, a good smile.

"How do I look mommy? Do I look good?"

"Yes sweetie, to me, you look like my beautiful son, my beautiful, fourteen-year-old son."

Carol dropped her head and sighed, still sobbing quietly, rubbing Earl's back in little circles, like she used to.

"Is C really an angel mommy, like you thought?"

"I'm not sure sweetie, I wish I knew. I wish I had the answers, but those things, the things he knows, I don't. The things he might be able to do, I can't. I'm not sure he even knows those things; I don't think he does. He plays by different rules and answers to different people, or things, something; he has a different *feel*, I'm not sure if he even knows, or ever will. I know he has rules he has to follow, *lots* of rules."

"Well, if he's an angel, maybe he can help me? Maybe he can save me, like Chick."

Carol smiled sad at Earl, and scrunched her face, crying quietly.

"I think he's here to save Lilly sweetie."

"Why? What's wrong with Bibby? Is she okay?"

Carol bowed her head.

"Yes sweetie, she's okay. But I asked, don't ask me who, because I don't know; you don't really ask, it doesn't work that way here, you just think, in a certain way, which can only happen when you care about something so much that it hurts, and I asked for help, for Lilly, because she was gonna need someone strong, someone good, on the inside, to help her, when you came to see me....today. So I asked, and then C showed up. I don't know if he's here because I asked, and I don't know who sent him, or what he *really* is, if he's anything at all, but I think Lilly's gonna be okay. She's gonna miss you, sweetie, so much that it hurts; but I think, with C by her side, she's gonna be okay."

"The water is *so* warm; hey mom, can we hang around and fish with Al and feed the ducks, and put our toes in the water like we used to, can we?"

"Yes sweetie, we can watch Aloysius fish and we can feed the ducks whenever you want; Al will never leave you *ever* again; he'll be here, with us, forever."

Carol started crying quiet again, looking at her beautiful son.

"I missed you so much sweetie, but I wish you weren't here, not yet, not now....not ever."

"Is this heaven mommy?"

"It is now."

CHAPTER 415 – SPOKEN BY A PUPPET-POSSESSED: *HOWDY DARLIN*

She was riding a bike, not hers - it wasn't pink - and it belonged to someone else - but it felt like hers; it felt like she should own it.

She was riding fast, trying to gain speed, heading up a small incline, to a crest she couldn't see beyond. An unknown. But as she approached, she spied an ominous gray building taking shape on a far slope, beyond a chasm she couldn't possibly hurdle, no matter how breakneck she sped.

But she tried anyway, because in situations like this, when it simply doesn't make sense to try, you still do. She pedaled faster and faster still, until she began to lose control, the handlebars jerking reckless left and right. She was going too fast and couldn't stop.

She lost control of the bike and found herself hurtling off the road, falling through the sky, her stomach in her throat, plunging from the height of a plane and clenching the bars in a death-grip, knowing for sure she was going to die when she hit the ground. Her brain raced for a solution to slow herself down, to figure some way to halt the hurtle; she twisted and yanked on the handlebars for some magical fix, some brake, but none could be found. And as she agonized, pushing and pulling in a panic, passing through the clouds, knowing she would soon be dead, the bike somehow slowed to a crawl, and landed softly on the ground, with nary a bounce.

She was safe, not a scratch. And from nowhere, she donned a backpack; what it held, and why she now wore it, she had no clue.

Things like that happen here, in places like this.

She turned to look around; as she did, the bike, the backpack and everything about her, dissolved into nothingness.

She found herself prone under too-white covers, pulled tight to her chin, on a bed in a room cloaked mostly in darkness, cut by a distant, dim light, diffused, from a source unknown, maybe the moon. It had the look of moonlight, grainy and opaque. She wasn't sure if that light was welcome or unsettled, as if it hadn't yet decided what it would be. The phosphorescence was enough to see shadows and endless shades of gray against furniture, clothes and other shapeless objects that melted together in an amorphous blob, which stretched from left to right, just beyond the edge of the bed.

Involuntarily, Lillian half-sat; as she did, the bed covers partially fell away.

She was naked.

At the far end of the long room, thirty feet beyond the bed in which she now sat, was a second-story window, framing a distant park; with it, she gained her bearings. She now knew where she was; it was *the* Park....*her* Park, the Courthouse Park in Belvidere. And from her vantage, she realized she was in Carol's house; she must be sitting in Carol's bed.

She looked about the room; she hadn't been in this house since she was a kid, when the veterinarian owned it, Dr. Beaumont. She always thought the house was haunted growing up, all sorts of animal ghosts in there, the pets who never made it out of Doc Beaumont's basement exam room alive.

She breathed deep and recognized a woman's scent on the sheets; it was faint, like some warm body had laid where Lillian now lay, but the fragrance was thin, about to disappear. She breathed deep and recognized the balm of Earl, a familiar aroma of forty years, a fragrance that felt safe.

It too, was fading fast.

And she felt utterly alone.

Lillian was uncomfortable; she didn't want to be here. She needed to leave, to run away, to find Earl, to find Cord….to feel *safe*. But she was naked, glued to the bed beneath the sheets covering her lower half. And even if she could move, she suddenly didn't know where to run to, or how to get there.

Just then, the slightest draft slithered through the dark, seemingly birthing from nowhere. Lillian got a chill of death, or what she thought death must feel like; it tingled through her arms, like pins and needles, raising upright the tiny hairs on her limbs.

She sat staring blank at the far window, into the gray shades of the space about her, as if she was waiting for something to happen.

Soon enough, it did.

A single cricket chirped outside the window. Then silence. Then came a second chirp, a final one, for none followed. But this trill wasn't outside anymore; the cricket was now in the room, and it was close. She suddenly realized that insect was somewhere in the bed, beside her, hiding beneath the sheets. And for reasons unexplained, she found herself terrified.

More silence, which seemed to last forever; waiting. And sure enough, it came.

Lillian heard it, distinct; it came from the second floor hallway of Doc Beaumont's old house. She couldn't see it from her vantage, but she knew it was there from when she was a kid, running around this haunted place; it was just off stage, to the right.   And the noise was unmistakable; a single shuffle of a shoe on the hardwood floor, by something that was trying not to be heard.

But she heard it, and *it* knew it, and it stopped. And they both waited for the other to act.

Lillian was frozen in fear, unable to move, straining to hear something, anything.

Another single shuffle; this one was a bit longer, as if purposely drawn out, and a bit louder, because whatever it was, was a step closer to where she sat.

And it was clear; this second shuffle was *meant* to be heard. She heard a muffled sound; it sounded like the titter of a child. Her limbs went numb.

Maddening silence ensued, coupled with shifting shapes in the ocean of grays that surrounded her, followed by another deliberate, scraping step.

She could tell it, whatever *it* was, now lay just beyond the corner in the wall, just about to turn and face the bed, framed by the window and the Park beyond. It was close, *very close,* and there was no escape.

Another long shuffle of its shoes.

And then she saw what looked to be a small leg, like that of a tiny child in dark pants; it just began to peak the corner. And as the leg appeared, she heard the faint, high pitch of a child's snicker, the *click-click-click* of teeth gnashing, followed by two horrible words she had hoped she'd never hear again, spoken by a puppet-possessed:

Howdy Darlin

CHAPTER 416 – SHE WAS CRYING; IT WAS *PUMP-TIME*

The bedsheet slowly, ever so, began to banana peel, involuntarily away from her body, toward the foot of the bed, as if by some invisible string, some invisible hand. A slow-motion pornographic show. She tried to raise her arms to stop the unveiling, to re-cover herself, but her limbs were dead, useless, dangling by her sides.

The white silken sheet was halfway down her stomach....she opened her mouth to scream, but no sound emerged. Tears ran down her face as the sheet descended steadily, like a curtain drawn on a stage, revealing the mystery beyond, exposing her nakedness a fraction of an inch at a time.

She sat there, helpless, disrobed like a whore.

As Lillian was debased, the puppet turned the corner, herky-jerk, and stood silent, its grotesque, oversized head erect, but with eyelids closed and mouth shut tight. It didn't move, except the slightest of sways, left to right, as if being held stationary by invisible marionette strings.

The sheet continued its indecent slide, revealing ever more of Lillian's bronzed skin.

As it did, the outer edge of the puppet's painted lips glistened, as saliva built and began to spill from the corners, forming long strands of cloudy drool, extending from its head, to the floor, the puddled sputum grew, and slowly spread.

The sheet receded to her pelvis, with the first hint of pubic hair revealed. As it did, she felt her legs being pulled apart, slowly, like the stirrup-stance on an examination table. She tried in vain to hold them shut, but it was no use. The sheet continued south, as her legs involuntarily opened wide, in a pornographic-v. Her entire crotch was now exposed, her legs spread-eagle, till they could spread no wider, pulled high into the air.

She was ready to be taken.

Lillian felt her back arch and her mouth slowly open, the tip of her tongue slightly extend, like a slut about to take in and taste a cock. Lillian's tongue licked her lips seductive, a flag waving surrender, her mouth waiting to do its job. She could feel the lips of her vagina, they were vulnerable, swollen and wet....ready to be used, piston-fucked hard for as long as whoever fucked her wanted to fuck.

She was crying; it was *pump-time*.

CHAPTER 417 – VIOLATED OVER AND OVER, *FOREVER*

The bloodshot, spider eyes slowly opened, the puppet's lips parted; the breathing was steady and heavy.

Billy Bones spied his chattel and smiled, his teeth clicking sick, head turning left, right and back again.

What a lovely little prize for the puppet.

And Billy, along with the eyes behind him, beside him, within him, *thousands* of corrupt eyes, gaped at the whore spread wide on the bed. The minikin began to snicker and click its teeth faster and faster still....a ritual dance before the rapist's maul.

As the puppet slid its feet forward, across Carol's bedroom floor, as the impending molest festered, bubbled and boiled over, Lillian's eyes grew wide, for she knew what was about to happen. A bestial rape by thousands of corrupt souls, brutalized and violated over and over again, till she couldn't be savaged any longer....till there was nothing left.

She was going to die with Billy Bones and thousands like him on top of her, deep inside of her; brutally, sexually violated over and over, *forever*.

CHAPTER 418 – FOURTEEN, AND SMILING WIDE

The puppet was gone.

It didn't go left or right, up or down, it just disappeared, in a blink.

There, then gone.

Lillian was still frozen pornographic, unable to move.

She noticed a slight breeze blowing the white curtains in the far window, overlooking the Park. From her vantage, although she shouldn't have seen, couldn't have seen, she somehow did, as if looking around a corner – she saw the four benches in the center of the Square.

And they were all empty, except one.

It was her mom, sitting with Earl, rubbing circles on his back and holding his hand. At their bench. And she was smiling.

Earl was all of fourteen, and smiling wide.

CHAPTER 419 – I HAVE SOME SECRETS TO SHARE

It suddenly appeared again, and it was *so* close.

She could feel the rhythm of hot breath on her right cheek, spilling down her neck, bits of saliva stuck to her skin; its lips were that close. The flicker of it's tentacle-tongue, like a lizard, flicked and stuck to her skin.

Lillian couldn't turn her head to see, nor turn her head away; she simply watched her mother and Earl in the Park, as a foul exhale washed over her from the vile puppet.

She tried to scream to her mother for help, to Earl to save her, but the words spilled a hair above a whisper; they never made the window, they barely made it to the end of the bed.

And the teeth clicked, and the sickening snicker of a child burrowed in her brain, a worm she couldn't escape. Its tongue laid warm and wet in her ear, and the puppet breathed six ominous words, and only six.

"I have some secrets to share."

CHAPTER 420 – IF YOU *REALLY* DO....THE POSSIBILITIES

What is love?

A wisp you can't touch, taste, see….smell. Something that only exists in one's mind, a hypothetical. Except when it's not.

How does it *really* work? Why is it *so* important?

How can something so speculative, a ghost that can come and go without rhyme or reason, move mountains. And why can something so tenuous, be so surefire....so unshakable. Such that one would wither without it, or die for it. Regret is surely living a life never having felt it.

Oh but if you do, if you *really* do….the possibilities.

CHAPTER 421 – UPON THIS WOMAN'S HEAD WAS WRAPPED A RED SILK SCARF

Billy Bones slowly pulled his serpent tongue from Lillian's ear, ready to spit terrible tales of him and her mother: their undying love, their years of obscene, raw sex, their little baby-on-the-way, and all the other lies, real and imagined, all rolled up and ready to be dished to Lillian, to out the mother and devastate the daughter, after which Billy and the thousands squirming inside him would ravage and rape Lillian raw.

Billy Bones hated Lillian so much, he could taste the disdain. And he hated her more now than ever and couldn't wait for her to hear his filthy secrets and then finally die with him and thousands of others inside her, violating her forever.

But as Billy pulled back his elongated tongue, and as the others inside him, defiled and foul followed, the puppet stood tall between the whore's legs, ready to mount, when Button noticed a not-so-subtle change.

The naked body atop the bed, still spread-eagle and ready to be taken at will was similar, but not quite the same as it once was.

It *was* beautiful, as before, but now, it was more so. And the face had changed, and upon this woman's head was wrapped a red silk scarf.

CHAPTER 422 – THE CARNIVAL RIDE WAS OVER, YET AGAIN

Others above self, regardless of the cost; shoulder-to-shoulder, right or wrong. Such was a fallen mother's love for her broken daughter, a daughter she had broken, so many years before.

Not again.

Lillian always said when mom wore that scarf, it was gonna be a good day. Whenever she wore it she would never yell at us, and we never got in trouble or anything; it was good luck, that's what Lilly would say, and Lilly was always right about stuff like that.

The puppet was frozen in fear.

Billy Bones, for the first time in twenty-five years, was standing beside what he cared about more than anything, *ever,* what he missed more than life itself.

It was her, it was *really* her, beside him once again, in bed. He could see her, touch her, sense her. And she was his to take, to ravage, over and over, for as long as he wanted. *Forever,* whatever that meant in this place.

But Billy Bones *wasn't* stag, and the prize was not his alone for the taking. For a *thousand* lustful eyes, rather a thousand upon a thousand, buried deep within him, sharing space in the puppet's malevolent frame, leered venereal over her helpless, naked body, ready to rape her.

And Carol turned her head and looked directly into the puppet's eyes, into the brain of Button Pierce. And she saw not a malicious, vengeful monster, but a scared and skinny little boy, unsure of what to do.

But the vile souls inside him knew *exactly* what they were going to do. Yet Billy Bones would share Carol with no one; *no one* touched her but him. And as he tried to turn his head, and thus their primal eyes away, the turmoil inside the tiny wooden body roiled, spinning out of control, shaking the manikin as if it was ready to explode from the chaos of corrupted souls.

And as the puppet quivered and shook, its teeth clicking uncontrollable, a large powerful hand grabbed the head, another cinched the chin, and clamped the mouth shut, like a vise, as it began to twist the grotesque figurine apple-core in a gruesome distort.

Billy Bones was powerless against the hand on his body. And as his head twisted, and the wood splintered from the force, he focused on Carol, trying in vain to stop her from leaving.

But he couldn't; all he could do was watch her slowly fade away, falling further and further into a black background, until what he desired most was just a speck of light faint on the horizon, which flickered once, then disappeared. Billy Bones eyes narrowed and the lights dimmed, as the powerful hands upon him squeezed and twisted, until the teeth stopped clicking and the venal eyes went gray.

The head stopped talking, the eyes stopped looking, and a thousand-plus souls drained away, as the puppet's head snapped from the body and fell harmless to the floor….a pile of dirty clothes adorning a broken marionette.

The carnival ride was over yet again.

CHAPTER 423 – THE RULES HAD JUST BEEN BROKEN BY A LITTLE BOY

This was no longer Lillian's dream.

Lillian was gone, saved by Carol through some means Carol didn't understand; she knew Lilly was in trouble, she heard her call, and somehow willed what happened to happen.

There was no other explanation.

Yet she and Earl were now left alone, standing side-by-side in a place that was no longer part of Lillian's dream. Lillian had moved on, like disjointed dreams do, and this was what happened to those tableaux in those dreams when the dreamer presses onward, the old scenes somehow stay, as vacant whereabouts, a stage-set with the lights dimmed and the audience gone.

But Carol sensed she and Earl were not alone. And Carol began to shake uncontrollably.

Because she knew what was in this space with her and Earl was something to be feared, something she didn't understand, something that was going to punish her, or worse, punish Earl for what had just happened.

The puppet lay prone, silent, dead, whatever that means here, in a crumple on the floor beside them. A pile of broken wood.

And *It* was now nearby, a presence occupying space between the puppet and Carol. Silent and unseen, but most certainly felt.

And *It* wasn't happy or sad, angry or otherwise, because it didn't have emotions, it didn't possess anything like that.

But it did have the game, and the game had rules. And
the rules had just been broken by a little boy.

CHAPTER 424 – WHY ARE YOU CRYING?

Carol didn't speak, because *It* didn't speak; that was not how it worked.

She just thought.

And she thought hard, in her fear for Earl, as to how she could sacrifice herself for him, for she knew bad was to come of this, and she had waited too long for her son to join her in a place she never wanted him to be, to see him go away again, forever.

"Please! Please take me, don't take him, don't hurt him, he's just a little boy, trying to protect his mother."

But it was all for naught; Carol had no say in what was to happen to Earl, no bearing on the outcome….*It* made that clear to her, without a word.

And *It* had already decided what to do, there would be no change to those plans, and the game would go on.

Carol closed her eyes. Earl reached over and held his mother's hand, which was trembling.

"Mommy, are you okay? Why are you crying?"

CHAPTER 425 - FEED THE DUCKS FOREVER

She heard a blue jay squawk, just once, then the lilt of a downy woodpecker, hiding in one of the majestic towering trees surrounding them in the Park. The sun kissed her cheek; it was warm, a welcome summer smooch.

Carol opened her eyes; Earl was asleep, his head gently resting on her shoulder. She was safe, Earl was safe; they were all alone.

She looked about, happier than she could possibly be, for what had happened, and why, and how, she didn't understand, nor cared to. Earl stirred and raised his lazy head, looked at her and smiled.

"You're so beautiful mommy; I love when you wear your red scarf....you know why?"

Carol smiled and nodded yes; but Earl explained anyway, as if he had never told her the story before, as she knew he would. And she loved him for it.

"Lillian always said when you wear that scarf mommy, it's gonna be a good day, it was good luck, that's what Lilly would say, and Lilly was always right about stuff like that, wasn't she?"

Carol started to cry as she slowly shook her head a silent yes.

"Earl, I'm sorry you had to see me like that, in the bed, but I had no choice, I had to help your sister; I'm so sorry."

"I didn't see *anything* mommy; I was scared and had my eyes closed the whole time! I didn't see a thing! No way! Too scared!"

"Not a thing?"

"Nope, not even that stupid puppet, but I knew he wasn't nice. C told me all about him, and I knew he wasn't supposed to be there. The puppet broke the rules! *I* know the rules; he's C's puppet, he's supposed to scare *him*, not Lilly, or you, or me! The dinosaur is supposed to scare me, not the puppet; he wasn't playing right, he broke the rules, so I just kinda felt around and grabbed him. He's not very strong you know, and he smells kinda funny, like stinky fish, but not anymore. I think C will be happy he's gone, at least I hope he's gone. I'm not sure about that, he might come back, but he's not gonna bother you or me or Bibby anymore, that's for sure! He's not part of *our* game, I made sure of that, right?"

Carol just looked at Earl, shaking her head.

"How do you *know* all that sweetie? Did somebody tell you that?"

"Nah, I just kinda felt it; it just feels right, what I just said. Why were you crying before mommy, did I do something wrong?"

She kissed Earl gently on the head.

"No, you didn't do anything wrong; I'm just so happy to be with you....I love you Earl."

"I love you too! Hey mom, can we go back to the boat ramp and say hi to Aloysius and listen to music and stick our feet in the water and put bread between our toes and feed the ducks, can we? *Can we?*"

"Sure sweetie, we can feed the ducks forever."

CHAPTER 426 – THE FAINT BRUSH OF A BONY FINGER

The dream had moved on.

Lillian found herself in a familiar second floor hallway; she was still in the Beaumont house, Carol's house, she knew that, because she had run this hall before, as a little kid, with Earl, chasing the ghosts of animals past.

Why she was now standing here, she did not know.

She was wearing a loose thin tee-shirt and soft cotton underwear, both hopeful white and years old....her favorite set of sleepwear. Her feet were bare; the worn oak floor was smooth and warm beneath her soles.

And she was at the end of a horrid scream.

It was not for something *now*, but rather for something *before*, or so it felt. But what that horror was, she had no idea. She didn't remember where she was before, nor how she ended up here, in this hall; this journey seemed to start here, the spook she just felt a remnant from a journey past.

But the scream ended abruptly, the period at the end of a sentence started on a previous page. Lillian found herself standing alone in the dark, in the silence of the second floor, peering over the mahogany railing to the empty stairs leading to the stately foyer, a long floor below.

And she could feel it, distinctly; there was *something* down there....waiting.   There was someone, or *something*, in the house, down those stairs, lurking; Lillian felt it. The hair on her arms rose in primal warning.

Lilly flipped the hall switch, expecting the lights to flicker then fail; they never work when you're scared, when you are in situations like this.

But to her surprise, it did, or at least one did, a lone, ornate Victorian fixture set atop a newel post, far below her, at the bottom of the grand staircase run. It responded to her flick of the toggle, casting a dim yellow orb about the bottom step, as if waiting for her, a sign-post pointing the way to go....the way to come.

Her hand faintly riding the rail, she lightly tread to the top step, dropped three risers and turned one-hundred-eighty on the mid-landing; the newel post waited patient at the far end of this last stretch of staircase. Lillian was nervous; she knew what was biding below was not a person, but rather a thing. It had that feel, and the feel wasn't good.

A silent glide commenced down the carpeted stairs, forever anxious, waiting for something bad to jump, to show itself. Lillian's heart was racing. But from landing to light, nothing happened. Whatever it was that lay in wait decided to stay hidden.

For now.

Lilly stepped off the bottom riser, onto the hardwood foyer floor, safe within the amber arc of lamp-light.

There wasn't a sound, save the muffled metronome of an unseen clock, hiding somewhere in the darkness beyond her. Such a soothing sound can signal relief, or a sense of forebode.

Which would it be?

The stage was set; something was about to happen.

The dining hall lay across the foyer, through immense chestnut double-doors, open; beyond was cloaked in darkness. The light she stood within feebly fingered through the doors to expose amorphous the leg of a chair and the near-corner of a table....she sensed it was large and long, but couldn't be sure. And she saw nothing else.

The ticking clock called from deep within this hollow.

She slid across the hall as if on rollers, through the massive double-doors; she wasn't sure why she felt the need to go in that particular room, but somehow, she did. Dreams rarely give away such information.

And as Lilly crossed the threshold, her legs went dead, and her arms suddenly hung useless at her sides. The air was thick and murky, as if trying to navigate through suspended soot.

The fright set in cold.

She couldn't lift her legs to run; the best she could do was slowly shuffle. The faster she tried to move, the slower she progressed, with each passing second becoming more vulnerable to whatever it was that hid in that immense room, and whatever terrified her was moving in, gaining on her, getting ever-closer; she could feel it tingle her skin.

Lillian found herself looking around, waiting for the bad to happen, she could feel the veins in her neck bulge as her heart pumped piston.

She thought she saw a flash of white to her left, something that looked like a head of translucent hair, obscured by whatever it was she was passing through. It was less than an arms length away, getting closer.

She was a step away from the exit, a side door to the kitchen, an escape from this horrid space.

When she felt, on her cheek, foul, stale breath from a cackle exhaled, along with the faint brush of a bony finger.

CHAPTER 427 – SHE STOPPED, DEAD IN HER TRACKS

Lillian fell onto the safety of the kitchen floor. The green granite was cool to the touch; the air was fresh and clear; the room was dimly lit by under-cabinet lights, indirect, warm....welcoming.

She could move her arms, her legs; she knew she was safe here.

And she found herself in a rage.

She jumped to her feet and charged the threshold between where she was, and where she had been. She was going to confront what she left behind; she was going back into the dining room, scream at the top of her lungs and kill whatever it was that terrorized her.

She was tired of being afraid, tired of being hurt; she was tired of it all.

And just as she was to step back into the abyss, to confront whatever it was that haunted her, a low, familiar voice came from behind.

She stopped, dead in her tracks.

CHAPTER 428 – HE BEGAN TO CRY

"She won't hurt you; she's here to see me."

Was all C said in resign; his voice a low monotone, almost as an aside.

He stood at the kitchen island, shivering uncontrollable in his boxer shorts, sopping wet, head-to-toe. He was cutting carrots with a broad, sharp knife, a bit faster than he should have been, just fast enough to be dangerous, just close enough to his fingers to be in jeopardy.

He looked up at Lilly, still chopping furious, and he began to cry.

CHAPTER 429 – IT DIDN'T TAKE LONG, AND HIT LIKE A WAVE

"I tried sweetie, I tried my best, but I couldn't find him, I couldn't save him."

C said, tears streaming his wet cheeks, looking at Lillian while still chopping frantic, chopping blind.

"Save who? What are you talking about? Why are you shaking? Why are you all wet?"

Lillian asked, confused.

"*He* asked me to go; *your mom* asked if I wanted to go! I didn't know it was a test, I didn't know it was a punishment. I didn't know it was….already too late."

C's voice trailed off, as he kept cutting, automaton, with pieces of carrot falling like dominoes, faster and faster still, his hands and the knife blade becoming nothing but a dangerous blur.

Lilly stood, mouth agape, trying to process what Cord had said.

It didn't take long, and hit like a wave.

CHAPTER 430 – IT'S THE WRONG HAND

"Earl? Earl! Where's Earl?!"

C stared at her, as life seemed to slowly drain from his eyes.

"What happened?!   Where is he?   ***Where's my brother?!***"

And as Lillian irrupted in a scream, she noticed a pool on the island, spreading like spilt milk. The liquid was dark, amorphous, a slow-motion roll across the soft, veined surface of smooth, green marble. The fluid was Cord's; his blood flowed thick from the cloven ends of what used to be fingers on his right hand. He had sliced them off clean, in perfect circles, roundels lying like cleft carrots.

He stared blank through Lillian and kept chopping frantic, his hand slowly disappearing beneath the blade, slick and thick in a spreading sea of red.

"Stop it! **Stop it! What are you doing?!**"

Lillian screamed at Cord, as he continued to stare blankly into the void beyond her, while the mutilation played on, faster and faster still, as his appendage disappeared in a flurry of red beneath the blade.

It was all he said, then he said nothing more.

"It's the wrong hand."

CHAPTER 431 – OUT IT CAME, IN A SOFT NAVY WRAP

It was on the island, off-center.

Lillian was *sure* it wasn't there but a blink before, for she would have surely noticed it. And she hadn't, but now she did. A blink later. That's how dreams tend to work.

And it was familiar.

And it was open, the worn and bent cardboard flaps peeled back, the imprinted side facing her, the words taunting her, as they had for twenty-five years.

Open When You're Ready

Cord watched her eyes read the words, and he silently mouthed them to follow.

"Open when you're ready."

He reached deep, like a magician; his mangled and missing bloodied hand, and entire right arm, disappeared into the void, as if the box was bottomless, and pulled the rabbit she recognized.

An envelope.

He held it in a now perfect right hand, with perfect fingers, sans red; it had nary a scratch. The knife was gone, as was the blood, the mess....all of it. Gone.

Beside the box he carefully laid the sealed, white envelope, just as she expected, based upon the ritual, based upon his story. It was set parallel to the edge of the island, precisely placed.

She looked for the cellphone; it had to be near, for it was next. But she didn't see him fish back into the box, and it wasn't on the island. She looked up and saw that C held it to his ear; from where it came she didn't know. He was speaking low into the receiver; she couldn't hear what he was saying, but she didn't have to, she knew the message.

"Stop! Stop talking!"

She lunged at him and grabbed the phone; she expected a struggle, some sort of fight to wrest control, but got none....C let go of the phone as easily as if he handed it to her. He stood statue with his hand still to his ear, as if the phone remained.

Lillian unleashed a guttural scream into the unknown on the other end of the phone, connected to some unknown machine, in some unknown place.

"No one is going anywhere!"

She turned and heaved the phone into the ink of the dining room. The soot swallowed it whole. The room briefly lit, like distant sheet-lightning brightens a dark summer sky for an instant, then fades back to black. She knew it wasn't lightening, it was something else, but that was the look. And in that lick of luminescence, no longer than a blink, Lillian eyed a frail figure standing at the far end of the room, and she heard a faint laugh, a short snicker from beyond. But the mock wasn't far, it sounded very close, as if right beside her, a waft of bitter cold blown against her ear.

It wasn't a good laugh; it had bad intent. And she knew to whom it belonged.

C bent over and placed the phone he no longer held perpendicular to the envelope; he fiddled with it a bit, adjusting it a bit left, then right, so it sat perfect. But nothing was there; there was no phone. So he stared hard at nothing, fussing as to whether it was placed correctly, and whether he could proceed. This was too important a step to skip, but Cord was befuddled, as if something was awry, but he wasn't sure what.

He must have satisfied himself, because Ay reached deep into the void of the box once again. Lilly was close enough to stop him, but she didn't. She wanted to, but somehow couldn't get her arms to move.

So out it came, in a soft navy wrap.

CHAPTER 432 – IT FAILED HIM, AND SAVED HIM, FOREVER

As she expected it was neatly wrapped in a navy velvet sleeve; he handled it with great care, reverence, guiding it slowly to the stone surface, and slowly peeling the sheath.

Lillian knew what would be revealed.

Cord was right; it was beautiful, a piece of art. And she hated it.

But the loathing couldn't wrench her eyes from its lithe body, the smooth nickel surfaces - the body, the barrel, the frame - fingered and rubbed over endless years of worthless use.

She saw the intricate carved ivory, and remembered Cord's distress, for an innocent animal that gave such a sacrifice for such a useless object.

And when she looked upon it, Lillian no longer saw an object of hatred, of disgust. Instead, she saw a friend, Cord's only true friend through the years, one who put up with all his antics, his nonsense, his bad deeds with nary a word of advice or admonishment. It waited for him patiently, year after year, traveled the globe by his side, and always obeyed the rules.

The lovely, dreadful device stood with him, side-by-side. It failed him, and saved him, forever.

CHAPTER 433 – A SINGLE WORD, OVER AND AGAIN. PLEASE

Lillian simply watched in silence; a front row spectator, forbidden to interrupt the play.

C swung open the cylinder and eyed the single bullet that was always there, waiting for him to play. It was patient; it had all the time in the world. And it never tired of trying.

Cord smiled sad and gave the cylinder a hearty half-spin. It rotated a bit shy of two full turns, as usual. The same every time.

C lightly placed the revolver on the island, with the barrel facing away, folded the box flaps, cracked his knuckles one last time and inhaled deeply, as he quietly closed his eyes.

But there was to be no walk in the woods this time; no rambling conte through memories-past....just a long slow tired exhale.

Ay secured the revolver, raising it to his temple, barely opened his eyes, slits really, and pressed the cold nickel of the barrel end against his skin. He seemed to notice Lillian standing nearby for the first time, as if she was a welcome arrival to a party gone on too long....a party long past stale. He smiled kind, a genuine shine, an Earl-smile; it was clear he was happy to see her.

Lillian stood silent; tears streamed her cheeks as she mouthed quietly to C a single word, over and again.

"Please."

CHAPTER 434 – THE NIGHTMARE WAS FINALLY OVER

There were rules. So he had no choice.

Despite Lillian's plea, C slowly squeezed the trigger to end the ride. The snap of metal startled Lilly; she trembled uncontrollably at the sound.

But the explosion that reverberated in the kitchen as the bullet left the chamber and entered Cord's brain was simply not to be.

Denied once again.

So Cord broke the rules....*again*.

In rapid fire, without time for thought or consideration of consequences, he flexed his trigger finger four times and four times the nickel snapped impotent. He smiled throughout the exercise, knowing full well it would come down to chamber number six, the last chamber, where the odds were no longer seventeen percent. They rose just a bit in C's favor, to *one hundred percent*.

There was no turning back; there was no more doubt. C smiled satisfied; the nightmare was finally over.

CHAPTER 435 - THE TRIGGER DEPRESSED
AND THE ROOM EXPLODED

Cord's eyes rose to meet Lillian's and he mouthed four simple words, as Winston did, in *1984*.

"We are the dead."

"We are the dead."

Lillian dutifully replied for Julia, but it was against her will. She tried to keep her lips sealed, but the words were forced by those in control.

"You are the dead."

Echoed a dreadful voice from behind Lillian, from the room beyond. The hag stood at the threshold, slumped shoulders, enveloped in a swirl of blinding soot, her mouth open wide, revealing nothing but an expanse of endless black.

"I suppose we may as well say goodbye."

It was Julia's line, taken by Cord, in a whisper. And in that one sentence, life was over.

"I love you!"

Lillian screamed at Cord, crying. It was the last time she would ever say it.

"I've *always* loved you, and always will."

C whispered, as the trigger depressed and the room exploded.

CHAPTER 436 – *RUN!*

The blast shook Lillian conscious.

She was damp in sweat, breathing short and fast. And for that instant, in the foggy micro-moment when you first blink awake, Lilly was unsure what was real, and what was imagined.

And as the fear receded, water down a drain, it was replaced by a warm blanket, the satisfaction that the fright and dread was simply a bad dream.

Lilly breathed easy and collected herself.

She was lying prone on cool, damp sand, the river's edge gently lapping the bottoms of her bare feet. The water was springtime cold, countered by a bronze mid-morning sun, warmly kissing her cheek.

She was safe.

She blinked a few times, gaining her bearings. A familiar song brayed to the right, on a radio she couldn't see.

"It's *Juice Newton, Angel Of The Morning,* number twelve this week. I like her Bibby, she's pretty, like you. But you're prettier, and you sing better too, but I still like her, don't you?"

Lillian turned her head toward the sweet young voice, a bit scratchy, with a bit of a squeak, one pulled from a life long ago.

Earl was sitting in his favorite beach chair, the front legs sunk in the sand by the water's edge at the boat ramp, like always. He had bits of bread stuck between his toes, surrounded by mallards and wood ducks, picking away at the bread crust, like minnows. He laughed as the ducks plucked his toes, as happy as a fourteen-year-old could possibly be.

The beach chair beside him was empty.

"Where's mommy, Earl?"

Lillian asked.

He pointed excited across the river, but there was nothing there.

"Wait, she'll be back!"

Earl said, his legs swinging lazy amongst the dozens of ducks.

Lillian followed Earl's pointer, staring at the rolling blue water, when all of a sudden the surface broke, and up popped Aloysius with a catch, happy as a clam; quick enough, the minnow went down the hatch.

Earl clapped happy at the show, then just as quickly stopped, as if he was listening intent to something in the distance, something Lillian couldn't finger. Then he turned worried to his sister.

"Mommy said you better run Bibby, run as fast as you can, faster than you've *ever* run before! He's on his way, and he's almost there! You *have* to beat him! You have to save him; mommy's knows you can do it! And Bibby, when you get there, be sure to....oh no!"

She looked at him anxious, waiting for the rest of Earl's story to spill.

But he just looked at his big sister, with a sense of dread and urgency that a fourteen-year-old boy shouldn't have.

He screamed at his sister, yelling but one more word, and Lillian, without question, did as she was told:

" Run! "

CHAPTER 437 – NO CHICKEN, NO CORD....NO NOTHING

The sensation was that of a sprint on a *walkalator*; a mad dash on an airport moving walkway, doubling Lilly's speed, tripling it. Her bare feet scarcely touched the road; it was if she flew on a cushion of air, elevated inches off the pavement.

She had never run faster, her heart hammering hard.

But she never saw Cord, and she never passed him, as she raced the length of South Water Street, up Greenwich, to the *Palace*. Not a soul occupied the street; she heard not a sound, no traffic, no birds, no rush of the river, nothing but a run through a wispy light fog, slowly burning off in the late morning sun, on its way to a beautiful day.

She bounded the long flight of stairs, two at a time, till she reached the peak, and shouldered the front door open, slamming it against the kitchen wall.

And there she was met with silence.

No Chicken, no Cord….no nothing.

Lilly stood statue, waiting for something, anything, to move, to give her direction, to tell her what to do.

Earl told her to run, but not to where, not to who. She assumed it was C, she assumed it was here, but maybe it wasn't, maybe the save was meant for someone else, somewhere else that she hadn't figured.

Maybe she was lost. Maybe she failed.

But this had the right feel. And for that reason alone, she still stood sculpture, and waited.

"Be sure to what?"

Lilly whispered to herself, and to whomever else may be listening; her words floating down the empty hall.

No response.

"Earl, ask mommy what I should do; what do I do now?"

But Earl didn't answer. Her mother did.

"Just a little further, almost there sweetie, come on."

Carol's voice swam sweet down the hall, from around the corner, sight unseen. Lillian's lower lip began to quiver, as her mother's familiar words softly soaked in, from a dream long, long ago.

"I don't understand, what do I do mommy? Help me, help me!"

It seemed like eternity, and nothing happened. So Lilly asked again.

"Mommy?"

"You already did it sweetie, you already did. It's done."

"Did what? What's done? What did I do?"

And her mother's voice was trailing away, getting softer, floating further from Lilly.

"Stop, don't go….wait for me!"

Lillian pleaded with her mother, as the voice slowly melted away.

"It's time. Just do it sweetie, go ahead and do it; you're ready. I'm so proud of you, you're finally ready."

"Ready for what mommy?

Lillian whispered.

"Open when you're ready."

Her mother whispered back.

"Open what mommy?"

Carol softly smiled and whispered whist to her daughter.

"Your eyes."

CHAPTER 439 – FINGERS PROBING INSIDE A BROWN BOX

Lilly blinked. Then again.

She found herself alone, standing on step forty, at the very top, looking between the wooden Venetian slats. They lined up perfect with her eyes, but the window was streaked and smeared with grit, dust and cobweb remnants; all she saw was the soft glow of mid-morning light and the hazy details of the gravel parking lot three stories below. It looked like the beginnings of a pretty day.

She knew where she was.

She gazed at her feet, still tucked in flats from the trip to New York City, the *Log Cabin*....last night. The hallway top landing outside Cord's apartment door was spotty-wet, trace remains of former footprints, fresh footprints....*his* footprints.

Her eyes ran up her bare legs, past her short black skirt, creased crooked and deep from a fitful sleep. Her white cotton top was turned corkscrew, pushed up a bit to reveal the soft skin of her belly, just above the skirt band. A few stray blonde strands stretched pipe-cleaner and blurry across her face; she could feel her bed-head; mussed, with some strange cowlick.

This place felt much different than all the strangeness that had come before. This place felt concrete. She was no longer dreaming; this was *real*.

A muffled tussle leaked faint through the apartment door, and she knew then, for sure, this was reality.

And she knew exactly what it was, fingers probing inside a brown box.

CHAPTER 440 – SLOWLY SHAKING HER HEAD NO

Lillian sighed sad and grabbed the brass door handle, time-worn, smooth and cool, and gently turned it quarter-right and stepped quietly into the darkened kitchen. He didn't notice her entry, his head buried south, fumbling for what she knew he longed.

A smear of water mixed with wisps of blood shimmied the wood in the long hallway, dead-ending into an expanding puddle in the front room, by the table where the box sat, and to where Cord stood, shivering uncontrollable in his boxer shorts, soaked head-to-toe.

And she knew then it was true, after forty short years, he was gone, forever.

She hung her head, briefly, then raised it strong, stronger than she'd ever been. She owed them that, both of them.

And once again, she watched the familiar scene slowly unfold.

Cord was mumbling staccato to himself; she couldn't hear what he was saying, but it wasn't kind.

Like a man possessed, he flung angry in all directions foot powder, darts, maps, clothes - worn jeans, shoes, a travel-weary navy blazer; she could hear them, out of sight, hit walls, furniture, the floor.

He threw the envelope on the floor and yanked the phone from the box, shoved in the battery and flipped it free, jamming his finger hard on *Speed Dial No. 2.*

"Fuck you! *Fuck you!* **Fuck you!**"

He screamed at no one and anyone who cared to listen; he figured they were all listening, laughing at him, waiting to see how the scene played. But then again, they already knew.

But regardless, C **knew** how this was going to end; his own surprise for the lot of them....*game fucking over*.

He mumbled and paced as the phone slowly awakened and ramped to life. It didn't care about C; it took its time. He strode across the living room, out of sight, but she heard him clearly, when the voice-mail beckoned. It wasn't his usual cocktail:

'Heh, it's time, no word in a half-hour, you know what to do....be good."

Instead, Ay made it clear things, this time, had changed:

"I'm done! No call back; get your ass here and clean up the fucking mess!"

He flipped the phone shut and hurled it across the room, smashing it to pieces.

Cord strode back to the box and thrust his hand in again, ripped off the delicate navy velvet sleeve, tossing it aside.

He eyed the Colt and held it to his temple, never taking the time to spin the chamber. It didn't matter, he already decided how this one would end. There was no more seventeen percent, *this* was one-hundred fucking percent; *this* was a God-damn given.

And as he raised his head to whisper *Kristine* one last time, his eyes trailed the long hall, till they fell upon Lillian standing alone, tears tracking both beautiful cheeks, slowly shaking her head no.

CHAPTER 441 - BEFORE HE PULLED THE TRIGGER, HE SMILED SMALL

He spoke first.

"I tried sweetie, I tried my best, but I couldn't find him, I couldn't save him."

C's voice cracked as he began to cry for his best friend, looking at her with the cold nickel of the revolver pushed hard against his temple.

Lillian didn't ask who, what or why; there was no need.

"*He* asked me to go; *your mom* asked if I wanted to go! I didn't know it was a test, I didn't know it was a punishment. I didn't know it was….already too late."

C's voice trailed off.

"I know sweetie; I know he's gone."

C's hand dipped a bit, the barrel still glued to his head, but at an angle with the floor.

"*How?* It *just* happened; how do you know?"

"*You* told me."

Was all Lillian said, sad.

He stared back, blank, shaking his head negative.

"Oh sweetie, I can't stay - I just can't; *everyone* around me always dies, all the time. I never used to care, but now I do. I have to end this; *I am the dead.*"

"You are *not* the dead; don't let them tell you that, don't let them tell you *anything!* Don't listen to them anymore! You have to stay, for Earl, for my mom, but mostly….for *me.*"

Lillian walked slowly, calmly down the hall, watching C shake in terrible fits, the gun wriggling spastic against his brain, his finger hard on the trigger. He tried, but couldn't stop crying.

Then she saw it; the beginnings of a slow burn.

The faint preface first formed on the periphery of his face; the lines and wrinkles tightened, deepened, and the disease spread like a pebble-ring in a pond, to the slit of his eyes, the wrench of the jaw, the purse of the lips, the flare of his nose. And Lillian knew that C wasn't listening to her any longer, she was already tuned out. This was a one-way ticket; the first subtle changes from sadness, helplessness and despair to anger, hatred and rage....it was inevitable, a manifest before her eyes. And she watched helpless as the bile and venom grew and boiled, the violence building within to that point just before irruption.

So she stopped.

C knew there was no save. He *was* the dead. He knew how it ended wherever he went, whatever he did, it was always the same; a fate set long ago for a twelve-year-old boy.

Always the same; always a mess, always bad, always dead.

And because of it, his best friend was gone, and, even though he didn't yet know, so was Martin and Ji-Sue....all of them gone, all because of him.

And he wouldn't let them take Lillian too.

So he would end the game, Lillian would live, and maybe, wherever the bullet finally took him, he would be happy, and free, forever.

Maybe Kristine was in that place, maybe she had been waiting all these years for him, just hoping he would finally find the courage to simply hop off the carousel, and join her.

He was about to find out.

And for an instant, before he pulled the trigger, he smiled small.

CHAPTER 442 – WE'RE ALL THE OTHER HAS LEFT

The revolver clicked impotent, as he knew it would.

The first one was always a throwaway; it had been for years, *forever*, every game he had ever played. Why would today be any different? Why would today, of all days, be a winner? He knew they gave it zero chance, and he knew they were all laughing.

He shook his head negative in disgust….*fuck them.*

Lillian shuttered at the sound of the single metallic snap; a ripple of movement swayed her left to right. It was reflex. She couldn't believe C pulled the trigger in front of her; that he actually tried to blow his brains before her eyes. And because of it, she should have been anything but calm; she should have been furious, screaming profane and charging Cord in a rage. That was Lilly.

But somehow, this Lilly was calm. Because she too knew, that he knew, the snap would be nothing but toothless.

The first one would never go off, it never had, and of all days, it certainly wouldn't go off today. It just wouldn't. Lillian somehow knew that.

She shook her head negative in heartache for C; he didn't deserve this.

She slowly, quietly spoke in comfort to her best friend.

"The game's over C, and you're still standing, you win; just put it down, please, it's *over*."

Cord looked at her with distant eyes; it was if her words drifted over his head without interception, without recognition.

She noticed he was no longer shivering. It was as if a blanket had suddenly been thrown around his shoulders; he stood perfectly still, the revolver end dimpled into his temple. She could see him pushing it harder and harder still, as if he was trying to pierce his brain, to push the barrel clear through.

And she realized it wasn't over.…*not yet.*

She had stopped any forward momentum, standing a mere ten feet from C, maybe less. But she dared go no further. Whatever was to happen, would happen here, like this. And she resigned herself to same.

He spoke slow and pacific as they faced off in the hall.

"You shouldn't be here; no one is supposed to see this *[C shook his head hard in the negative].* Whenever I open the box, I'm always alone, always; that part of the game is always solo, always, has to be. That rule is never broken, *never,* it just can't be, it's not allowed; that much I know."

Lillian responded in a voice that began to slowly rise, began to belie the calm.

"You've been doing nothing *but* breaking rules. And I frankly don't care about your rules, or their rules, or anyone's fucking rules. All I care about is *you*; that's all that matters to me - *you and me* - just you and me. Don't let them take that away C; we're all the other has left."

Four rapid revolver clicks and a cortege of bullets. The barrage lasted less than a second.

But there were no bullets, of course. The foursome that followed was as effective as the first, which was not effective at all.

C eyes briefly tilted toward the ceiling as he smiled evil.

"More broken rules. As if I didn't know *that* would happen. But now we're at the last chamber, *last one*, one bullet and one chamber left. The odds, I suspect, have tilted quite a bit in my favor; *now* it gets interesting."

CHAPTER 444 – THE FINAL CHAMBER EMPTIED. STORY OVER

C's finger was pressed light but firm against the trigger; the smallest twitch, the slightest flex of his pointer, and the last chamber, holding the so-patient bullet, waiting years for just this chance, would do the do.

It was that close, finger close, to being over. For real....forever. And C was relieved to finally bark at this door.

And as it was that very first day, through the plate glass door at Sam's Market, much more than a lifetime ago, Cord Brin and Lillian Liddell stood silent, eyes locked, waiting for the other to do something, whatever that may be.

And both their lives changed forever.

And here they were again, same set-up, but with slightly higher stakes.

C spoke first.

"I suppose we may as well say goodbye."

It was Julia's fateful line, pinched by Cord, delivered monotone.

And as Lillian stared at Cord, she again felt the pang of what Earl had told her she felt all along. That she had fallen in love, that Cord Brin was finally the right man, for her, standing together, forever.

"I love you."

Lillian whispered his way.

"I've always loved you, and always will."

C whispered back.

"Earl told me that your mom said that I wouldn't believe in her, at first, but I hopefully would, eventually. Well I do, I *really* do, and if I'm lucky, *really* lucky, I'll get to meet her, very soon. Your mom also said I had something to tell Earl, *when I was ready;* well, I'm ready."

Cord blinked, locked eyes with his best friend, and spoke slowly, a tribute to a kindred spirit....a brother forever.

"Earl is in my heart;
And I love him very much;
He will never die."

And before she could react, before she could do a thing to stop him, his finger squeezed and the final chamber emptied.

Story over.

CHAPTER 445 – A SINGLE LONELY BULLET

The metallic click was followed by nothingness.

The room, the hallway, the entire show was blanketed in an sea of silence, a fog swallowing the duo whole.

Cord slowly removed the Colt from his temple, mouth agape; he eyed the revolver as if some foreign object, beyond comprehension, was glued to his hand. He released the pin and the beehive rolled open in a single snap.

There was no malfunction to blame, no shell to be scolded, no explanation to be had.

Six chambers, all empty. No bullet to be found.

It was only then that Lillian felt the warmth of something small, something smooth, quietly cradled in the fold of her hand. It was only then that she realized why Earl had told her to run, and what she had done, and why her mother was *so* proud.

Lillian quietly whispered to herself:

'Open when you're ready'

as she turned her left palm upward and unfurled her fingers, like the slow spread of morning petals from a lovely *Lemon Bell.*

And there, in her tiny palm, it quietly lay, a single lonely bullet.

CHAPTER 446 – YOU DON'T NEED THAT BOX ANYMORE

C dropped where he stood, sheer exhaustion; the revolver clung impotent in his hand. His eyes were closed as he quietly cried, crumpled in defeat on the living room floor.

Lillian saddled up and knelt beside him, cradling his head in her lap and hugging C tight to calm the shiver that returned, letting the remnants of the river on his bare skin slowly soak into her skirt, her blouse. She ran her fingers softly across the stubble on his face, tracing tiny circles with the lightest of touch, as she rocked him gently, as a mother would.

She felt warm and safe, and his shivering stopped.

She closed her eyes, bent and kissed him long on the forehead, remembering the call he had to make, the phone he smashed, and the bowl of blood they had dealt with at *StoryCorp*, seemingly ages ago, less than twenty-four hours before.

She spoke quietly, as if in a church.

"You need to make a call, tell Selena that there's no mess for her to clean-up; you're my mess now. You can use my phone, yours is a bit distressed."

As Lilly eyed the fragments of C's phone, scattered across the living room floor. She kissed him again, gentle on the brow.

"And I'm calling a new doctor tomorrow; doctor's *can* be wrong.…they're *always* wrong."

She raised her head and stroked his forehead.

"And *I'm* throwing the box away, the game's over, for good, forever. No more game."

And Lillian raised her head, barely moving it left and right in a cadenced *no*, and looked at him with eyes that loved.

"You don't need that box anymore."

October 14, 2006; a sunny Saturday in Belvidere.

It had been one-hundred seventy-seven days since Cord Brin stepped off the *Greyhound*, staring at *Luigi's Rancho*, wondering what kind of hand he had been dealt, in some bum-fuck New Jersey backwater.

It had been one-hundred seventy-six days since he first met Earl Liddell.

It had been seven days since Earl left Belvidere for the first time in his life, to save *Louie the Lobster* and his friend, discover Skeleton Island, solve some mysteries, meet some dinosaurs and explore the big City. It had been seven days since his birthday bash at the *Cabin;* seven days since his marriage to Carol Crowe.

It had been six days since he drowned in the Delaware River, just above the *Foul Rift.*

It had been three days since the Delaware finally released him.

The River Patrol found his body at the downstream end of the *Rift,* washed ashore, shoe-less, in a quiet little eddy that formed a spit of river beach, only exposed when the river ran low. The beach was a mix of round river rocks, assorted sizes from pebbles to cobbles; hundreds of tan, black, gray, green and white stones - *over-sized marbles* - that's how Earl would have described them, with coarse dark brown sand trimming the beach edge, pushed up against the toe of the bank. Earl was seated, heels dug in the angular sand, in a bright morning sun; he was propped against a solo sycamore, rooted precarious at the base of the cliff, directly below *Couch Rock,* where the ducks float lazily by all day long. Earl used to smile at that sycamore when he laid on *Couch Rock,* upside down and backwards, lazing many an hour away, watching the river forever roll by.

It was a good spot to sit on a beach along the river; Earl would of thought it was the best spot ever.

Carol's *Actaeon Bacchanal* had been scheduled for today; it had been planned meticulously for six months – over two hundred gilded invitations had been returned as-attending. Earl had been marking time, a not-so-patient one-hundred-twelve days since he received the invitation in the mail, counting each off, one day after another, anticipating with bated breath his first *royal reception*, his first sleep-over party at Carol's.

Earl ended six days shy of a royal reception that never arrived; but he still got the best part....he got his sleepover.

Saturday, October 14, 2006; day one-hundred-seventy-seven. The weather was simply gorgeous, surely one of the best days of the year, so far.

Cord glanced at the small oiled bronze timepiece, atop the glass and worn green wicker side table; he and Earl had eaten breakfast here all summer long, trading barbs with Carol and smiles with Ji.

It was 11:34 am. He quietly sighed.

The drone of crickets filled the early Fall air; C never realized that they'd be out in the morning, in such force, so loud. Although they likely were just as loud yesterday, and would be just as loud tomorrow, and had likely been so all season, it took till today for Cord to take notice. And now that he noticed, he could focus on nothing else, as you sometimes do with the background din that, for some reason, becomes foreground. The cricket whir was soothing, and didn't seem to upset the headache that was starting to get behind his eyes.

A lone yellow-jacket hovered alongside the window to his left; he glanced at it, then away, and it was soon gone. He took a first sip of his Earl Grey tea; maybe the caffeine would help his head. There was no coffee in the house. There was no breakfast. There was no grocery shopping done. There wasn't much of anything done.

Because there was no Ji-Sue.

C shook his head, simply amazed at how loud those damn crickets were. There had to be hundreds of them in earshot, all safely hidden away. Above it all, he heard a lone bird call, every few seconds; it was one he couldn't identify, and that bothered him for some reason. A few crows joined in; they sounded a bit away, perhaps a half-block or so down Hardwick, away from the Park.

He looked skyward; it was a beautiful, even shade of blue – the color blue that *sky blue* is, because it was.

And it was marred by nary a cloud.

He smiled small.

Because he knew today was the kind of day that Earl would constantly tug on C's shirt sleeve, saying over and again that this was *exactly* the kind of wonderful day made just for the two of them, to go on an adventure, to solve a mystery, like Sandy Allen and Ken Holt would, like they did in the *Secret of Skeleton Island*. And they shouldn't waste it, they needed to do something, and do it *now*! Because mysteries are meant to be solved, right C?

And C would always agree.

Earl would rattle off the list of potentials:

- lay upside down on *Couch Rock*, watching the river slide by as the blood rushed to your head; or
- laze at the boat ramp, stick their toes in the water, feed the ducks and wait for Aloysius to catch another fish; or
- sit on his mom's bench and stare at the porch, waiting for Carol to wave them over for breakfast, with Ji-Sue smiling and serving plate after plate after plate; or
- whatever else would dance into the big man's head, and there were no bounds in that regard....which made Earl, Earl.

C took another sip of tea; his headache in reverse, slowly receding. Maybe he would finally read the *Secret Of Skeleton Island* for himself, after hearing non-stop about that damn book for the last six months. Maybe he would do that today. Or maybe not.

C shifted in his favorite chair, Carol's chair, rolling thoughts of Earl round his head. The noon Belvidere sun already washed his lower half bright; the mercury had climbed to eighty degrees; too warm for October 14th. He could feel the first trickle of sweat soak his pant legs.

He looked out over the Park, a myriad of colored leaves, dappled in light; he was surprised the trees were still mostly green....more than half. But a wave of yellow, orange and crimson swabbed the over-story in the beginnings of a broad brush of color, wicking capillary, working from leaf tip inward, toward the trunks, a liquid called autumn. In a few more weeks, the leaves would have already turned full and dropped, the doorway open for the cold to come. In Belvidere, word on the street was a brutal wintertide approached; the *Farmer's Almanac* confirmed it: *super-cold, with heavy snowfalls.* And as the Almanac goes, so goes the weather; at least that was the belief in Belvidere.

Cord wondered if he would ever see it, or would he be somewhere else....far, far away.

But now, the thought of winter seemed silly.

He shook his head a bit, to be sure; yep, his headache was gone. The tea must have done the trick.

He shifted in his seat a bit to better eye the benches at the cross-mark, center of the Park. They were obscured by a potted fern and the immense head of the southern seated bronze lion guarding *L'antre du Lion.* He imagined Earl sitting there, on the bench, looking back at him across the leafy green.

He glanced over at Earl, sitting quiet on the love-seat to his left; he was going to crack a joke about the queue of cars saddled up to St. Mary's Episcopal, like they did every Saturday, drunks in the process of reform, shuffling quiet into the church mess hall for their weekly

Saturday group fix. Earl would scold C and his drunkard jokes; they were *trying hard*, Earl would say....he knew most of them, since he knew most everyone in Town, including the drunks. Christ, Earl was becoming a drunk himself, *thanks to C,* that's what Lillian would always say.

But Cord didn't talk to Earl; Lillian wouldn't have approved - she'd be upset all over again, and he wouldn't do that to her. So he just smiled to himself and had the conversation in his head. Earl sat silent, acknowledging C's smile.

Lillian was standing at the railing, her back to Cord, staring blankly across the street, into the glade. He heard her sigh, her shoulders slightly raised and fell in concert. She was two feet from him, and a million miles away.

The mail truck pulled up to the *Sykes* house, a stately, red-brick mansion, catty from Carol's porch; the mailman hopped out with a bundle of deliveries under his arm and soon disappeared down the sidewalk. Hunter was splayed belly-up on the porch deck to C's left, fast asleep in a small spot of sun, twitching her paws, the offshoot of the dreams of a fat, happy cat. Zeke had been lounging, stretched-long, all morning, moving around the porch, following the sun. C looked about, but there was no Zeke to be seen – he was holed up somewhere out of sight. He'd surface soon and land on C's lap, if Hunter wasn't already there, covering him in cat hair; that seemed to be the recent drill. And C didn't mind a bit.

The Park insides were empty, not a soul to be seen. Lillian, for no real reason, tracked right-to-left a lone woman walker, a middle-aged pear, skinned in black nylon yoga tights, a purple tie-dyed tee and shoed in bright pink sneakers....a motley montage. She power-walked past, water bottle in hand, earbuds socketed, oblivious to all around her. A long, lazy ponytail swung slow across her back, in concert with her lazy arm pump; she turned the Park sidewalk corner at Hardwick and faded up Third Street, anonymous.

Normally, Lillian would comment on her God-awful outfit, her pear shape, her slow pace, her anything-else-that-annoyed-her at the moment. But she remained silent; she said nothing at all.

In the opposite direction, an old couple, shoulder-to-shoulder, heads cocked toward the ground, like seniors often do, circled the Park sidewalk slow. Both wore long casual pants, too short, revealing black nylon socks and new white no-name sneakers, fresh from the discount store box. Soon enough, they too were gone, and the Park sidewalk was empty again.

Time passed and Lillian stared into the void; there was no exchange between C and Lilly save silence, her back to his front.

"What time is it?"

She finally said, sans turn.

C glanced at the table clock.

"12:15."

Lillian didn't respond, didn't turn, didn't do anything more, but continued to stand statue, looking away at nothing.

Then something caught Cord's eye.

He looked to Lillian's left, less than a foot from her hand resting light on the porch rail. It was a *huge* spider, ash-black, crawling away from her, atop the same rail she gripped. *Jesus – where the hell did that come from?* Cord thought to himself. It must have crawled along the bottom of the rail, under her hands, outside her ken; no way it crawled atop the rail and over her knuckles, no way she ever saw it; she would have screamed and run, it was *that* big.

Cord leaned forward to get a better look; he hadn't seen a spider quite that large in awhile, or that shape, or that color, come to think of it. It was *that* unusual, lumbering along in no particular hurry, as if waiting, expecting, hoping, to be seen; and seen it was.

CHAPTER 449 - THE ENDLESS DIN OF THE INVISIBLE

C leaned further forward in his chair, eyes squint to slits, to get the beast into better focus.

His eyes slowly opened wide, as he sat quietly back in his chair.

That was no spider; it was a huge, black cricket. And it didn't make a single sound as it continued to crawl slowly south, away from Lillian, toward the corner post and rain-chain off the end of the porch.

When do you ever actually *see* a cricket? Especially mid-day, under a hot noon sun. The hair rose on his arms as if iced, and he expected harsh words to follow, or a vile snicker, born deep in the folds of his brain….Jenny, the hag, the puppet, or that worst voice of all, which wasn't a voice as much as a thought. The one he feared like nothing else.

But no words, nor thoughts, followed, no sick laughter tickled his brain. Nothing. He shook his head, left-to-right, as if trying to dislodge them, to root the rot out. Expose them. Still nothing, silence in his head.

Maybe it was *just* a cricket, walking by, on its way somewhere else, with no meaning other than that.

No way.

He looked to Lillian, to share his thoughts with her, but decided against it.

He looked back to the cricket, but it was gone….disappeared. He stood up to look around the post, up and down the rain-chain, on the prehistoric cryptomeria tree nearby, but of course there was no cricket to be seen; wherever it had come out of hiding, back it went.

It would never be found, so he didn't bother to look any further.

"What are you doing? What are you looking for?"

Lillian said, eyeing him, indifferent.

"Nothing."

Was all he said, which was apparently a good enough answer; she turned back to stare blank at the Park beyond; further words weren't exchanged.

The Box, and all its contents, were gone, collected curbside by the Belvidere Department of Public Works, transported, burned and turned to electricity at the Warren County incinerator, in neighboring Oxford, five miles away. The remnants ran live through the wires overhead.

And visits by the neighbors in his brain had ended, at least for the last seven days; a period of calm ensued.

So maybe it really *was* a strange fluke; maybe it was just a random cricket; maybe the game was really over. Maybe *this* cricket was a portend of *good* luck:

*In scattered areas around the globe, from Barbados in the Lesser Antilles, to China in the Far East, to Zambia in the Sub-Saharan Dark Continent, to find a lone cricket in your home is considered a harbinger of good fortune, needed rain, financial windfall....**hope**.*

That is what he told Lillian and Earl many months ago, when he first told them the tale of the puppet, the crickets and the flies. He closed his eyes, leaned his head back and trailed to thoughts of hope, as he listened to the endless din of the invisible.

CHAPTER 450 – ASH, MIXED WITH TINY BITS OF TOOTH AND BONE

It was 2:20 pm and Carol had still not emerged; neither C nor Lilian had seen her all morning, just the sound of footsteps on hardwood, the open and close of wooden dresser drawers, the running of water, belied her invisible movements far above and behind them, on the second floor.

Sam, Buck and Martin's father had already collected and set, in neat rows, all the folding plastic and metal chairs they could muster from The Legion Hall, all six churches in Town, the elementary and high schools and the firehouse. The total stood at well over five hundred, and it would not be nearly enough.

Marty and Ji-Sue's service was held joint the day before, Friday afternoon; three hundred plus attended, including law enforcement from nearly every town in Warren County, dressed in formal blues.

A small group of Koreans, a half-dozen Catholics from Ji's church, outside of Hackettstown, arrived, all clad in black. They kept to themselves, speaking their native tongue in hushed, reverent tones. All were strangers, and none were family. No one, including Carol, had ever met a single one; they had never been to Belvidere before yesterday; they would never be back again.

And with that, Ji-Sue's chapter closed....forever.

No family claimed Ji-Sue's ashes, and Carol couldn't bear the thought. So Martin's father kept the two urns in the living room, on the mantle, until he could decide what to ultimately do with Ji-Sue and his son's ashes. After a week, he mixed some ashes from each urn in a third covered porridge bowl - a cheap, white porcelain knickknack that was Martin's favorite as a small child. His mother had kept the bowl in a dusty vitrine in the hallway, by the basement door; the top knob had been broken off by Marty when he was still in a high-chair, throwing the top across the kitchen in a tantrum, not wanting to eat his mother's sweet potato puree. His father would smile remembering the day it happened, because he too didn't want to eat his wife's sweet potatoes, and wanted to throw his bowl too. Martin Sr. figured part of Marty would like to be in that bowl with Ji-Sue forever, until he could find a place to gently spread them, maybe on the farm, maybe on a beach somewhere.

Somewhere good....somewhere nice.

Martin Sr. would have to think about it some more, pick the perfect spot to spread his son's ashes, both their ashes, to do them both justice, so they'd be happy together, forever. It was important....to be reverent.

So he thought about it for awhile, until he didn't think about it as often, until he didn't think about it at all, and it quietly fell off the *to-do* list.

The two urns and the broken porridge bowl sat trio on the mantle for twenty-odd years, dusted once every two weeks or so, until Martin's father died. The pair of urns sold for ten bucks apiece at the estate auction; the porridge bowl was tossed in the trash as worthless.

The auction staff swore all three vessels were already empty when they arrived, although there were family doubts.

In the end, no one could say for sure who did what, or what ever happened to Marty and Ji, reduced to three petite piles of ash, mixed with tiny bits of tooth and bone.

CHAPTER 451 – HUNGRY, THIRSTY AND SCARED, WITH NO END IN SIGHT

Loki wasn't buried.

He was fetched from the woods by the police the day Lloyd killed him, dropped and zipped in a large body-bag due to his size and weight; for a two-hundred-twenty pound English mastiff, nothing else made sense.

The work crew down at the maintenance yard drove the garbage truck up and threw the dog in; Loki was burned in the Oxford incinerator on Wednesday, the day they found Earl; he was mixed with Belvidere's weekly municipal trash run. One of the garbage collectors who rode the back of the truck pulled a muscle shifting the body-bag off the vehicle, and kicked Loki in the gut with his steel-toed boot in disgust. He took the next two days off, watched television, drank beer and fucked his fat girlfriend, complaining about the pull in his groin.

Loki traveled all alone, up a long conveyor run, into the burner, followed before and after by a never-ending line of garbage that fed the flames.

And because there aren't any rules for who is allowed to have a dog, including white trash, by Friday, less than five days after Loki died, the dirt-bags living at the dump at 260A Depue Street got another dog, a mixed-breed pit bull, a sweet six-week old puppy, which they tied up in the yard on a too-short heavy metal chain, left to pace endless in a round dirt circle-rut, with no grass, no trees, no shelter. He had been there for less than twenty-four hours and had already been beaten twice, whipped with a stick across his head and kicked in the stomach and back legs. He couldn't stand, his legs were too bruised, so he laid listless, shivering alone in the mud.

The fucks named him Loki.

And the trailer-trash kids on Depue had already thrown rocks at him, rattling the chain-link every time they passed. And they passed every day, all day long.

Loki was only six weeks old, and already hungry, thirsty and scared, with no end in sight.

CHAPTER 452 – A CHORUS OF CRICKETS

The afternoon sun, on a downswing, bathed the Park in long rays of speckled light, filtered through a canopy of greens, mixed with a medley of burnt color. There were well over a thousand people in the Square, all facing the Courthouse, spilling into Second Street, which was closed, barricaded to thru-traffic.

Carol, Lillian and Cord sat in the front row, side-by-side; they spoke little to none, listening in the afternoon glow as Ryan, the Episcopal minister that married Earl the week before, finished his eulogy. It was short, sprinkled with stories of Earl as a child, Earl as an adult, Earl as a friend. Fully every person sitting and standing in the Park could recount their own memories, everyone had a favorite Earl-tale to tell. The memorial could have lasted a week on that leg alone.

Ryan folded his notes and nodded to C, who stood slow and walked to the lecturn. His own jottings were stashed in his jacket pocket, but he failed to fetch them. No need.

Lillian and Carol, sitting beside one another, both quietly crying on and off all day long, began again. Who would imagine the two girls together as best friends? Who could have imagined such a thing more than a week ago?

Carol reached over and and put her hand on Lillian's, giving it a long squeeze; Lillian fell slowly to the side, her head coming lightly to rest on Carol's shoulder. And that is the way the two of them stayed, sisters....glued together.

The Park was hushed, save the shifting of bodies in chairs, the rustling of memorial papers in hand, and the gravelly murmur of suppressed coughs and stifled throat-clears, scattered amongst the throng. A tinny bark hailed from a micro-dog on the far side of the Park, which unleashed a chain reaction of whines, hoarse barks and extended howls from other dogs, all unseen, in the blocks beyond *Garret Wall*. It dimmed after a bit, but the volleys continued as Cord quietly turned from the crowd, pulled Lillian's phone from an inside pocket, fingered in the number and simply said *five minutes*. He flipped the lid shut.

The crickets were still singing strong, as they had all day, without rest. But the birds were in siesta, and the distant dogs finally calmed.

C turned and gazed upon a sea of forlorn faces, many of whom were raising glasses in salute to Earl and Carol at the Cabin a week before. Tears already tracked Cord's cheek, before his first word was uttered. He still could not believe he was here....alive. Why? He looked to his brother, his best friend, his kindred spirit, set beside him, let go a long sigh, and began to speak above a chorus of crickets.

CHAPTER 453 – I CAN'T THINK OF A BETTER WAY TO SAY GOODBYE

Cord had a dozen good stories to tell, and a dozen atop that, and those were the just the Earl *best-ofs*, they didn't include the countless snippets of life with Earl that made the one-hundred-seventy days they spent together the best of times, bar none. He had scribbled reminders on a handful of favorites to share, to make them laugh, to cry, to remember Earl as a man who comes along but once for each of us.

But as he scanned the mass of faces spread before him, spreading deep into the Park, most of whom he didn't know, he realized they all had their own nuggets, their own *Earl-isms;* they didn't need to hear his, they needed to savor theirs….they *all* did.

He left his pocket-notes untouched, and recalled his many past visits to his parents, slamming an open hand hard on the granite face of the mausoleum wall to get their attention, to wake them up from their slumber, and then sitting quietly, feet propped on the stone facade, and forging a leisurely mind-ramble with the two of them, reliving a lifetime of good, better and best. He always thought there was no better way to share time with those that were somewhere else; it didn't get much better than that.

Cord cleared his throat.

"Most of you probably don't know me; my name is Cord Brin. I met Earl six months ago, by chance, in the middle of *this very* Park. Unbeknownst to me, I was sitting on his mom's bench, so he sat beside me, and as simple as that, so began the journey. And the next six months, these past six months….what a ride. I can't imagine knowing Earl for years, for decades, as most of you probably have. Some, like Sam, all forty years that Earl walked around this little Town. In Earl, I found the brother I always wanted, the best friend I never had, a kindred spirit that few of us are ever lucky enough to meet, all wrapped in an unbelievable package....so sweet, innocent and good. I never deserved an Earl, most of us don't, yet we all got him....I suspect most of us are here today because of it. So rather than listen to me recount my own Earl stories, and in six months I have more than a lifetime's worth, please just close your eyes for a long moment, all of you, and take Earl along for a jaunt: remember the good, the better and the best of times with him, be it a day spent, or simply a glance exchanged. There are well over a thousand of us here today; there are *ten times that* in stories we all share in common....how Earl touched us, made us think, made us feel, made us *better*. To a friend, I can't think of a better way to say goodbye.

CHAPTER 454 – WHAT A RIDE

In that beautiful Park, a thousand plus were swept in a hush, collective eyes closed; a mix of wry smiles, trembling lips and tears drifted through the mass, and as they did, Earl was streaming live through all their minds, snippets of forty years....videos loops in a thousand imaginations.

Earl was *everywhere*.

And there he was, a fourteen-year-old boy, sitting quiet, swinging his legs on his favorite bench, smiling wide and listening to his best friend and looking over a sea of people while holding his mother's hand, drinking it all in.

They were all there for *him*, they were all thinking of *him,* and Earl could see *every* memory, all at once, sprinkled on a thousand screens in everyone's mind.

What a ride.

CHAPTER 455 – WAITING FOR THE RIGHT MOMENT TO PULL THE TRIGGER

C slowly opened his lids, as the best memories of Earl faded to a wisp; he blinked in the afternoon sun and watched as an ocean of eyes began to unseal, accompanied by small smiles, dressed in melancholy.

"I bet Earl enjoyed that; I know I did. One last thing I'd like to do, before I stand down. Whenever Earl was sad, or happy, or anywhere in-between, he would sing a familiar song, one he shared with his sister, and his mother. It was his favorite, his mom's too. Now I can't sing, not a lick, and every time I tried to sing this song, to practice - and Earl would always encourage me to practice - he would roll his eyes, cover his ears, and tell me to please not ever sing again….it was *that* bad. Anyway, I would practice a lot, on my own, so I could hope to surprise him someday, to let him know that maybe I could get just one stanza out before he begged me to stop.

Well, now he can't stop me, so please, let me do one stanza before you boo me to sit down; it means the world to me, and I want to do this for him."

Cord bowed his head, so they couldn't see him cry, but they heard it in his voice. He tried to compose himself, but it wasn't easy; it seemed like forever before he could steady his voice enough to give it a try.

While C had been speaking, a lone, thin black man took a long last drag on a half-smoked *Lucky Strike*, then flicked it indifferent to the road, where it once-bounced off the curb, landing in leaf litter accumulated in the gutter. The young man stood straight and stretched from his lean against his beat-up car, idling Park-side in front of the Presbyterian Church along Mansfield Street, about two-thirds of a football field from Cord. He shuffled a few steps, slowly opened his trunk, unzipped the large duffel bag, assembled his gear and quietly clicked it shut. He walked a half-dozen steps in army boots and stood alone in the grass, about twenty feet into the Green, partially obscured by a large sugar maple. No one saw him, no one paid attention, all eyes were directed at the Courthouse, to the lectern, and Cord standing behind it.

It only took a few moments before he was fully outfitted and ready, standing silent. He eyed Cord in the distance through a squint, biding his time, waiting for the right moment to pull the trigger.

CHAPTER 456 – AMAZING GRACE HOW SWEET THE SOUND

Cord Brin stood alone at the ambo; the crowd sat silent, watching him. He didn't see the young man two hundred feet away, eyeing him intently from behind the immense trunk of the maple. But he knew he was somewhere in the Park....he felt him.

And that was a good thing.

C raised his head to speak, but before the first word left his mouth, the young black man exhaled as he squeezed his fingers, and a haunting shrill drifted through the Fall air in the Park, wafting toward the thousand-strong.

Once the sound was heard, was recognized, a collective cry rippled through the crowd.

Except for Earl; he smiled wide, squeezing his mom's hand. She squeezed back, and they were both smiling broad.

The Scottish bagpipes came alive, as the first stanza spilled from C's trembling lips:

Amazing grace how sweet the sound

CHAPTER 457 – IT WAS BAD; BUT HE WAS SAVED

It was bad; but he was saved.

CHAPTER 458 – IT HAD BEEN TOO LONG, AND IT FELT GOOD

Cord reduced his voice from a boomlet, to a whisper, to nothing in the span of six words, as he coursed the second stanza:

that saved a wretch like me;

Because her voice took over.

It filled the Park and blanketed the crowd with such beauty, mixed bittersweet with overwhelming sorrow, that no one, not even the young black man, accompanying her on the bagpipes, could claim dry eyes.

I once was lost, but now am found;
Was blind, but now I see.

T'was grace that taught my heart to fear,
and grace my fears relieved;
how precious did that grace appear,
the hour I first believed.

And as Lillian continued, she never stood, nor opened her eyes; all she did was sing to her brother, to her mother, in the most beautiful voice anyone in earshot had ever heard, as she squeezed Carol's hand, for strength, the lilting bagpipes followed for the ride.

Earl had said that his mother had the most beautiful voice he ever heard, except for Lillian. Lillian sang like no other. And he was right as rain.

Earl sat, chin high, abeam, as he held his mother's hand, and they both sang with Lillian, the three of them, singing together….for the first time in twenty-five long years.

It had been too long, and it felt good.

2718

CHAPTER 459 – THIS IS THE BEST FUNERAL *EVER*

Through many dangers, toils and snares,
I have already come;
Tis grace that brought me safe thus far,
and grace will lead me home.

And with *home*, as Lillian finished the word, came the first bark, a thunderous percussion, coughed on Mansfield, less than fifty yards away, near the Post Office that Earl and Cord visited that very first day together, just out of sight.

But not for long.

It was inescapable, and unmistakable.

And the rasped gnarl of the engine grew louder and louder still, the bluster a constant bellow belched by the black *Knucklehead* with the red seat.

Earl's *Knucklehead.*

It stopped Lillian and the bagpipes cold. The concussion echoed through the Park; the crowd was rapt silent, as the bike slowly rolled up Mansfield, past the Presbyterian Church.

The chopper wheeled just half a block before the deafening cloud of the rest followed. Cord looked on in awe as a mass of motorcycles, locusts, like no other anyone had ever seen, slowly queued down Mansfield, following Mac and Lucien. The air in the entire Square vibrated as the first hundred bikes strung a third of the way around the Park, growling, a pack of rabid dogs, seven across, countless deep. The most bikes circling the Green numbered two-hundred-fifty during *Rolling Thunder*….the most *ever*.

The bike-count hit two-hundred-fifty before Mac had even reached Carol's house.

The noise was ratcheted to ear-pierce – Belvidere had never seen the likes before. Three hundred became four hundred, which swelled to five hundred, choking all four sides of the square, dozens of police choppers mixed in and amongst, paying respect. Two motorcyle patrolers, beefy white and blue enduros, friends of Martin, officers in blue, brought up the rear as the mass of leather and metal engulfed the Square.

Final tally: five-hundred-thirty-two bikes, all revving as one, the windows in every building around the Park shook in their frames, all in honor of Earl.

By this time Earl was standing tall on his bench, beside his mother, the percussion buffeting him in an endless sea of sound. Earl's mouth was stretched mile-wide in a smile as big as they come; his eyes sparkled, awe that only a fourteen-year-old can lay claim.

He squeezed his mom's shoulder, his face beaming, as he breathed to her, barely above a whisper.

"This is the best funeral *ever*."

CHAPTER 460 – WATCHED ONE TIN SOLDIER RIDE AWAY

Mac and Lucien ponied slow to the podium; the only bike allowed inside the white sawhorses cordoning off Second Street, in front of the Courthouse.

The remaining five-hundred-thirty-one hogs idled-in-wait, barking, coughing and pulsing as one, a thousand-leg centipede wending the remaining planes of the Green.

Lucien's eyes were bloodshot, her face wet with tears; Mac was scrunching his face, trying not to join her, and failing. His red eyes were hidden behind mirrored shades.

Cord looked at Earl, placing his hand gently on the urn.

"Time for your IOU buddy; and you got a bit of a train to follow."

C said, he scanned the endless mass of metal encircling the Park.

"It's a beautiful day; enjoy your ride my friend."

C whispered.

And with that he handed Lucien the urn. She quickly cinched it with a lanyard around herself, and pressed it between her and Mac, a tight threesome on the bike. Mac, who never uttered a word, simply nodded his head in agreement, revved the *Knucklehead*, and raised a single arm, hand clenched in a solemn fist, punching the sky, a tribute to Earl Liddell....*Billy-Jack* style. He kept his arm raised, as did Lucien, and he quickly skipped past the Courthouse, straight for a block and took a left onto Greenwich Street. In less than twenty seconds, he, Lucien and Earl were gone, on the ride of Earl's life.

It was then the centipede, five-hundred-thirty-one bike
links long, followed single file past the podium, each
rider, each passenger, with arm raised, fist clenched,
punching the sky in honor of Earl.

It took a full fifteen minutes for the last police bike to
pass; not a single person spoke, not a single person left.

Five-hundred-thirty-one choppers followed as the crowd
of a thousand plus watched one tin soldier ride away.

CHAPTER 461– YOU NEVER HAVE TO HOLD ON AGAIN

Earl stood tall on the bench and watched in awe, both fists clenched, pushing the sky above his head, a mimic to the parade that was there for him. His smile was a mile-wide.

His mother looked up at him, lightly rubbing his leg; a proud visage creased her face.

"Hey mom, can I ask you something?"

Earl said, still tracking the line of bikes passing Cord.

"Sure sweetie."

"Is that *your* bike, your *Knucklehead*? Is *my* bike *your* bike? I bet it is, isn't it? I betcha it is!"

Carol smiled sad, and sat stoic for what seemed like forever. Finally, she barely shook her head in a twice-nod.

It was a yes.

"**I knew it!** Lilly didn't believe me, but I just knew it! You used to ride on that *same* bike....*my* bike!"

Carol smiled and shook her head, more forceful, this time.

"Yes sweetie, many, many times, it was my favorite; I loved that bike."

"Oh boy, I knew it! Did you ride with my dad? Did he look like Santa Claus? I always pictured him like Santa Claus! Was he jolly and fat? Did he wear a red suit? Was it his bike? I bet he rode it the best ever, even better than C can; I bet he could even beat the dust, right?"

And the joy drained from her face, and Earl saw it. And he wanted to un-break the egg. She saw the worry in his little face, and couldn't stand it; Earl should never have to worry again.

She decided there would be no more lies.

"Sweetie, the man who owned that bike didn't look like Santa Claus, and he was not your father, he was a good friend, a very good friend of mine, at one time, who treated me very badly in the end, so I left him. And to hurt me, he took my baby away, and gave me a new baby instead, thinking it would punish me, and make me sad. And I was, sad, to lose my baby....but he never realized he did me the greatest favor in the world sweetie....he gave me *you*."

Earl just looked at Carol, face scrunched....processing.

"Where did I come from then, the grocery store?"

Carol smiled and laughed through a cry, a little snort of a snicker.

"I don't think so. You just have a dad that I never met, and a real mom, that I didn't know either, but that doesn't matter to me, it never did; I hope it doesn't matter to you. I'm sorry I never told you; I was ashamed of myself. I wasn't a good mother that way; I'm sorry Earl, you deserved better than me."

Earl bent down and touched his mother's face, her cheek was wet, and she was trembling.

"You're my real mom, you always have been, and always will be....forever. And you were the best mother ever, ever, ever, ever....*ever!* You still are. I love you mommy."

Carol cradled his hand in hers, and the two were silent on their bench, in the middle of the Park, as the engines roared all around them.

"Mac said the man who owned the bike, who sold him the bike was named Jones, is that right mom? Was that your friend? Was he your boyfriend?"

Carol shook a mournful yes to all the above.

"Hey my lizard is named Jonesy! Isn't that funny, that I named him Jonesy? I don't know why I did that, when C gave him to me; I looked at that poor little wrinkled, shriveled lizard and poof – the name just popped in my head - just like that! Isn't that funny mommy?"

Carol just smiled wry.

"Yes sweetie, sometimes things like that just pop in your head."

Carol stood up and hugged her son hard, sucking him in so close, trying to absorb him into her.

"Hey mom, I got a good idea."

She pulled away and looked up at him.

"What?"

"Wanna go for a ride?"

Carol just smiled.

"You can't just do what you want Earl, not in this place; it doesn't work that way."

"Sure it does!"

He said with the confidence only a little boy can have.

"Go ahead, grab my hand mommy."

Earl extended his to hers, she touched it lightly, and in an instant, they were there, front of the line. She was amazed; he just smirked at her.

"Do I hafta be careful? Do I hafta hold on?"

Carol smiled, knowing Earl already knew the answer. She shook her head a slow no.

"No sweetie, you never have to hold on again."

CHAPTER 462 – WHAT A RIDE

Mac found himself grinning, the first time he had since he got the news. Lucien hugged him tight from behind, Earl's urn snug between them. He knew that hug; he knew she was beaming too.

Why, they no idea.   But it felt good.

And they couldn't shake the smiles, at the head of five-hundred-thirty-two bikes, snaking the highway, the convoy stopping traffic in all directions.

Earl, all fourteen years of him, stood tall atop Macs shoulders, arms touchdown over his head, the wind whipping his clothes. His mother saddled at the rear, arms around Lucien's waist, head resting gently on her shoulder, looking up radiant at her son, her hair waving wild in the wind.

God, she loved this bike, and she loved her son; she could simply stay here forever.

What a ride.

CHAPTER 463 – THERE WAS PLENTY OF ROOM FOR FOUR FRIENDS

Just over two hours had passed.

It took that long for the crowd to disperse, for the last stragglers to offer condolences to Lillian, Carol and Cord.

Buck was last to leave; like a puppy, he didn't want to go, shadowing C's side on an invisible leash. He couldn't stop crying; it wasn't full bore, just a still whimper now and again, followed by quiet, accompanied by a non-stop shake of the head, a nose sleeve-wipe.

All those years he was mean to Earl, for what? He wished he could take it all back; he wished he was dead too. Cord told him Earl didn't give a lick about any of it, all he cared about was Billy in the end – that they were good friends again, and that Billy loved Chicken, that's all that mattered. Buck wanted to believe it was that easy, but he just couldn't shake all the memories of bad behavior – a stain he couldn't erase.

But now Buck too was gone, and the Park was empty. The urn was on its ride, and the three sat alone, squeezed tight on Earl's bench, heads looking at the leaves surrounding their shoes. Carol and Cord were bookend, with Lillian between. Carol and Lillian held each others hand; C was hunched over, fingers folded on his lap.

And they shared the silence, as the crows and the jays squawked incessant, unseen overhead.

"What am I gonna do?"

Carol asked the ground, shaking her head, not wanting an answer. No one obliged.

They had all been sleeping at Carol's since last Sunday. Lillian refused to sleep in the apartment, and C had no interest in occupying that space. Carol had set up a room for Lillian and Cord the first night, but they didn't sleep together; Lillian wandered the house alone, and finally crawled into bed with Carol sometime early Monday morning. They both slept till close to noon the next day. Cord crashed on the sofa, in the rear parlor, with Chicken and a revolving door of Carol's cats on his chest and at his feet. Chicken couldn't get close enough to Cord; he shook his head at the irony. Always second fiddle, till he was the only fiddle.

Carol hadn't been to work, and had no plans on returning anytime soon. The office ran itself; she had a good staff, and let them take the reigns. For now....until when, she didn't know. And she didn't care. It mattered that little; she wasn't sure when it would matter again....eventually, she guessed. But not yet; not even close to yet.

"We should go tomorrow, it's supposed to be a nice day; he said he wanted to go on a nice day."

C said to the two; neither answered.

"Well?"

"On a bus? *Why?*"

Lillian said, deflated and annoyed at the same time.

"Because that's what *he* wanted; he always said he wanted to see the levee rim road, to beat the dust, and to do it by bus, just like how I showed up here....same exact bus. I don't know why he wanted that, he just did. He asked about it all the time, like he always does when he wants something real bad. So that's what I'm gonna do, simple as that. If you two don't want to go, fine, no problem, I'll go alone. I'll just take a bit of him with me, and be back....later."

Lillian looked up at him with wary eyes; the words snapped more than she expected.

"When's *later?*"

C's immediate thought was the real answer: *there likely isn't going to be a later.* But that's not what he told Lillian.

"When it feels right to come back."

Was all he said, and he said nothing more, staring blank at his boots.

She was in no mood to argue, so she let it drop. He figured she didn't really care, and he congratulated himself for being right.

"I don't even know how to feel, or what to say, or what to do, or anything. I've never felt so helpless, so….*lost.*"

Carol said, still having a conversation with herself.

"I just wish I could talk to him, to have him tell me he's okay, wherever he is, because I know he's *somewhere.* He's not in that urn, I know that, I believe that more than anything; I just hope it's a good place, and that he's happy, and that he's with your mom."

Carol looked to Lillian and whispered so low, the two of them barely heard her.

Lillian squeeze Carol's hand, and placed her head gently on her shoulder. Cord reached over and put his hand atop theirs, a pyramid of fingers interlocked.

"I know he's okay, I just know."

Lillian whispered and smiled in a way that one does when one truly understands what others only hope.

And with that, Earl smiled and kissed his big sister on the forehead, put his enormous mitt atop their three, a pancake of hands, and easily squeezed between the three of them on the bench.

The four friends sat quiet, and for a bit, anyway, things for Lillian, Carol and Cord seemed closer to okay than they had in days.

Because on that bench, there was plenty of room for four friends.

CHAPTER 464 – ASS-SORE, IT WAS TIME TO BLOW THE BUS

Fuck.

The word bounced about his brain, for no particular reason.

Typical.

The bus hummed along at a good clip; the grass median was a blur and the season's corn stalks drying in the fields passed by - an endless line of silent sentries. He stared blankly at the kinetic scene, his head lightly touching and then lifting off the glass, on and off, as the bus gently rocked along. It was a beautiful sun-splashed day; it shouldn't have been.

The destination was fast approaching.

He cracked his knuckles; half responded loudly, like oft-cracked knuckles do; the others were blanks. He stretched his legs and frowned a bit, then casually looked to the middle seat of the row; the porcelain urn sat beside him, safe, secure, pushed snug against the low, steady purr of the Sherpa bag, still always together, inseparable. She knew, Chicken knew, Earl was in there. He smiled to himself at the thought....that little uptick smile that accompanied pursed lips.

The aisle seat was empty, as was the near-seat across the aisle. Both were still warm; bodies there, no longer were.

Three rows from the front.

Six months of lost weight was certainly visible, must be thirty-five to forty-odd pounds, he figured. A lot. He's not sure why it came to mind at this point, but it did. He could see it, or lack thereof, in his face, in his stomach. He was donning a new outfit, the first change in travel-wear in years, but there was no choice in that regard. His old habit: comfortable blue blazer and green, linen button-down, his faded jeans, a favorite pair, thread-worn, with the beginnings of a frayed hole in the crotch, and the tried tassel-loafers, which shined with a rich gloss, sporting remnants of white *Ammens* foot powder, which also faintly colored the tops of his feet, were, in toto, long gone, burned in the incinerator, converted to electricity, pulsing through overhead wires.

His new outfit fit well, better than his old one ever did; the shoes were shined to an even luster. Newly shined shoes usually put him in a good mood, but not today.

Certainly not today.

He felt apprehensive, tired and not particularly proud. But he knew this conte was to be expected all along.

But he never figured it would end this way, not this ending....never.

He quietly closed his eyes and extended a long exhale as he settled back in his seat, alone, rocking gently with the sway of the bus.

In a moment, Carol and Lillian were back in their seats beside him. The tired *Greyhound* crossed the cable-stayed Emerson Memorial Bridge, leaving the Illinois farm fields behind, the chocolate waters of the mighty Mississippi flowing slow and south, far below them. The bus routed past the River Campus of Southeast Missouri State University, along Shawnee Parkway, taking a right, and weaving through *historic* downtown Cape Girardeau, Missouri which was just a much larger version, half a country away, of *historic* downtown Belvidere. A tired, Midwest town, blue collar, trying to do better, but pocked heavy with worn, empty storefronts: *coming soons* that never came, and modest homes, a mix of ramshackle and not.

The bus ambled slow through blocks of weary buildings built along the river, wending its way until they found themselves on Broadway. Lillian spied one of the many orange, blue and green telephone pole banners, snapping light in the breeze, each pronouncing:

Great
American
Main Street
Community
Old Town Cape
Cape Girardeau, MO

Live….Work….Play

"Live, Work, Play? ***In this*** *[Lillian pointed out the window at the passing sorry street scene]?*! Christ, we came all this way for *this*? I can be a part of this crap in Belvidere."

Lillian spat the words invective, peering out the window at the depressing scene.

"Almost there."

Was all C said, in a tired voice; Carol was silent, eyes half-closed, an ongoing interrupted sleep.

The dusty bus rolled to a quiet stop at 937 Broadway; the remaining handful of passengers stood, stretched and gathered whatever it was they brought along. For each of the three, it was simply a small travel bag, accompanied by Earl-in-an-urn and a dozing Chicken-in-a-Sherpa.

After sixteen long hours, and a day later, ass-sore, it was time to blow the bus.

2734

CHAPTER 465 – DESTINATION ARRIVED: THE MIDDLE OF NOWHERE

As expected, the sleek, black stretch limousine was idling in the Broadway Plaza parking lot. Carol walked to the window and spoke monotone.

"Waiting long?"

He shook a no, exited and opened the rear door; the four and Chicken silently slid in.

"All the bags set? In the trunk?"

Carol asked.

The driver simply nodded yes.

"Regional airport in Scott City, off 55, just south of here; can you find it?"

C said.

Again, the driver didn't speak; he simply nodded a yes, punched it in, and with that, the stretch retraced the bus ride through downtown, and wended its way toward Route 55, southbound, no more than a ten minute ride.

They motored silent along Route 55 South; Lillian closed her eyes for a bit, and seemed to doze. Suddenly, in a bit of a jolt, her eyes opened wide, the little body-shift that accompanies a startled wake. She looked at Carol and Cord; neither noticed the event. She stared across the back seat of the coach, at the side of Cord's face, on the far end of the bench seat; he seemed lost in thought. What was going through his mind, she thought; to this day, she *still* had no idea who he really was.

In just a few miles, the signpost ahead signaled the next stop:

Missouri AB, Nash Road, lay perpendicular, off the end of the ramp. To the right, and a quick left, dumped the car onto Airport Road; in less than a minute, they found themselves in the small parking lot aside a spit of an airstrip, set in the expanse of gray floodplain mud flats of Scott City, a piss-ant to which few paid attention, at the top end of the Missouri Bootheel.

Destination arrived: the middle of nowhere.

CHAPTER 466 – IT WAS A GIVEN, BECAUSE SHE WAS NEVER WRONG

The custom, private jet was pulled into a T-hanger, off the tarmac; the pilot and assistant waiting patiently beside.

"There it is."

Carol said, pointing.

"You think it's okay?"

Lillian asked, politely.

"Yeah, my office took care of it, took care of everything; there won't be a problem – there never is - they're very good."

And she was right.

Earl's *Knucklehead* was already unloaded, fully fueled and polished high, the sun glinting off the black body, laying in wait beside the plane.

The stretch limousine idled nearby; the driver, with shades, stood stoic, looking straight ahead. It was Carol's limousine, her personal driver, her personal plane, along with her dedicated pilot and crew. Never once had she mentioned to Earl, Lillian or Cord she had any of them.

"Are you sure you want to do this now? You must be tired."

Carol asked C.

"No, I'm doing it right now; it's a beautiful afternoon, just the right kind of day, just the right time of day. Dusk is coming; the sun's gonna disappear soon enough. Everything's right….it's time."

"Do you need the bolt-cutters? They should be in the trunk."

Carol said, looking to her driver; he nodded yes.

"No. We passed the access road when we got off the ramp, it's right next to the ramp – forgot just how close. I looked and the old gate is still there, but it was swung open....unlocked. It was never unlocked – never. But then again, I haven't seen it in twenty years, so maybe it's always unlocked nowadays, or maybe it knew we were coming."

C continued.

"Hey, in my bag there are four books; the two Ken Holt's I owed Earl for lost bets awhile ago: *The Riddle Of The Stone Elephant* and *The Black Thumb Mystery*; plus I got him the next two, numbers four and five in the series, I will owe him for this ride, when he beats the dust: *The Clue of the Marked Claw* and *The Clue of the Coiled Cobra.* He always loved the titles; he'd say them while he twiddled his thumbs like he did whenever he got over-excited; God I miss that....who would ever think you'd miss someone twiddling their fucking thumbs. Anyway, I wish I gave him the first two, but I never did, and he's gonna earn the next two. Maybe you two you can read them to him, keep them by the urn; I know he'd like that."

C grabbed the small cardboard box of ashes, a subset extracted from the porcelain urn, to ride on his lap. Funny, he remembered telling Earl, on the bet for Holt book numbers four and five, that the only way he would ever beat the dust is if he *rode his fat ass on C's lap....and that wasn't happening.* But Earl took the bet anyway, because his mother told him the bet was sure, and she was always right in such matters; in fact, she was never wrong. C shook his head sad at the memory; his mother knew about *this* day way back then, months ago; she knew this day was coming, that C would be standing here, today, with her son's ashes in his hands, all along.

Cord frowned.

He was sad at losing his brother, sad for Carol, and for Lillian; but he was happy, because he was sure he was going to see Earl soon.   *Real* soon, as in *a-couple-minutes* soon.   And if he was lucky, maybe he'd meet Carol too, for more than just a fleeting squeeze of the hand in the *Jenny Jump* barn that morning, maybe a real face-to-face, whatever *real* meant.   In any event, it would make all this nonsense worthwhile.   He had tried a hundred times over to beat the dust when he was here twenty-odd years ago, and always failed.   But not this time, he knew he was going to beat the dust; that was a given.

But he also knew another given, because he also remembered the last thing he told Earl that day:

"I still don't believe it, it's a good bet; your mom's going down on this one. The only one to beat the dust is me, and I'd probably fucking die doing it."

It was a given, because she was never wrong.

CHAPTER 467 – AN EYE BLINK AND THE SLIGHTEST, SINGLE NOD

With that, Cord straddled the bike, sans helmet, and kicked her to life. The engine coughed and pulsed, vibrating his body. He donned his cheap black shades, the ones from the Mustang, and turned the bike for the short ride up Airport Road, to the gravel Outer Lane, which ended dead at the gate to the levee rim road, skirting the Castor River Diversion Channel.

"We'll follow you in the limo."

Carol said, gesturing Lillian to join her, the driver politely held the door open for the girls. But Lillian stepped away from the limo, toward the bike, and started to straddle the back, behind Cord.

Cord shot her a look, tipping the bike away from her.

"Whoa, what the fuck are you doing?"

"Going with you."

Lillian said, *adaman*t was clearly in her voice.

"No you're not, no fucking way, not a chance; *way* too dangerous."

"I'm going with *my* brother, which means I'm going with you. You don't have a fucking choice, you don't have a fucking say; and if you don't understand that by now, after all we've been through, if you *really* think this issue is up for a fucking debate, then you really don't know me."

Lillian wasn't even close to joking. He had too-many-times seen the dark side of Lilly, the *don't-fuck* side that was scary – and the look she was giving him now didn't come close to that. It was worse.

He took off his shades and just stared hard at her, and she back at him....harder.

Without a word, he leaned in ever-close to her, so close their noses lightly touched, and even then, C spoke so soft that Lilly barely heard his words.

But she did.

Cord asked if she had talked to her; Lillian answered with an eye blink and the slightest, single nod.

CHAPTER 468 - HER JAW SET HARD

Cord had no idea what that meant, or what her mother had said to Lillian. It couldn't have been good; Lilly didn't have anything close to a good news face on.

Would one die? Or the other? Would they both die? Would they finally be together, all of them? Was this *always* meant to be the end? Was this why he came?

It all raced through his head in the milliseconds that passed after her blink and nod.

At this point, he figured it didn't matter; what would be, would be....events were out of his hands. C didn't say another word; he simply tilted the bike toward her, and she straddled the ruby-red seat, sucked up tight against Cord, her arms cinched around his waist.

Carol was utterly distressed.

"Don't worry, I'll drive safe, we'll be fine. Just drive up with us to the ramp, and then meet us at the other end; it's three miles down Nash Road. Follow the cloud of dust and meet us on the other end. About five minutes; we sat for sixteen hours on a shit-ass bus for five minutes on a bike....crazy, right?"

C tried to make light, but Carol wasn't buying. But she knew she had no choice – she saw Lilly on the bike, her face hard, looking straight into C's back; she was done talking. Carol put her head down and disappeared into the back of the limousine.

C handed Lillian the box.

"I assume you want to hold him; it'll be better for me to concentrate on the gravel path. I haven't been on this stretch for twenty years; I assume nothing has changed, but I could be wrong, there could be surprises. It's a long, quick three miles. Also, there's a *nasty* ninety degree turn halfway down the road, crossing over a set of active, rail tracks, although freight trains rarely use these tracks, maybe once a day, maybe less. But that dog-leg over the tracks, even without any trains coming, is a fucking bitch; if we get in trouble, it could be anywhere, but it'll likely be right there. So just hold the fuck on, and don't let go for *anything;* this is gonna be one fucking ride that…."

C didn't finish the sentence. Lillian took the box and gripped it tight....a death-grip.

"I'm not gonna ask what your mother told you, and I don't want to know; the table's set - it is what it is."

C revved the engine loud, so he couldn't hear her answer.

But there was nothing to hear; Lillian didn't say a word, she just held on tight to C's waist, her jaw set hard.

CHAPTER 469 – IT WASN'T PUT THERE FOR HIM....BUT FOR THEM

The dusty, gray gravel spoke low as it pinched under the bike tires; it mixed with the hum of spotty traffic, tractor-trailers mostly, on nearby 55, the rustle of leaves in the trees between them and the Diversion Channel far below and the din of afternoon Missouri crickets. The *Knucklehead* slowly rolled under the low-slung power lines, through the unlocked pasture gate, and climbed the steep gravel road facing the levee, slipping and gripping the loose rock. They slowed to a quiet stop as they crested the levee top, thirty yards past the unsecured security gate.

Before them lay a narrow, twelve foot wide gray ribbon of rock, strung atop the levee like an ever-long string. The green-tinted, muddy river lay far below them to the right; fallow fields and an endless row of nondescript, low-slung industrial buildings spread far below to the left. C slowly raised his head and stared down the raceway before him; he had scorched this strip a hundred times in his silver Chevy, maybe more, blasting the radio....and he *always* lost.

He's not even sure why he played the game with the dust; he just made it up one bored day in his twenties, and it soon became an obsession. But maybe he never made it up, maybe it was all part of the other game, the *real* game. Maybe it was just as he thought, a grown-up version of those dam-scampers he made as a kid, outrunning the park rangers, when he skewered himself on a fence at twelve and was made a player in a game he still didn't understand. Maybe it had been decided then, as he struggled on those spikes that he would end up here, thirty-one years later. Maybe this levee meant something more than simply a cloud of stone dust.

He shook his head; it had been twenty-one long years since he last stood on this levee, looking down the pike through through twenty-two year old eyes....Christ, if he only knew then what those eyes would witness, the carnage, in the coming years; a lot of water under the bridge, a lot of bodies left in the wake. What a fucking mess.

But this run was decidedly different; he wasn't alone. And that part, he didn't like, not one bit. Especially when *that part* was Lillian, sucked up behind him.

As if on cue, his favorite stanza from *Sunset Grill* played in his head:

Respectable little murders pay,
They get more respectable every day;
Don't worry girl, I'm gonna stand by you,
And someday soon,
Were gonna get in that car and get outta here.

He looked down to his right; going over the levee edge was a one-shot deal – there was no recover if you went south – you'd be done. In this case, they'd *both* be done.

The October *Bootheel* sun was beginning to set, pushing through loose-knit wisps of clouds, low on the horizon; it was still hot and humid - the air was thick, vintage *Mizzou.*

Just as he cranked the throttle to rev the engine, the bottom of the sun kissed the horizon and the sky turned orphic, the cloud edges were on fire with sunlight, white hot embers, glowing across the horizon. He was sure no one else was looking at that sky right at that moment, no one had the vantage he had, and saw what he saw - it was set there just for him.

And right at that moment he wondered if the good times, the very good times, that he felt were coming his way twenty-one years ago would ever show, because they certainly hadn't so far. At least not in the way he imagined. He always believed it wasn't a matter of *if*, it was simply a matter of *when*. Back then, in 1985, the premonition felt providential, not in a religious way, but rather in a sense of peculiar good fortune.

Good fortune that, in the way he expected, had yet to show its face. Maybe it was just a bad joke, and he was the only one who hadn't yet gotten it.

But at what point does one say to oneself: I'm satisfied, I'm fulfilled, I'm not interested in the better times that surely await me around the next bend – for what I have already experienced *is* the *good* in the good times – more isn't necessarily better, it's just more.

And for some reason, at that moment, he turned and looked at Lillian. And he saw she was staring in awe at the same sky, the same orphic Missouri sun.

And he realized then that it wasn't put there for him….but for them.

Just as Mac had promised, he hit the black button on the dashboard console, and the lyrics began, as the rear tire spun and spit gravel skyward, high behind them. Without warning, he gunned the bike, like he always did the Chevy, just as the song was beginning to play:

Sunset Grill

After twenty-one years, the game was finally replayed.

The *Knucklehead* quickly climbed past eighty in the first fifty yards; Lillian was holding on for dear life. Cord looked in the rear view and the dust was spiraling high behind them; it was still on its way up, curling and wafting lazy with the afternoon breeze. Lillian didn't dare look left or right, her eyes were squeezed shut and straight ahead, into Cord's back, just as her mom told her, and she gripped Earl tight, squeezing the box with all her might.

The bike clipped the half-mile mark in just under eighteen seconds; the speedometer topped one-hundred miles per hour and was still climbing. The first straightaway, until the first gentle curve north, to the right, tilting toward the Dutchtown Ditch and Ranney Creek, was exactly 1.6 miles into the run; they would have to hit that break at just under the minute mark, it would have to be that fast, if not faster, to beat the dust. The bike was clocking one-hundred-ten miles per hour; Lillian couldn't see, but felt Cord lean slight to the right, and she leaned with him, as the engine roared hot between her legs.

He yelled to her that the ninety-degree dog-leg, just over the rail tracks, was coming fast, it was ten seconds away....less. He had to slow down fast, crossing the tracks, or they would never make the dog-leg-left, they would sail straight off the levee rim and end into the canal far below – you simply die at that dog-leg if you don't make that turn.

There was no alternative.

And the canal waited patiently for them to die in her.

But Lillian didn't hear a word C said; her eyes were squeezed shut, her head buried in his back, as she was told.

Which was good.

Because in the hundred-plus runs Cord had made on this rim road, the hundred runs that he always lost to the dust, he had to slow too much to navigate the ninety-degree dog-leg-left....and that slowdown, to survive the canal, would spell defeat to the dust.

Every time.

But in the hundred-plus runs he had made in the past, when he invariably slowed at the rail crossing before the dog-leg, instinct more than anything else, he never once had to take an outlier into consideration.

Because there never once was a freight train coming up on the crossing.

But there was now.

CHAPTER 471 – COULDN'T MOVE HIS EYES
OFF WHAT HE SAW....JUST COULDN'T

The *Burlington Northern* and *Sante Fe Pacific* railroads merged in 1995; from it, *BNSF* was birthed, and with it forty-three thousand employees and twenty-two billion dollars in revenue....a spidery conglomeration of three-hundred-ninety rail lines merged, morphed and molded over one-hundred-sixty years into one behemoth.

It was a monster.

There were thirty-two-thousand five-hundred miles of track in the *BNSF* web, wending over two-thirds of the western United States, Canada and Mexico. And one of the oldest rails in the *BNSF* fold was the *St. Louis – San Francisco Railway* line, known simply as the *Frisco*. And the *Frisco* checkered the *Mizzou Bootheel*, winding its way through every too-small farm town in Missouri, and had for the past one-hundred-fifty years. They were the oldest, loneliest rails in a remote corner of nowhere.

Two monster yellow-jacket engines, painted black and gold, pulled a line of eighty-seven beat-up, open-top boxcars, stretching behind them for a full mile. Even empty, the snake weighed in at a shade above three-thousand tons....over *six million pounds* of moving steel on wheels. Even at thirty miles per hour, it would take no less than ten football fields, over a half-mile, to stop six million pounds of train in motion.

About thirty minutes prior, as the *Greyhound* crossed the Emerson Bridge into the Cape, the yellow-jackets were chugging north at fifty miles per hour, half-way between Sikeston, to its rear, and little Morley up ahead, rolling mindless through a patchwork of brown and green farm fields....sameness miles on end. The engineer, elbow out the open window, gazed glassy as the endless ribbon of rail slipped below the belly of the train, and spit out the other end.

Nash Road and the Diversion Channel lay in wait, just twenty-four miles up the track.

The Nash Railroad Bridge on the old *Frisco* line crossed the Castor River Diversion Channel in Scott City less than four-hundred feet east of the levee rim road dog-leg. It was a two-span through-truss, built in 1928, and it looked the part. It was old, rusted, and had the precarious look of a decrepit span standing on last legs. It had replaced a bridge that crumbled earlier that same year, 1928, when a freight train derailed as a two-hundred foot span of the bridge crumbled, plunging the freighter into the swirling waters of the Diversion Channel far below, killing the engineer and brakeman. A nasty mess, never forgotten.

It was almost eighty years ago, but train engineers *never* forget the places where engineers before them died. And they died just up ahead, round the bend.

So when the glassy-eyed engineer at the helm of the *BNSF* rounded the long curve into the portion of Scott City that ran along Nash Road, he slowed the belching yellow jackets just a bit, to thirty miles per hour. He wasn't focused on anything other than that rickety Nash Railroad Bridge spanning the Diversion Channel, the one he hated to cross, which lay less than five-hundred feet ahead, approaching fast. That put the head of the snake less than one-hundred feet from the gravel levee rim road that cut across the tracks, which, less than fifty feet later, dog-legged to the left.

The yellow-jacket would slice the rim road in less than three seconds.

So the engineer could be forgiven.

Because he never saw the hazy cloud of road dust off to his right, nor the cause for same, until he was upon it. So there was no braking, not as if it would have mattered, but he did get a fast hand on the whistle, one long blast, a concussion in the air the train was breaking before it.

And at that instant, just a flash really, he saw something, a blur of black, a shadow, crossing the nose of the yellow jacket. And he heard the slightest tick, an almost imperceptible bump, the kind you might hear when you hit a small animal on the highway, but you aren't really sure.

He turned quick, as the mile-long snake slowly slithered over the levee rim road, and headed for that fateful bridge.

And he couldn't move his eyes off what he saw….just couldn't.

The shame of it was that he could have survived, both he and Lillian could have lived to tell the tale.

If C had braked hard right at that instant, when he first eyed the yellow jacket barreling toward the crossing, and could somehow control the bike inside the safety of the twelve- foot cart-way, he could have stopped; Cord could have avoided hitting the train.

On loose gravel, at one-hundred-thirteen miles per hour, his speed into the turn, he would have needed over six-hundred feet to stop, and he had about twelve-hundred feet to play. He didn't know those numbers in his head, he just knew in his gut he had enough room.

And he was right.

But C also knew he had less than a few seconds, three seconds to be exact, before the bike ate up the excess yardage, and the decision would be made for him.

Three seconds in such situations is eternity.

And Cord didn't need eternity.

The full two-minute wait necessary for the length of boxcars to pass was a death sentence - it might as well have been two hours. To stop and wait those precious minutes would be to lose to the dust. And that simply wasn't in the cards he'd been dealt that day.

He hadn't figured how he would navigate the deadly dog-leg-left fifty feet beyond the rail crossing….he had a monster train to deal with first, and there was little time or distance past the train to figure a hard turn left, so the dog-leg would just have to work itself out. Either that, or he and Lillian would drown together under the still, green waters of the canal, far below.

Drown just like Earl.

Maybe *that* was the plan; maybe Earl was waiting down there for the two of them. In any event, he'd find out soon enough, with Lillian in tow.

So he didn't hit the brake; he tossed that ticket to live.

Instead, he ratcheted the accelerator and rocketed the *Knucklehead* on adrenaline to one-hundred-twenty miles per hour; it actually climbed beyond that, but Cord never saw just how fast he was going when he reached the crossing, because he turned his head and stared down the steel snake as it closed the gap fast from the left, the dog-leg-left laughing at him, straight ahead, a stone's throw beyond the tracks.

He screamed at the top of his lungs to Lillian:

"Hold on tight! No matter what happens, don't let go!"

But she never heard a word Cord said, his voice absorbed and vanished in the roar of the engine and the hurricane swirl of wind. She never even knew a train was in the works, and coming on fast.

Instead, she was jammed hard against his back, in a death-grip around his waist, listening on the *qui vive* to the whispers in her ear.

CHAPTER 473 – THE ONLY THING LEFT WAS IMPACT; THEN IT WAS OVER

It was a surreal feel, being nigh to the face of an oncoming train.

It obliterated the field of vision; the entire sky consumed by an enormous yellow, black and orange insect, its face full of twisted, rusted pipes and hoses – feelers, antennae, with dirt and grime smeared all about. Four white-hot lights glowed pyramid on its face – warning all to stay away, its two tiny glass eyes were set high above, looking far down the tracks, no attention paid to whatever lay below. The entirety engulfed them, breathing hot diesel, inches away. With no choice but to kill.

Cord took it all in, but the time elapsed was a mere fraction of a second.

C still thought he might just squeeze past, but he was wrong.

The last act, just before impact, was the belch of the *BNSF* horn, a sonorous eruption, an extended, ear-splitting, elephantine trumpet that rattled and shimmied the bike. Lillian screamed into the void, but never lost her iron-grip on C's waist, never disobeying what she was told to do by her mother.

But Earl somehow shimmied free between them and the box flew skyward, exploding into the face of the beast. Lillian knew she lost her brother, but she had no choice but to let him go, and to hold on tight to Cord Brin and weather the storm.

The only thing left was impact; then it was over.

CHAPTER 474 –TO *NOT* DIE, BUT LIVE; IT WAS THE ONLY OUT TO WIN

There was no rational way to explain what happened.

An uneven rail tie, an out-of-level section of spur, the buffet of the *BNSF* air horn, an involuntary shift in weight by Cord, or Lillian, or both….some combination thereof. Or simply something else.

Whatever it was; *something* happened.

And that *something* somehow lifted the front wheel of the *Knucklehead* off the ground, the bike inclined like the beginning of a wheelie. But the back tire, somehow, also barely unglued from the ground, just the thickness of a sheet of paper. But the air beneath the spinning rear rubber was just enough; there was suddenly no friction to hold it still while the train flattened it, and the two of them with it....end of story.

Instead the entire *Knucklehead* was airborne; a horse with no hoof touching the Earth.

And that was all they needed.

The yellow-jacket's massive, pocked black-iron V-angle, low to the ground, meant to clear debris from the tracks ahead of the ongoing engine, clipped the rear-most part of the *Knucklehead's* back tire, the very last half-inch of rubber.

C came that close to missing the train.

And in *missing* the train, he and Lillian would have sailed past the dog-leg at one-hundred-twenty miles per hour, off the rim road, landing, and dying, in the Diversion Channel far below, less than five seconds thereafter.

Both of them, less than five seconds to dead.

The yellow-jacket saved them; they needed to be hit by a
train to *not* die, but live; it was the only out to win.

CHAPTER 475 – ON ITS WAY ELSEWHERE....PURE NIRVANA

Pinball.

When you play a flipper-bat game on a classic *Bally*, the silver ball sometimes rockets out of the shoot, careens off a bumper, fatefully finding its way into a shallow, recessed cup, where it nervously sits for a second or so, while the bonus digits go crazy, racking up points, ringing bells, flashing lights and spinning numbers ever-higher, a sure path to extra balls and bonus play. Then the silver ball is suddenly rocketed, like a bullet, out of the cup, sailing across the slanted, flashing board, on its way elsewhere.

Nothing feels better; pure pinball wizard nirvana.

That's what the *Knucklehead* was, a silver ball, and that's what the *Knucklehead* did - sailed across the board, on its way elsewhere....pure nirvana.

CHAPTER 476 – IT PROBABLY COULDN'T HAVE *REALLY* HAPPENED. BUT IT DID

Three-hundred-eighteen feet.

No one ever measured it, but that's what it was when the wheels finally touched ground.

And no one would ever believe it actually happened, except the two people that witnessed it: Cord – through the air, and the yellow-jacket engineer, over his shoulder, as the engine rolled on, toward the Nash Bridge. And he wasn't sure what he actually saw; to this day, he still wasn't.

The *Knucklehead* sailed airborne in an arched trajectory, down the levee rim, somehow landing square on the gravel path a football field plus from impact.

What were the odds?

It clearly *shouldn't* have happened; it probably couldn't have *really* happened.

But it did.

CHAPTER 477 – MIXED BITTERSWEET WITH A BOX OF ASH

The final one mile plus stretch of rim was a straight shot; and Cord barreled it at a shade under one-hundred-thirty miles per hour. Lillian never unburied her head, not once. It was still glued to C's back, eyes shut, as he finally let up on the throttle and the bike coasted to a long, slow stop. She never asked him what happened, or how. It didn't matter, she knew, she truly believed, everything would be alright, if she just did as she was told.

And she did, and so it was.

As he crossed the finish, Cord looked over his shoulder, back a full three miles, an uninterrupted view, to the far end of the rim, where their conte began, just minutes ago.

And he smiled sad, for Earl had earned his prize.

For the dust from the gravel all the way back to the start still hung lazy in the air, mixed bittersweet with a box of ash.

CHAPTER 478 – CONTINGENCY PLAN

"Oh my God, we never thought you'd beat that train! Was it close?"

Cord just smiled at Carol and answered deadpan.

"Nah, beat it easy."

"But I lost the box, I lost Earl; we didn't really do it C, Earl wasn't with us, not in the end. We didn't win; we failed."

Lillian said dejected.

But Cord didn't seem to mind the infraction.

Instead, he quietly reached into his front pocket and pulled out a micro zip-lock, the kind you use for pills. It was carefully taped shut. But through the opaque plastic could be seen a light-to-dark gray ash, mixed with tiny bits of white. The packet was neatly labeled in black marker:

Open When You Are Ready....

———

The Clue of the Marked Claw
The Clue of the Coiled Cobra

Earl's fat ass was sitting on C's lap the whole time, the whole trip....start to end.

And Cord closed the chapter with two words, as he held up the packet and smiled wry at Carol and Lillian.

"Contingency plan."

CHAPTER 479 – GO WITH THE FLOW

The three lounged silent in the steamy Jacuzzi, fingers waterlog-wrinkled from the bubbling jets of chlorine-pickled water. They were the only ones in the cavernous room; the sun had long set on the wall of windows, which were steamed opaque. The clock on the wall read 9:48 pm - the pool facility closed in twelve minutes. The Sherpa was set beside them, Chicken fast asleep. Earl's urn was between Chick and Carol, her fingers lightly stroking the porcelain face, as if she was touching him.

"Wow, the Drury Hotel; you sure bring us to the best places."

Lillian said snarky, out of nowhere.

"It's the Drury *Suites,* and I told you, this is about as fancy as it gets in the Cape. Anyway, I have memories of this place from the '80's – it wasn't a Drury then – something else, can't remember what, but the same old bargain chain shit it is now. But I *do* have a great sex story to share, when I was twenty-two, right here in *this* Jacuzzi."

"*Ew!*"

Both girls cried collective, rising vertical from the tub of hot, musky water, waking Chicken in the process.

"It's not like it's the same water."

C smiled deadpan.

"I'm not so sure about that."

Carol said disgusted, refusing to reenter the now squalid *aqua pura* and quickly drying off what she was convinced was a recirculated stew of water and spooge.

C reluctantly exited the froth and the three stood in silence, each going through their own drying process ritual with over-sized white cotton towels snagged from the plastic bin by the door. Carol and Lillian slipped on loose workout pants and cotton tops over their bathing suits; C just slid on his loafers and headed for the door, towel draped over his one shoulder. They had gotten two rooms; Cord put his bag in one, Carol the other; Lillian kept hers in the limousine....she apparently hadn't decided where she was bedding that night, the thought of which elicited a wordless *whatever* shake of the head from Cord - he was beyond trying to figure her out.

"What are we doing tonight? Are you going to eat? What's the plan?"

Carol yelled nonchalant to C's back, as he shuffled toward the door.

"I'm gonna take a quick shower, then I wanna head out and check something out. You guys can go ahead and eat; I'll get something on the road. Can I use your limo guy, or are you going out somewhere to eat? Otherwise, I'll just get a taxi, no big deal."

Lillian looked at him incredulous.

"What the fuck are you talking about?"

C stopped and turned, still annoyed at the luggage issue, although neither of them knew that.

"What?"

He said, feigning innocence, mixed with mild annoyance; a classic C face.

"*What?* You drag us half-way across the country, to this dump, and then you say: *have fun at dinner – I'm going out.* Really?"

Lilly barked, more than a bit annoyed.

"I have to go see something."

"Like what? What can you possibly want to go see in this bum-fuck place at 10 o'clock at night? Some wrinkly, old, fat Jacuzzi girlfriend from twenty years ago?"

Lilly snarled.

"Why are they always *wrinkly*? Well, at least I graduated to seeing a wrinkly, old fat girlfriend, as opposed to a wrinkly, old gay boyfriend; I guess I should be happy about that."

C said, condescending.

"Enough."

Said Carol, shaking her head, acting referee.

"Where *are* you going at ten at night in this place, if you don't mind me asking?"

Carol said politely, maybe a bit too politely.

C just shook his head; there was no easy way to answer this one, without begetting a dozen more questions.

"I left a car here, last time I was here; I just want to see how it is."

Now they both looked at him incredulous, each with hands placed firmly on hips. That wasn't a good sign.

Lillian was the first to bite, of course.

"Seriously, *that's* your story? You're going to see about a car, from twenty years ago; did you forget to feed the meter?"

C huffed. He should have just said he was going to bed.

"You don't believe me? Fine, you're welcome to come. I didn't think you'd be interested; it's not a big deal."

"Oh we're coming, whether you *'invited'* us or not *[Lilly used air quotes – since she knew it annoyed C when she did that - and apparently decided for Carol that she too was coming along for the ride].*"

Cord looked to Carol, to see if she agreed with Lilly's *plan*; she offered neither resistance nor approval – she apparently decided to go with the flow.

CHAPTER 480 – RIGHT HERE, THROUGH THAT DOOR....ROOM 101

The limousine drove slow toward the approach to the Emerson Bridge.

"This is all new; we need to get down to the water somehow, down there."

C was leaning forward in the front seat alongside Carol's driver, whom still Cord had yet to hear utter a single word. The girls were in the back, whispering amongst themselves, and generally annoying Cord in the process. It was dark, with the side road entrances hard to see.

"You better take this left, or we're gonna be heading back over the river."

The limo banked a quick, last-minute left onto South Fountain Street and found itself approaching the Southeast Missouri River Campus, which looked to be under construction.

"Christ, this is *all* new; none of this was here. It looks like a campus or something."

C said, mostly talking to himself.

"Hey, go right, off this circle; we'll have to run into the river at some point. Yeah, yeah, holy shit, that's the old bridge ramp, they tore it down; okay, can't go that way, take a left here, yeah, Spanish Street, don't remember that one. Head toward the old Downtown; okay, I think I know where I am, but maybe not *[C said, rubbing his chin]*. No fucking street signs! Okay, stop, take a right here; ah, there it is! You can't see it, but in the blackness ahead, that's the Mississippi, right in front of us. Okay, now this should be right, stop take a left here, this should be it. Where's the fucking sign? *Aquamsi* Street? What the hell is that? This is supposed to be....they must have changed the name....this has *gotta* be Water Street."

That caught Lillian's attention.

"Water Street? We're on Water Street? That's kinda weird, isn't it?"

Lilly said, from behind Cord.

"There's a lot more than one Water Street, sweetie; Belvidere isn't the only town on the water."

"I *know that,* but it's just funny to hear Water Street and not think of home."

Actually saying the word *home* was strange, because she was never anywhere *but* home for most of her life. And saying it aloud made her think of Belvidere, her apartment, and her brother....and a sadness suddenly engulfed her, like a wave. Lillian's stomach sank as she slumped back in her seat. Carol witnessed the process, quietly saddled beside her, and neither said another word, as Cord navigated the driver along what he remembered as Water Street for a long, single block.

And suddenly, there it was, adjacent to a ratty building now used as a muffler shop - he couldn't remember what it used to be, maybe it was always a muffler shop.

"Holy shit, I can't believe it; *there it i*s."

C whispered to himself, looking in awe out the left side of the windshield. It was nothing special to see....a single story, non-descript, neat-as-a-pin red-brick building, sans a single sign, nary one indication of its use, nor what lay inside. They rolled to a quiet rest at the Stop sign.

"Take a left and pull onto that concrete apron, by that first white bay door, right there."

C whispered to the driver, who silently obeyed. He had to pull catty, since the limousine was too long to get its tail out of the roadway perpendicular. Two other bay doors existed further down the long, low-slung building. It was quiet, not a soul to be found.

C shook his head in the negative to himself, recalling all the miles, all the unmitigated mess of a life that had passed between this, then and now.

"Come on."

C mumbled hush, exiting the car.

"Where are we going?"

Carol said.

C pointed to a single incandescent bulb, which cast a dull, yellow arc on a simple, five-step masonry stoop, covered by a shingled overhang, protecting a white-painted door, with a three-digit number over top.

"That's where we're going, right here, through that door....Room 101."

CHAPTER 481 – THE GOLDEN KEY NEEDED TO OPEN THE DOOR. *OUI*

The door was locked; he suspected as much. So he gave it a brisk three-knock with the meat end of his fist, hoping a certain someone was home.

And C waited.

In the bowels, he detected the faint sound of a presence. But it didn't move much.

So he did it again, another rap trio, harder still.

And he heard the faint screech of a wooden chair push back against a concrete floor, followed by a slow shuffle of steps, getting louder as they approached the other side of the white, wooden door. The noise stopped at the threshold; whomever it was stood the thickness of the door away. They made no sound, they just waited for something else to happen outside, hoping whatever it was had gone away.

So *whatever it was* spoke.

"Bonsoir, Monsieur."

Was all C said.

The two words were greeted by a second of silence. He knew the mind on the other side was processing a greeting he never expected to hear, certainly not without warning, certainly not after 10 pm, on a cold and lonely Monday night, on October 16, 2006. But the voice was familiar, a voice the other side of the door most certainly knew.

Slowly, an accented response emerged from within, with an inflection flavored of both surprise and disbelief.

"Monsieur Majoric?"

And a single word followed, which was the golden key needed to open the door.

"Oui."

CHAPTER 482 – WHAT WAS WAITING ON THE OTHER SIDE OF THE DOOR?

As the doorknob jiggled, but before the curtain was cast aside, Carol spoke softly.

"Si, parlez-vous Francais epicerie garcon?"

Cord turned to her and spoke smoothly.

"Je ne parle un peu francais, desole....apres tout, je suis juste un epicerie garcon."

"Uh huh."

Carol said deadpan.

"Okay, enough of that shit, speak fucking English!"

Lillian yelled, annoyed at their affront.   Carol apologized, turning to Lilly.

"Sorry Lilly, I simply asked him how a simple grocery boy found the time to learn to speak fluent French....and he replied, in perfect form and accent, that he only speaks a little French, after all, he's just a grocery boy."

And with that, Carol raised her eyebrows, and they both turned to Cord.

"Oh, and he answers to *Mr. Majoric,* so I guess that's his name, this side of the river anyway."

The swing of the door saved him, for now.

A slight, slender and short, clean-shaven man filled the frame, sporting wire-rim spectacles. He had a refined appearance, a cultured veil that affirmed Old-World. He was wearing navy, thin-wale corduroys, a comfortable gray wool cardigan, fully buttoned save the bottom loop and a crisp, solid-crimson silk tie. He finished the look with highly polished obsidian tassel-loafers, and red argyles, only visible when he sat, hiking his pant leg enough to reveal the pattern. He loved all types of colorful socks, especially argyles – he had a bit of a sock fetish. He was in his mid-fifties and generally well-preserved. He eyed Cord up and down, clearly in awe of some sort of rarity.

"De vous rencontrer, enfin [To finally meet you]."

He whispered.

"Please speak English my friend; my friends prefer English."

"So sorry, of course, of course. Welcome....to you all. I apologize; I was not expecting visitors, especially the uncommon kind that stand before me, so I have nothing to offer, no food, I'm afraid, save half a sliced-cucumber sandwich, a late snack, before I retire. My God, you are not as I expected."

The man said, gazing carefully, thoroughly, at Cord, as if an antiquity.

"And you, are *exactly* as I expected."

C said in retort, placing a gentle hand on the small man's shoulder, and giving it a single squeeze.

"May I introduce my friends: Lillian Liddell and Carol Crowe."

And then Cord turned to the girls.

"And my trusted acquaintance, *Monsieur Roy.*

The little man extended a delicate hand to the girls, whom each shook gracefully. Lillian didn't like the limpish grip, and quickly released with the slightest acknowledgment....*yuck.* Carol was accustomed to the dead-fish handshakes common amongst the white-collared gentlemen on the party and investor circuit; it didn't phase her in the least.

"Plaisir de vous recontrer, Monsieur Roy [pleasure to meet you, Mr. Roy]."

Carol said, with perfect inflection; she wanted the gentleman to know she too was fluent in French....C wasn't going to label her an American bumpkin.

"Le plaisir est pour moi; un ami de Monsieur Majoric est un ami a moi [the pleasure is all mine; a friend of Mr. Majoric is a friend to me]."

Lillian shot Carol a wicked glance.

Carol knew that was coming, but she had to do it, to save face in front of Mr. Roy. Now she would knock off the French; she made her point.

"Thank you, thank you for your kind words."

Carol said, just to say something in English, to smooth the Lillian feathers.

"We don't have long; I just wanted to see my little girl. We'll, she's not so young anymore, is she?"

"No, afraid not, all grown up; but still looks as pretty as the day she was born."

The girls looked at each other odd; what was waiting on the other side of the door?

CHAPTER 483 – THE REAL PRIZE HID
BENEATH HER BEAUTIFUL GOWN

Mr. Roy walked them through his small billet, past his carefully creased newspaper, the *Southeast Missourian*, set beside a fine porcelain plate holding a half-eaten crisp cucumber sandwich, to a weathered, wooden, non-descript door on the far office wall. It creaked a bit as old doors do; he swung it open into a vast, black void. The air was decidedly cooler and still….undisturbed.

He reached his hand left and flipped a single switch.

And there she shone, in the distance….Cord's little girl.

She lay prone, solo, as if on stage, basking in a single, white spotlight, at a distance no more than sixty feet. The bath of light fell from her flanks and faded to gray, then charcoal, into the room. From what the girls could see, as their eyes adjusted to the dim, was a singular, cavernous space, stretching over a hundred feet long by fifty feet wide, five thousand plus square feet, and the room was entirely empty, not a box, not a broom….not a thing. Nothing. Just empty space, with a beautiful girl set smack in the middle.

C smiled in a way he rarely did. It was a good smile, pure and genuine. She deserved that.

The girls stood silent, not sure what to make of what they saw.

She was a long muscular cat, sinewy and sleek, dressed formal in an ever-dark forest green, a color she called *Sherwood.*

But the real prize hid beneath her beautiful gown.

"That's yours?"

Lillian said softly, sporting a cocked-eye at C. He simply smiled a yes.

Carol's mind kicked into overdrive, already formulating fast, plausible explanations, none of which included Cord actually earning the prize. Parents, or some rich uncle, died? Inheritance, lottery or quid pro quo for a secret kept? Possibly some combination thereof. Wealthy people always did that, quickly discounting how *someone else* got something valuable as some sort of gift, quirk or oddity. No one earned it like they did, no one worked as hard for it, or deserved it, as much as they did....everyone else got it easy. So goes the thinking.

Inheritance....someone definitely died; that was the ticket Carol quickly settled on. And Carol's whole analysis of the prize in the spotlight lasted less than five seconds – between the time Lilian asked the question and Cord smiled his answer.

"Who died?"

Carol asked dismissive.

Cord looked at her funny; surprised she hit it on the head – first try.

"Very good."

Was all he said, smug.

The foursome approached silent to her flank, settling beside the driver's side door; Cord bent over, looking, in awe, through the window.

"5.2 miles per day, seven days a week, twenty-one years, but no rain, no snow – she's never seen either, not a drop, am I correct *[Mr. Roy nodded affirmative]*? Some sick days thrown in, I'm thinking 30,000 miles, give or take *[Cord had already done the math before he arrived]*."

Mr. Roy smiled wry.

"28,202, as of today; she was out in the sun stretching her legs earlier this afternoon."

"Just the Broadway run right? To Wimpy's and back....same old loop?"

"Yes sir, every day; it's a given, like the striking of the church bells on Sunday. Needless to say, I've become something of a local legend; to this day, so many years later, people still ask the who, the what and the why....the papers have done stories, more than once."

Mr. Roy added a trailer.

"But of course, I say nothing, not a word of explanation, as per your instructions."

C nodded in appreciation.

"Thank you, Mr. Roy."

"You've been very good to me *Monsieur*, the thanks are extended to you; a treat to do so in person.....*merci.*"

C smiled, and nodded once again, which resulted in an annoyed huff from Carol, which Cord summarily ignored.

"Can I sit in her?"

"But of course, Sir; after all, she ultimately answers to you."

Ay depressed the driver's-side thumb-latch and the heavy door opened with the feel of a precision instrument. He slid in and saddled behind the leather wheel; it was a right-hand drive, as he ordered.

"You know, I've only sat in this car once before, in '85, when she was delivered, uncovered and rolled off the flat-bed. I felt the same way then as I do now. Thank you *Monsieur*, you have done well."

Mr. Roy nodded and smiled.

"Do you want to take her for a ride, sir?"

"Nah, this is good enough....but I would like to hear her purr."

"Certainly."

Mr. Roy swept his pocket and presented Ay the key; C slid it in, gave it a quarter-turn, and she sprang to life. It was simply beautiful. He gripped the wheel and squeezed tight, closing his eyes and smiling faint, trying to conjure good memories of this place....there were a few, but just a few. But that was a few more than most. For a moment, he forgot the girls were even there, but was soon reminded.

Mr. Roy smiling like a queer at Cord; Cord smiling with his eyes closed in the car....Christ, what a gay-hump love-fest Carol thought to herself, stewing silent over this whole stupid episode.

Lillian decided to share her thoughts aloud.

"Excuse me *Monsieur*, what the fuck!?"

Lilly yelled into the car, in an exaggerated accent she thought sounded like pretty good French.

It didn't.

Cord opened his eyes; reminiscence time was apparently over.

"Sorry, sorry."

Was all he said.

"Give it up."

Lillian ordered, thumbing him out of the cab. And he did, exiting the car without protest.

Lillian quickly slid into the large driver's seat, grabbing the wheel and turning it in an exaggerated way, like a little kid on an amusement ride."

"I can drive this!"

She yelled.

"I'm sure you can't."

C said, matter-of-fact.

"Why not? I'm a good driver!"

"Really? Have you ever driven anything, *ever*?"

"I drove Marty's tractor all over the farm, in and out of the barn, and he let me drive his cruiser once, at midnight, around the Park; I didn't hit anything!"

Lillian smiled, then frowned, because Marty was dead. Then she pushed it out of her mind. She was tired of thinking about dead people.

"Uh huh."

C said.

Carol was standing, fuming, beside C at the driver's door; *this must have been one big inheritance.* And she finally blew, her words dripping sarcastic.

"Just curious, this car has been parked here twenty-one years, in an empty building, with *Monsieur [spoken with a perfect accent]* Roy driving it around town once a sunny day, between newspaper interviews, eating sliced-cucumber sandwiches and reading the newspaper, on someone else's dime, I suspect....what's the fucking point? And who fucking pays? And I'm not asking your driver, since he is apparently committed to pinky-secret silence, I'm asking you, *Monsieur Majoric.*"

C's shoulders dipped; he knew this was coming. He exhaled a long sigh.

"Por favor nos da un momento; voy a estar de vuelta en decir adios en un poco [Please give us a moment; I'll be back in to say goodbye in a bit]."

Carol's ire spiked instant to red.

It *wasn't* French; she knew it was Spanish, because she recognized some of the obvious words, even though Cord spoke them *very* fast, fluent-fast. But she couldn't speak Spanish, so she didn't know what he said, and that enraged her. She was not illiterate, but she felt that way now. She made her Spanish house-staff, when she employed them in the past, speak English only; if they spoke Spanish, even once, in her presence, they were immediately discharged. She hated Spanish; she considered it *low.*

"Now you speak Spanish too? French and Spanish, fluent, and you have a *Bentley Turbo R [Carol spoke as if she was familiar with the model, but she only guessed that was the name, since she spied the insignia 'Turbo R' on the back]* that you've never driven, since you were what? Twenty-two years old? **Come on.**"

Carol said, with a healthy mix of disbelief and disgust.

Lillian looked at C, still gripping the wheel, still turning it left and right, like a kid, flipping and twisting all sorts of buttons on the dash and console, hoping something exciting would happen.

"Yeah!"

Lilly added, for good measure, like a dutiful sidekick, but barely paying attention.

"Ladies, if you'll excuse me."

And with that, Monsieur Roy quietly retired to his billet. The door clicked shut and the three were alone, accompanied by a low, powerful purr.

Carol didn't say another word. She simply waited for the explanation she knew he would try to worm out of. But there would be no worming, not tonight; she was tired of the whole charade. For six months, Cord was always a mystery, but now he was also one big fat lie.

Cord saw it in her face, her eyes; so, for once, he didn't play the worm.

"You're right, I bought it when I was twenty-two, in '85, a kind of present to myself. You don't buy a Rolls at twenty-two, not cool, so I bought a Bentley. It was new, a new model that year, just came out; only seven-thousand, two-hundred-thirty of them produced. It looked just like the Rolls, except for the grill, and the hood ornament, of course. I was told this was the ninth sold in the States, the other eight were pre-orders a year earlier. So, I was the first customer to buy after the doors opened, so to speak, and certainly the youngest. I'm sure that was some bullshit story to make a twenty-two year old feel special and help close the deal. Maybe it was true, maybe not, but no matter, I believed it at the time, and was going to buy it anyway. So I did."

"Of course you did."

Carol said, snotty. To which Cord answered indignant.

"What are you so mad about? What, you're the only person in our little group allowed to have money? Infringing on your *territory*?   On your *position* as the smart, rich one?"

"No!"

Carol immediately protested, but that was *absolutely* the problem, at least part of it anyway....most of it, actually. But Carol would *never* admit that to Cord; instead she skewered him with the other problem, the much bigger one.

"You know what I'm mad about, what my *problem* is? *You [she stabbed an angry finger in his direction]!* I've known you six months, and we've gone through a lifetime's worth of shit together in that time, and I might as well have known you for six minutes, because I don't know you *at all*, not one fucking bit, not even your real name, just made-up shit you dish out now and then, if you can't dance around the question in the first place! You don't add up, and I'm tired of it, of you, not adding up! If I'm really your friend, I deserve more, I deserve better, so does Lilly....we deserve fucking answers! I think we've both *earned* it."

By this point, Lillian had exited the car, and stood, shoulder-to-shoulder with Carol. C looked from one to the other − scowls looked back. There would be no more dancing.

"Okay, okay, ask away, your one shot to ask, till I get annoyed with you and stop answering, which feels like it will be in about two minutes, maybe less, because you are fucking annoying me, and I was in a good mood, for once."

"Oh, I'm annoying *you?!*"

Carol snapped.

"Now you have one minute."

A quiet huff followed, which he let slide.

"Did you pay cash?"

A single nod yes.

"How much?"

"$201,000; it was $193,000 base, but I kept adding shit, extras, to get it over two hundred grand, just because I wanted to....I was twenty-two and that somehow mattered, at the time."

That got Lillian's attention.

"Two hundred grand, for *this*?!"

C didn't answer.

"And Monsieur Roy, I'm sure he does this for fun; I'm sure he's free, right?"

Cord shook his head in a single, negative nod.

"Didn't think so. So you've been paying him for what, twenty-one years?"

"Uh huh."

C said, indifferent, looking around the warehouse, bored.

"How much?"

"Is this really necessary?"

"Yes, *very much so.* How much?"

Carol asked sharply, as if in court.

"Two-thousand."

"Two-thousand dollars?"

Carol repeated.

"Yes."

"Two-thousand *what*? A year? A month?"

C sighed.

"A week."

"*A week?!*"

Carol responded, an octave higher.

"***A week? Two-thousand a fucking week?***"

Lillian screamed.

"To eat sandwiches and drive a car five miles! I want that job! Fire him....***now***!"

Lillian was positively beside herself.

"So you pay him over $100,000 a year, cash I assume, for the last twenty-one fucking years?"

Carol spit the words. C shook his head; yes to all-the-above.

"And you work in a grocery store?"

"Enough with the grocery store bit, it's boring."

C snarked. Carol got pissed at the rebuff. She took a deep breath and sighed, a visible annoyance she blew into his face, long and slow.

"Okay, so how much is the rent?"

He didn't answer fast enough.

"Okay, okay, that's what I figured."

Carol said, shaking her head angry.

"Figured what?"

By this time Lillian had moved to C's far side, an uncomfortable female sandwich.

"He doesn't pay rent, because he knows the landlord *very* well."

"The Jacuzzi girl; I knew it!"

Lillian yelled, mystery solved! Carol never took her eyes off Cord, watching for any twitch in his silent face.

"No, not the Jacuzzi girl, someone much, much closer to our mystery friend here, someone who knows *all* his secrets. Am I right *Monsieur Majoric?*"

"The black girl?"

Lillian guessed again.

"Nope, not the black girl either; care to solve the mystery?"

Carol tilted her head to Ay.

He didn't answer, but the purse of his lips signaled she was dead-on.

"How much did it cost? Cash I assume?"

"Less than the car."

Was all he said.

"And taxes, insurance, upkeep? I assume you've never rented it out to anyone....empty all these years, except for your *little girl* and Mr. Roy, of course."

C nodded another bored yes.

"Wait a minute, you own this building? You own this too?"

Lillian asked.

"Sure he does, just to house a car he's never driven, watched over by a man he's never met."

And then the gravity hit Lillian, and her arm hair tingled.

"C, is Mr. Roy *Speed Dial No. 2?*"

Now it was Carol's turn for surprise.

"What's *Speed Dial No. 2?*"

C needed to jump in and stop this thread, immediately.

"No, Mr. Roy is **not** that guy; that's someone else."

"What's *Speed Dial No. 2?*"

Carol asked a second time, louder, to which C responded, in a more hushed, but firm, tone.

*"End of discussion on the phone issue; over, not debatable....**over!**"*

And it was clear C meant it. They both stood silent, arms folded across their chests, angry and pouting.

"Listen, that is a *very long story,* for some other day....*not* today."

"*Some other day* never comes with you....*ever!*"

Carol yelled.

"I'm answering questions, right?"

"Yeah, but...."

Carol said, before he interrupted.

"I'm answering questions about the car, about this place; and you're right, you both deserve that, but that's enough for today. The phone issue is *not* on the agenda today, agreed? Or we're done, *right now!*"

They both hesitated, then huffed a collective, reluctant yes. And then Lillian gave a second huff, just because she was Lilly.

Carol reset.

"Okay, car two-hundred grand, Mr. Roy, two-point-one million, building a hundred grand, and a guess for insurance, taxes, upkeep – for twenty-one years, say another hundred grand, maintenance five-thousand, no three-thousand a year, that's another sixty grand, add in stuff I forgot, add it all up, probably close to three million....*all for what?*"

Carol said, shaking her head at the so-bad-business of it all.

"For peace of mind."

C said, softly, through a blow of air.

"What does that mean?"

Carol asked, in a way that was more of a plea than a question. C cleared his throat.

"Every day, no matter where I am, anywhere in the world, no matter how much pain I am in, or what mess I've created, or what person I've hurt, or worse, I know that at 3:30 pm, Central Time, in a little nothing Mississippi River town in the *Bootheel* of nowhere Missouri, Mr. Roy is starting up my innocent little girl for a quiet ride around town. And it....*helps me;* it reminds me of a simpler time, when I thought life might hold some sort of....promise. But I was...."

His words trailed to nothing; C, staring at the floor, never finished the sentence, choking up, just a bit.

Lillian whispered, solving a mystery, for real.

"C, is that what 4:30 was all about? Earl said you used to always ask him what time it was: *was it 4:30 yet?* It was about Mr. Roy and this car *all* those times, for *all* those months, wasn't it?"

C just smiled sad and nodded his head, his eyes wet, with a tinge of red.

"I never told Earl, but only because, for some strange reason, he never asked. The one thing he never asked about. I'm not sure why, Christ, he asked a million times about everything else, but *never* that."

Lillian grabbed C's hand and squeezed it.

"I miss him so much it hurts."

"Me too."

C and Carol said, at the same time.

"You own other property don't you, not just this? That's how, that's why, you know so much about real estate; all our discussions about Brownfields properties, about Georgia-Pacific."

C nodded.

"Lots?"

A second nod yes.

"You must have inherited a boatload of money, not to work, to spend so….freely."

Cord shot Carol a wicked look.

"Who said I inherited *anything?* Who said I didn't **earn** it, just like you, I earned every *fucking* cent!"

And that ice cooled Carol's blood; the person who answered her was not C, nor *Monsieur Majoric,* it was someone else entirely.

"Sorry, you said someone died, so I just…."

"That's right, someone did die, more than one….*badly.*"

C whispered low at her. And then he stared cold at Carol, eyes locked hard on hers, enough to make her take a half-step back, for no reason other than instinct. Lillian missed the quick, wicked exchange.

"So C, how successful are you?"

Lillian asked, not-so-innocent.

"At what?"

"Well, we know the answer regarding relationships, a big fat no, especially with that *Whatever* girl, especially her; big zero strikeout for you on that front."

"Jesus, who's the *Whatever* girl?"

Carol asked, feeling she was out of the loop on everything: *Speed Dial No. 2, Whatever* girl.

"Yeah, especially her."

C parroted, looking at the Bentley. He always referred to her, the car, as *Kristine* in his head, for the last twenty-one years. When he spoke to the car, he called her *K*. He was glad that didn't come up in the volley of questions; that little bit was still only his to know.

"What about smarts? Are you smart?"

Lilly prodded.

"Somewhat."

C said, matter-of-fact.

"What about Carol, is *she* smart?"

Lilly delved.

"Less than somewhat."

Carol turned to C in horror.

"*What?!* Are you kidding me? You think you're smarter than **me**?!"

Before C could answer, Lillian drove the wedge deeper.

"Okay, what about money? Do you have a lot of it?"

"A bit."

C said, matter-of-fact. Carol huffed, a bystander to this ridiculous charade.

"And what about Carol?"

"Not *quite* a bit."

That was it, that drove Carol over the edge. She delivered a quick, two-handed shove to the chest, which drove C back on his heels.

"Wow, that's all you got? Lilly's way stronger than that!"

He teased, which made Lillian smirk and only enraged Carol further. She emitted some kind of low, alien growl....the sound of a cornered animal.

"No fucking way! How much? Prove it!"

"Enough that I don't have to prove it; *that* much."

He said calmly, which only egged her on.

"How do you know how much money *I* have? You have *no idea*!"

"Sure I do; you told me, bragging about it....remember?"

"No way! I would never do such a thing....gauche! When? **Liar!**"

Carol was screaming insane.

"You're right, it is gauche. But liar? Really? You sure about that? Remember our little conversations about real estate, your pictures in the *Times*, all my travels and how do I pay for it, my knowledge of couture....your little silk charmeuse too-short frilly white dress at the cocktail soiree on the Island? In the *Sunday Styles* section of the *Times*? Or how about shopping at Sam's, when I joked that I was buying groceries for a billionaire, and you said, and I quote: *not yet, but getting close*? Remember that? I do. And then you apologized for the brag and me saying: *No worries, you never know about people.* And you asked me what that meant? And I didn't answer. What do you think I meant *now*?"

And it all came flooding back, she did slip that she wasn't worth a billion yet, but getting close, and was embarrassed at bragging in front of someone who worked as a grocery store clerk, who now says he's worth a billion *plus*? Hogwash! She still didn't believe it.

As C looked at her, he saw the wheels spinning, the recollection coalesce, so he added the dagger.

"Remember Spanish Point? The story of the jagged glass? How you got so mad at me, thinking my penniless state was just because I was lazy….remember? And remember I replied: *Whoever said I was the jagged glass?* As I smoked a cigar on your porch? Are the pieces fitting together? Make sense now?"

And reality settled in; Carol's shoulders slumped, as if in defeat.

Lillian jumped in, dancing in a circle around Carol, pointing her fingers at her in a taunting playground tease.

"*I'm rich bitch!* I'm buying everything! The *Palace*, Sam's, the Park, the whole fucking Town! *I'm* the landlord now!"

Lillian raised her arms touchdown, as if the game ended, and she finished with the biggest pile of poker chips.

"Wow, look how quick *that* happened; I guess we're partner's now, or is it all *yours*? Can I have *any* of the money?"

C asked, in a state of mock incredulity.

Lillian cousin-hugged C, kissing him long on the cheek and left him with her trademark smile.

"Wow, that was the most expensive half-hug and sister-cheek-kiss any man ever paid for in history – *I win!*"

And C raised his hands in a weak, half-touchdown mock of Lilly.

"Hey."

Lillian pouted, as if she just realized all that money may not actually be *hers* to spend.

"Trust me Lilly, it's not all it's cracked up to be."

C said.

Lillian barked back quick.

"Oh bullshit! Rich people always say shit like that, but I don't see any of them giving it up! You're unhappy? I'll do you a big favor, for free....give me all your money, and then we'll both be happy."

Carol chimed in.

"C, I'd be a lot less happy without it."

"Unhappy is unhappy; are you happy? If you're so happy, then why are you so sad?"

"You know why."

Carol said, dropping her head.

"Of course I do. And you know what, Earl made you so very happy and it didn't cost you a cent, not a fucking dime. And he didn't have a cent. What you had, what you felt, had *nothing* to do with money, and because of it, it was priceless. Count yourself lucky, 'cause I've *never* had that."

Except for the memories of a skinny twelve-year old boy, and a twelve-year old knobby-kneed girl....except for that. But C kept that thought to himself.

"I miss him C, it hurts, and it's doesn't ever stop....it just doesn't."

Carol said, resting her head on Cord's chest.

"Me too."

C said.

"I wanna go home, *right now!* I don't want to be here anymore, not another minute."

Lillian said; the homesick came on all-at-once and she couldn't stand another second – it took hold, settled in, and ate her up.

**CHAPTER 485 – NOTHING BUT SILENCE
SURROUNDED HER**

The jet lightly touched the tarmac in Allentown, Pennsylvania just a hair past 2:30 am. A hired limousine picked them up curbside; they shuffled in silent for the half-hour ride home.

Chicken was fast asleep, and before they hit the highway, so were the girls. Cord was wide awake, regretting all he said, all he told them. It wasn't much, but even that was far too much, for it would only beget more questions, which would not result in answers he could share, so he would have to start lying, and once that began, he knew he would never keep track of the trail of lies, nor did he have any desire to try, it was simply too much work, and he became tired with the thought of same.

So he decided there would be no lies, because there would simply be no more questions.

About fifteen minutes in, the girls awoke. No one spoke, each looking out their window as the dark landscape silently passed. They passed a half-dozen opposite cars and saw a few deer frozen in the headlights, standing statue by the roadside; a single red fox dashed across Route 519 just a mile south of Town, well safe of the limousine, disappearing into a dried field of uncut corn. Other than that, they shared the road with no one, or no thing.

The town car made its way into Belvidere, past Saint Patrick's Church on the right; it came up to the Third Street and tapped the right directional. It clicked metronome – the only sound in the cabin.

"Drop me off at home please, straight ahead."

C said.

The driver hesitated, looking in the rear-view mirror to Carol for direction; she nodded affirmative, once. The directional clicked off and the limousine cruised quiet the three blocks downtown, turning left at the only light in Town, at Sam's, and saddled to the curb in front of the *Palace.*

"Night."

Was all C said.

"Goodnight."

Carol parroted; Lillian didn't say a word.

The trunk popped and the driver started to exit.

"Stay put, no worries."

C said.

As the driver resettled in his seat, Cord exited and pulled his bag from the boot. He was just about to shut the trunk when Lillian silently appeared by his side.

"I'm going to have to learn to sleep at home again sometime."

She said, somewhat in defense.

"Plus, I just wanna be in my own bed."

C just half-smiled and nodded, grabbing her bag in his free hand. Lillian carried the Sherpa, Chicken still fast asleep.

"She can sleep with me, if you don't mind. I would feel better if she was with me; reminds me of Earl."

"Sure."

C said polite, and he said nothing more.

The stairwell door closed behind them as the car K-turned and passed them, on its way to bring Carol uptown; neither she nor they turned to acknowledge the other leaving. Soon enough, Water Street was silent.

Cord and Lillian got to the first landing and Lilly pushed the door open and tentatively walked in. She had long since stopped locking her door, mirroring C. It felt different, knowing that Earl was gone, never to set foot in this space again. It was home, but it felt foreign. Home, but not really....kind of a fake home.

"This will be the first night here without Earl."

She stated the obvious to C, and the feeling between them could be best described as....awkward. And she wasn't sure why.

C didn't answer, placing her bag gently by her bed.

"Good night."

He whispered.

"You mean good morning."

She said clumsily. He just smiled, but it was a distant smile, at least it felt that way to her, and that made her sad. But maybe she was wrong.

She stared at the front door for a full half-minute after he clicked it shut, all the while she heard him climb the second flight, open, then quietly shut, his door.

Then, nothing but silence surrounded her.

CHAPTER 486 – SHOVED HER TONGUE DEEP INTO HIS MOUTH

He felt her warm breath on his neck; she was spooned behind him. He could feel her heat, it mixed with his and made a comfortable cushion in the sliver of space between their bodies.

He didn't know if she was naked, but he suspected as much. He was naked as well – he had decided to strip his underwear sometime after he got into bed, burying them with his feet amongst the crumple of sheets at the bed bottom. He rarely did that, but this time, the elastic was bothering his waist, and he began to obsess about it, laying in bed, staring at the ceiling. So off they went – problem solved.

At some point he fell asleep, till now, feeling her.

Her breathing was a metronome: soothing, comforting. He slowly moved his hand below the blankets and placed it lightly on her hip; it was bare, the skin smooth and warm….naked, as he suspected. He wondered the time; it was still dark, maybe 3:30 am, maybe 4. He wondered when she snuck in; he never heard her, which surprised him, since he usually was a light sleeper.

He hesitated a bit, then let his hand fall off her hip, following the contour, across her belly, to her navel. She was the temperature of toast, and ever-smooth. He traced the circle of her belly-button, and then gently flattened his hand, to feel her belly lightly rise and fall as she slept. He hesitated again, unsure if he should do what was next, but he did. His hand slowly traveled south, till his pinkie finger felt the first bit of hair at the top of her crotch. This was the same hair he saw when her sweats hung low on her hips, as she rushed into Sam's that morning after they first came close to sex, the night Button came home. The first time, the last time, he saw the wisp of pubic hair he was now caressing with his pinkie she was with Button. Now she was with him.

His dick slowly came to life, not quick, not immediate, more like a slow, uncertain march. His hand did not move further south; it stayed put, just barely touching her hair, waiting at the door, for what, he wasn't sure.

Then she lightly stirred and moaned softly into his ear; she wanted it, she needed it. That's what her moan meant, that was the cipher. He had never had sex with her, not once, and it was finally time. She rose off the pillow, just a sliver, and gently kissed his neck. Then she barely extended her tiny tongue past her lips and licked his neck, traveling slow, dripping sex, up his neck, across his cheek, searching for his mouth. And as she got close, he could smell her breath on his face; it was warm and moist….and foul.

It was then he saw, from the furthest corner of his eye, her straw-white hair, and felt the shiver of cold air between his body and her paper-thin wrinkled skin, just as the hag cackled and shoved her tongue deep into his mouth.

CHAPTER 487 – SWALLOWING IT ALL, TO THE VERY LAST DROP

Cord woke in a fright, but the hag was gone.

Behind him lay Lillian, as she just was, his hand where it previously lay, gently stroking the very top of her pubic hair. But now, he felt self-conscious, so he withdrew his hand a half-inch, away from her hair, further from her crotch, and with it, his dick shrank to limp.

That's when he heard the half-snort of a chuckle from the bedroom shadows, on the far wall, by his bureau. He knew that laugh.

"Couldn't fuck her before, and still can't, you little, limp-dick, pussy faggot."

And with that, Button slowly morphed from the shadowy edge of the room, toward the bed. He was naked, his body thoroughbred, his cock at full attention, larger than it ever really was. He smiled wise-ass as he strode around the bed, outside C's ken. And C, unable to move, felt Lillian shift her body away from him, sit up and slide to the edge of the bed, like a good girl, who obeys. He knew, without words, without instruction, that she opened her mouth wide and took his cock full-in; he heard her sucking, working her tongue, and moaning as she did, because she was rubbing her clit, masterbating, legs spread wide, all the while.

It seemed to go for eternity; C couldn't move, couldn't escape, mere inches away, out of sight, but well within earshot. And the sounds escalated, both of them ramping fast to finish, her telling him, as she slid his cock in and out of her mouth, that she was close, *so close*....and him telling her to *swallow it all, every drop, and that an ass-fuck was up next.* And then Cord felt the wet spittle hit the side of his face; a mouthful of chewed Muscadine grapes, spat on him by Button as he laughed and unloaded heavy in Lillian's mouth, her spread hips

shuddering involuntary as she rubbed her clit vigorous,
coming long and hard with him, and like a good girl,
swallowing it all, to the very last drop.

CHAPTER 488 – AS WENT THE TINY FLY: *TICK, TICK, TICK*

He now knew she was coming; it was inevitable.

And Jenny did, quietly whispering in his ear, like she had done, faithfully, hundreds of times before. He didn't pay much attention till the end:

And there will be trouble.

And with that, Cord cracked his eyes and felt the instant relief that comes with the realization that it was all just a dream, followed by the slow onslaught of dread that the game was far from over. Not that he really felt free, but the respite from its ever-grip for the last week gave him a glimmer of hope.

But in the end, it was nothing more than a cruel tease.

The hag never left; she was there, laughing, the whole time. And Cord felt it. He knew, somehow, that the puppet was dead, gone from the folds in his brain. How or why he couldn't figure, and didn't bother to try. But the void left by the evil manikin was replaced by something much worse....Button Pierce.

Cord shook his head; he was right all along, Button *was* the puppet, he always was, and he had to die, to then live, forever, in C's head. He wished the puppet gone for years; how ironic – he finally got his wish.

Be careful what you wish.

All the while, since he opened his eyes, the last thirty seconds or so, he didn't feel her presence, and that surprised him. But he did now.

Lillian was spooned close behind, and this time, the whole time, she was real. This was no dream. And he then realized the test that it was.

Another test.

He reached his hand back and felt her hip; he knew it would be bare, and it was. He didn't drop his hand to her crotch – he knew what waited below, his for the taking, for as much and as long as he desired. He could pound her all morning....all day; she had finally, fully, submitted.

His dick didn't react; it lay there, limp, impotent. Maybe Button was right.

He laid quiet, so as not to disturb Lillian; her breath, regular and warm against the base of his neck, felt good.

It was then that he first heard it: a *tick, tick, tick.* He knew immediately what it was, in the kitchen. He turned his head upwards, off the pillow and strained to hear better. And he did. And then he was sure.

He slowly, carefully, slid out of bed; Lilly never stirred. He quietly left his bedroom, naked, hooked a right, and found himself in the kitchen, leaning against the jam, mesmerized.

There she was, all alone, struggling, with no one to help....no one to explain the *why.*

He never understood why people got so mad, so immediately angry that they felt the urge to swat, to kill, a hapless fly. All she wanted was *out,* hitting the pane of glass endless, not understanding why she couldn't get to the outside beyond. And she would bump the pane endless, confused, frustrated, till she starved or tired out, and died. Just open the window; instead of killing her, why not just open the *fucking* window? Simple solution, let it out, let it go, let it live. Simple. But no one *ever* did that. No one, that is, but Cord.

But here, he faced a dilemma.

It was too cold on the other side of that glass; if C opened the window, the early morning October air would chill her lethargic and kill her but quick, much faster than the slow, confused, frustrated starve inside, hitting the glass over and again.

What was better? Free and quickly dead, or a trapped, safe but slow, demise. What was the right decision?

Cord stood and watched her in silence: the *tick, tick, tick* of his frustrated little friend.

His thoughts turned to Lillian.

He was gone, Jenny had made that decision clear. And he wouldn't deny her; he had seen the consequences in that. And no way would we risk Lillian....no way.

If Lilly left with him, she'd die, for certain. And likely quick. If he had any doubts before, the hag, and Button, were clear confirmation. But maybe she was dead already, maybe the hand had already been dealt and decided.

Maybe.

In that case, the little time she had left was best spent on the other side of the glass.

Maybe.

He shook his head; at this very moment, Lillian was lying in his bed, naked, and not drunk – her decision, and hers alone, to slide into his bed and open herself to whatever he wanted to do to her. And he got up; his dick was limp. He never had sex with her; it was his obsession for the last six months – he must have fucked her a thousand times, in a hundred ways, in his mind during that time, waiting for just this day. But now, it just didn't feel right; it was a little too little, a little too late. Maybe that was the hag and Button meddling in his brain, or maybe it was just him.

Either way, that's how it felt; it didn't feel right.

Lillian always had Carol, and Carol had her. Maybe that was enough, for both of them; maybe it had to be, whether it was or not.

And he always had Kristine; she was his safety, always was. Maybe *Kristine Whatever* won. He wondered again if she was still alive; maybe she was already dead, like him. Maybe that was why it worked. Maybe that's why women came and went, came and went, but at the end of the day, there was always Kristine, waiting for him, somewhere.

She had to be somewhere; even dead is somewhere.

Lillian, Kristine; Lillian….Kristine.

And with that, Cord made a decision, as went the tiny fly: *tick, tick, tick.*

The clock flipped to 4:17 am.

Cord survived, as expected, and stumbled drunk about the room, trying his best not to wake Lillian. A full hour had passed since he woke and heard the fly.

The fly was gone.

He went to say goodbye to Chick, but realized she was downstairs, in Lillian's apartment. He would swing by and give her a long kiss and belly-rub on his way out. She would stay with Lillian, or Carol, he wasn't worried about that – she would be in good hands with either. And she wouldn't miss him a lick; he was convinced of that. Cats, better than anyone, simply move on.

He slipped out the door, quietly and made his way down the steep flight of steps, holding onto the rail to lessen his drunken wobble.

He stopped dead on the second floor landing, ready to say his farewell to Chicken, when his foot slipped on the white envelope left askew on the polished wood floor, scrawled with a single letter: *C,* followed by a simple, urgent phrase:

Do <u>Not</u> Open When You Are Ready
Open Me Up – <u>Now</u>!

CHAPTER 490 – A SLOW UNCERTAIN SHAKE
FOR A BAD DECISION MADE

Cord sat on the step beside her door and finger-opened the envelope. Inside was a single sheet of white paper, neatly hand-written in blue pen. Not a single mistake or score marred the page.

It was perfect.

And so he read.

C:

I know that's not your name, but I don't care. To me you are, and always will be, C.

If you are reading this, alone, by my door, it means you are leaving, without me.

I want you to know, I don't care a lick about your money, I don't want a cent of it – I hope you truly understand that. You found me naked, in your bed, for one reason, and one reason only....I love you. I have since the first time I saw you through Sam's door; although I didn't know it then, I know it now.

And I know you love me....and I hope, I think, you leaving without me is some noble attempt to save me from some fate you are sure awaits me. You may be right, or you may be wrong....it's one or the other. But whichever door it is, I want you to open it with me <u>beside</u> you, holding your hand. That's what best friends do, they stick together....good and bad. You can't undo that glue. And you are, and always will be, my best friend....whether you leave with, or without, me.

I know you bought a new gun, new darts, new maps, a new box; she told me you did, and I found them....and she was so, so sad. She loves you C, as much as I do. She told me to tell you that, so I am.

I don't care about your past, all I care about is our future, and whether it's short or long, it will be together....forever.

I simply can't imagine living without you. I will never leave you; please do not leave me. Please come back upstairs and lay beside me.

All my love,

Bibby

C hung his head, cradled in his hands; a slow uncertain shake for a bad decision made.

CHAPTER 491 – CLOSED HIS EYES AND SMILED SAD

The morning broke and the sun began its slow, steady climb, nary a cloud marred the cerulean sky.

It was the beginning of a beautiful day.

Cord stared ahead as the bus rumbled toward the dart's destination, the first step in a long journey.

He looked lovingly to his right, at the seat beside his, closed his eyes, and smiled sad.

La Fin? Non.